A MATRIMONIAL MURDER

Praise for *A Matrimonial Murder*

'Just what the doctor ordered for a lazy Sunday. A deep dive into the great Indian obsession, marriage-making, the book is a sumptuous Gujarati wedding thali. All the flavours are served up—the base note of old relationships, the tanginess of sharp characterisation, the bitter-sweetness of romance and the mirchi of murder. What's not to like? A welcome addition to the growing tribe of Indian mystery writing.'

Ratna Pathak Shah
actor and director

'Meeti Shroff-Shah's *A Matrimonial Murder* takes us on a wicked jaunt through the world of modern Indian matchmaking. Shroff-Shah's likeable amateur sleuth investigates a killing at a glitzy matrimonial bureau in India's city of dreams, shining light on contemporary social issues as she goes. A gentle mystery with a murderous heart.'

Vaseem Khan
author of the Baby Ganesh Detective Agency novels

'A wonderful new addition to the canon of Indian mystery writers. Meeti Shroff-Shah tells a great twisted tale with acute observations about the people and the world she inhabits, all done with aplomb and assurance, keeping you guessing till the very end!'

Lillete Dubey
actor and theatre director

'*A Matrimonial Murder* is one of the funniest, heartfelt mysteries of the year. Meeti Shroff-Shah's gift for social satire mixed with humour and suspense makes Radhi's investigation of elite matchmaking in Mumbai an utter delight.'

Sujata Massey
author of *The Mistress of Bhatia House*

'A hugely enjoyable, atmospheric book. Such a vivid setting with a clever plot.'

Victoria Dowd
author of *The Smart Woman's Guide to Murder*

A MATRIMONIAL MURDER

A Temple Hill Mystery Book 2

MEETI SHROFF-SHAH

BLOOMSBURY

NEW DELHI • LONDON • OXFORD • NEW YORK • SYDNEY

BLOOMSBURY INDIA
Bloomsbury Publishing India Pvt. Ltd
Second Floor, LSC Building No. 4, DDA Complex, Pocket C – 6 & 7,
Vasant Kunj, New Delhi, 110070

BLOOMSBURY, BLOOMSBURY INDIA and the Diana logo
are trademarks of Bloomsbury Publishing Plc

First published in India 2024
This edition published 2024

ISBN: PB: 978-93-56405-45-5; e-ISBN: 978-93-56405-46-2
2 4 6 8 10 9 7 5 3 1

Typeset in Adobe Garamond Pro by Manipal Technologies Limited
Printed and bound in India by Thomson Press India Ltd

FSC www.fsc.org MIX Paper | Supporting responsible forestry FSC® C010615

In memory of Sushil mama;

I wish we could've taken that one last walk together.

1

Tuesday

On the quiet, gulmohar-lined slopes of Mumbai's posh Temple Hill, Sarla Seth is a powerful name. She doesn't hail from a Palanpuri family, which means there are no diamond factories chugging away in Seepz. Nor does she carry one of those mill-owning, Kathiawadi surnames, which come with prime real estate plots attached. Her late husband was a wholesaler of cloth. Moneyed, well-heeled and respected, of course, but cloth is cloth and however shiny silk may be, it can't possibly hope to out-dazzle diamonds. And yet, despite her largely ordinary background, Sarla Seth's presence at a party can cause a hushed ripple to go through the room. For she is the founder of Soul Harmony, the most venerated matrimonial bureau in the city.

As Radhika Zaveri waited for her meeting with Sarla, she watched the young receptionist talking softly on the phone. As the girl talked, she blushed and doodled, the pace of her pink pen slowing down and picking up in tandem with the tenor of her conversation. Every time she said something, she feverishly coloured the heart-shaped petals on the paper in front of her, and when she paused to listen, her hand moved slower, as if her entire being was focused on memorizing the voice at the other end. Radhi observed her for a few minutes before turning her attention to the heavy-set woman in a voluminous, fluorescent orange kaftan, waiting on the couch to her left. She had a creased forehead, a droopy mouth and the air of someone who had been here before because unlike Radhi she hadn't once glanced at the striking red wall with the gilded photo frames that dominated the waiting area. Nor had she picked up one of the glossy wedding magazines arranged in concentric circles around the vase of carnations on the table between them. She sat there staring at the floor, her face sullen, her arms folded protectively across her chest.

Radhi walked up to take a closer look at the red wall, which ran all the way down a narrow, well-lit corridor into what looked like the main office. The wall was covered in a dramatic yet elegant jumble of golden frames. Some carried magazine articles featuring Soul Harmony and Sarla Seth's clout over Mumbai's wedding industry; others were black-and-white photographs of happy couples on their wedding day. Inscribed under each picture were the names not only of the bride and groom but also of each of their parents. Radhi rolled her eyes and smiled — some things on Temple Hill would never change. A marriage would never just be about the two people who were getting married. It would involve each of their families, not to mention their hopes, fears and expectations, which would eventually find a way to seep into the new couple's married life. The young people in the pictures however were not thinking about in-laws just yet — they had their whole lives ahead to figure out those complex equations. At that moment, they were flushed with the attention from the hundreds of guests present at their wedding. And, of course, from their own, newly minted spouses.

One particularly tender picture caught Radhi's attention. The groom held a spoon in one hand and a tissue in the other as he gingerly fed his bride, who held up the huge ruby-studded gold nose ring that fell over her mouth. Her eyes were shut as she savoured the food. She had most likely fasted that morning and this was probably the first bite of food she'd had all day. But it was the groom's face that caught Radhi's attention. His mouth was slightly open, and his eyes were bright with wonder as if he simply couldn't believe his good fortune. Radhi felt a dull ache in her heart. And she was glad it wasn't more painful than that. She had a similar wedding photo with Bedi, her ex-husband. For a long time after her divorce, Radhi had found it impossible to look at other people's wedding albums without a pang of bitter envy. But that was many years ago. Now, that unhappy marriage was behind her, and Bedi and she were good friends — as they should have stayed in the first place.

'Bhavana ben?' Radhi turned around to see the receptionist address the woman on the couch. 'Kiran ben is free to see you now.'

The woman got up without a word or glance at the receptionist and walked down the corridor, her whole demeanour stiff and angry.

Radhi looked at the receptionist curiously. The young woman gave her a small, embarrassed smile. Just then the phone rang; she picked up the receiver and spoke into it before getting up.

'Come, ma'am,' she said addressing Radhi. 'Sarla ben is free now.'

She led Radhi down the corridor, which went straight down for a few meters before curving like a 'P'. This passage was lined with cabins that had frosted glass doors, with four desks in the open area in the centre. The receptionist led her to the largest cabin.

Sarla Seth was one of those rare small women with a personality so big it could fill the entire room. Her voice booming and permanently hoarse, her hair long, loose, reaching well below her hips, and the bindi on her forehead gigantic and magenta-coloured, each aspect of her person had a presence all of its own. And yet, they were but mere side notes to the woman. She was dressed in a cream organza sari with a loud print of peach roses and a matching sleeveless blouse. On anyone else the meticulously colour-coordinated outfit would garner comment, but with Sarla, one barely noticed her clothes. It was the woman alone you paid attention to.

Sarla beamed when she saw Radhi, getting up to embrace her before holding her at arm's length to examine her from top to toe.

'Just look at you! It's been what ten, no twelve, years since I last saw you at your sister's wedding? You've grown into a carbon copy of your mother!'

Radhi smiled and allowed herself to be kissed on the cheek. In reality, with her broad forehead, wheatish complexion and slender five-foot-eight-inch frame, she looked more like her dad. But she did have her mother's sharp nose and when she wore a nose pin, as she had today, people often told her that she reminded them of her mother. Radhi's parents had passed away in a car crash when Radhi and her sister, Madhavi, were teenagers. Sarla had been a close friend of their mother's, and over the years she had kept in touch with the girls.

'May I send something in?' the receptionist asked. 'Some tea or coffee?'

Sarla looked at Radhi, who answered, 'Tea for me, please.'

'Me too,' said Sarla. 'Oh, and, Juhi, did the printer-repair fellow come?'

'They've promised to send him by tomorrow, ma'am,' the young woman said.

Sarla nodded. 'And what about Amey Goradia's photographs? Did his mum send new ones?'

'Yes, they're better than before.'

'Good. I told her the Leaning Tower of Pisa was not the point of the photograph, her son was!'

Juhi grinned as she shut the door.

Sarla turned her attention to Radhi and shook her head. 'It's the funniest thing how often parents send me pictures of their son or daughter at some exotic foreign locale where the boy or girl can barely be seen. I have to remind them that I run a matrimonial bureau, not a travel agency!'

Radhi laughed. 'This is funny! I should be writing this stuff down.'

'I'm serious. I can't say, NAME: Rohan Shah, HEIGHT: 6 ft, EDUCATION: MBA and then attach a picture of the Eiffel Tower!' said Sarla grinning.

She leaned back in her chair and regarded Radhi with a sober expression. 'Now you tell me, how have you been? I know your divorce was rough on you. But that was a few years ago, no?'

Radhi took a deep breath. Ever since she had moved back from New York, she had been fielding questions about her divorce from the extended orbit of relatives, neighbours and acquaintances that surrounded her life on Temple Hill. She knew that most were driven to it by plain, bald curiosity, and she handled their attention flippantly. But when some, like Sarla, asked out of genuine concern, she felt compelled to attempt an honest answer.

'It's been a while. Many years, now. Doesn't hurt as much.'

'But what went wrong? Tell me, was it the vastly different backgrounds?' Sarla ventured. 'I always think that's the biggest risk with love matches like yours. I know your family didn't like you marrying outside the community.'

Unlike their cousins, neither Radhi nor her sister had had an arranged marriage. They had both picked the men they married, and coincidentally, both had chosen from outside their close-knit Gujarati community.

Remembering the time she had spent with her loud and boisterous Punjabi in-laws, and how similar they had seemed to her own animated gaggle of food-loving aunts and uncles, Radhi shook her head.

'Well, what then?'

'I think,' Radhi paused for a second to pick the right words before continuing, 'the problem with Bedi and me was not our differences but how similar we were. Our temperaments were very alike. We were both quick to anger and eager to take offence. I want to blame it on being young. But young is a euphemism.' She shook her head in disapproval of her younger self. 'We were just bloody immature! Always ready to throw the marriage away at any hint of a disagreement. Impatient to prove that we would be perfectly fine without the other.' Radhi gave Sarla a small smile. 'Does that make sense?'

The older woman scanned Radhi's face. Radhi could see that Sarla had more questions, but she held herself back. Then Sarla nodded, clapped her hands together and straightened up. 'Okay. Enough of the sad talk. If it's any consolation, divorce isn't as uncommon on Temple Hill as it was, say, a decade ago. Mind you, it still sets tongues wagging. But that's people for you. They'll always need something to talk about.' She flashed a smile at Radhi. 'Speaking of being talked about, Madhavi tells me you're quite the hotshot writer in New York now.'

Radhi rolled her eyes. 'Hardly a hotshot. You know how elder sisters are. She likes to talk me up, that's all. Also, I don't live in the US any more. I moved back to India in June to be closer to the family.'

A young peon in a white shirt and black trousers entered the room with a tray of teacups and a plate of tangy soya sticks and ragi chips.

'I'm glad to hear it!' Sarla handed a cup of tea to Radhi before picking one for herself. 'There's no place like home,

I always say. And no boy like a good Gujju boy, am I right?' She winked brightly at Radhi.

Radhi half groaned, half laughed. 'If you insist, Aunty.'

Sarla narrowed her eyes. 'I hope you're not dating one of those goras,' she said, wrinkling her nose in distaste.

A fleeting shadow fell over Radhi's face as she thought of Mackinzey. Kind, gentle, blue-eyed Mackinzey whom she had dated for a blissful two years after her divorce, before he suddenly disappeared from her life.

'No.' She forced herself to smile. 'No goras in the picture.'

'Good for you! Honestly, I just don't trust them. Who knows how many people they've slept with. Or how often they bathe!'

'Bathe?'

'Yes!' Sarla leaned forward conspiratorially. 'A friend of mine has a daughter who used to date a Frenchman. She told me that he didn't bathe for the whole week he stayed at their place!'

'Come on, Aunty, I'm sure she's just exaggerating!'

'That may be so,' said Sarla leaning back into her chair, 'but who wants to get close enough to find out?'

Radhi laughed despite herself. 'Aunty, that's ridiculous!'

Sarla shrugged. 'Is it? Well, everyone's thinking it, I just say it!'

Radhi had long abandoned trying to counter the classist and racist views she often encountered among the older folk on Temple Hill. The sense that they were 'purer' than the rest of the world was far too entrenched for Radhi to now take on the onus of changing their minds. Instead, she changed the topic. 'But, Aunty, are you telling me that the girls on Temple Hill are bringing their foreign boyfriends home to meet their parents? Have I really been away that long?'

'Don't be absurd, darling.' Sarla shuddered. 'This friend lives in London. She was just lamenting about the state of affairs there. Of course, our Temple Hill has also changed over the years, but not that much. Our Gujarati boys may sample their pasta and pizza outside, but when they come home, they want nice hot puran polis!'

'Eww, Aunty!' Radhi grimaced at the awful analogy.

Sarla cackled. 'Well, it's true! And you'll see for yourself when you conduct your interviews and spend a few days with us. I've asked Juhi to clear a desk for you.'

'That's perfect! Thanks once again for letting me do this.'

'Phishh! You can thank me when I find you a nice Gujarati boy to settle down with! Anyway, all that in good time. You tell me now why you want to write about matrimonial bureaus.'

Radhi was relieved to have the conversation move away from the subject of her love life. She had recently begun dating a good Gujarati boy, in fact, but she didn't feel like telling her mother's friend about it just yet. It would only lead to questions and conjectures, none of which she was prepared to deal with at the moment.

'You know that show, the one about matchmaking?'

Sarla made a sour face. 'Yeah, the one with that judgy aunty. Gave all of us matchmakers a bad name.'

'Well, it was hugely successful and generated a lot of curiosity in the West about arranged marriages, matchmakers and Indian matrimonial bureaus. People were keen to know more, and my agent thought I could do a collection of essays on why and how the system works, a sort of behind-the-scenes look into the different facets of matchmaking. I'll be doing an in-depth piece on you — what motivates you, some of the challenges you face, how you got started, that sort of thing. I'll also be speaking to other matrimonial bureaus and people connected to the industry like wedding planners, designers who put together wedding trousseaus, etc.'

Sarla nodded thoughtfully. 'Hmm . . . this could be good publicity for us as well. We're hoping to achieve a milestone this year — we are at nine hundred and ninety-four right now and by the end of December we hope to make that a thousand matches. If you like, you can talk to a few of our clients, as well.'

'That'd be great, actually!' said Radhi.

'Wait, let me jot down a few names. Then Juhi can help you set up a meeting with them,' said Sarla shuffling a stack of mail on her desk while looking for a notepad. Suddenly, her hands stopped moving, her face crumpled and a strangled 'oh' escaped her mouth.

'What is it, Aunty?' Radhi quickly scanned the desk to see what had caused such a reaction.

Sarla didn't answer. Her hands shaking, she picked up a red envelope that was lying face down on her desk. She opened it and then dropped it as if she had been burned.

Radhi picked up the fallen envelope, and when Sarla didn't protest, she peered inside and removed a cobalt card from it. It showed a dark figure holding a sickle, sitting atop a pale horse. There were people lying on the ground, around the horse's legs. At the bottom of the card was a single word: 'DEATH'.

2

'What is this, Aunty?' asked Radhi, alarmed. She turned the envelope over and checked it for a name or address. It had neither. She turned the card over. It had a fine geometrical pattern across the back in gold. She dropped the card on the table and checked inside the envelope again. A thin strip of white paper was stuck to its side. Radhi removed it and read the typed words out loud: 'All good things come to an end.'

Sarla, who had been sitting with one hand clutching her head, took the note from Radhi and read it before crumpling it and letting it fall to the desk. 'I don't get it,' she said, more to herself than to Radhi. 'Who's doing this?' She picked up the phone. 'Juhi, can you ask Hansa to come see me.'

Then, in response to Juhi's reply, 'I see . . . okay, ask her by when she'll be in office.'

She hung up the phone and turned her attention back to the card. 'This is the fourth one so far,' she told Radhi. 'The other three were equally terrible.'

'They seem like they are part of a deck. Do you have the other three here?'

Sarla nodded. 'They are tarot cards.' She rifled within her drawer and brought out three similar red envelopes.

Radhi removed the cards and notes from the envelopes. One card showed a tall tower on fire. It had been struck by lightning and people were jumping out of the windows to save themselves. The accompanying note read: 'The higher you climb, the harder you fall.' The second card had a blindfolded woman clad in white sitting on a beach with her back to the sea. In her hands she held two heavy swords crossed against each other. The note read: 'There are none so blind as those who will not see.' The third card depicted a swollen red heart pierced with three swords against a stormy background of grey clouds and needle-like rain. Radhi looked in the envelope for the note but couldn't find one.

'That was the first one. I didn't think to keep the note then.' Sarla looked distressed. 'It said something like "Every action has a reaction". I can't remember perfectly, but that was the gist.'

Radhi studied the cards briefly before handing them back to Sarla. 'When did these come?'

'Well, the first one arrived more than two months ago. Then the second one came two weeks after that. And the third and fourth have followed since.'

'What happened two months ago? Can you think of anything significant?'

'No! Nothing. I have racked my head about it!'

'But who in the world do you think it could be?'

'I don't kn—' The door burst open and a tiny, bespectacled woman in a yellow organza sari rushed in. She was skinny and extremely fair; her scalp showed through her thin, scanty hair, which was tied in a squiggle-shaped ponytail.

'Did you—have you also—' She spluttered to a stop when she saw that Sarla was not alone.

'Yes,' said Sarla looking at her unhappily. 'Yes, I did. Come in and shut the door behind you, for heaven's sake!'

The woman closed the door but continued standing awkwardly, conscious of Radhi's presence.

'Sit, Kiran, don't mind her. She's Radhika, the daughter of an old friend.' To Radhi she said, 'Radhi, this is Kiran, my partner at Soul Harmony.'

Radhi smiled politely at Kiran. She hadn't known that Sarla had a partner.

Kiran was clutching a similar red envelope. She handed it to Sarla and sank into the seat beside Radhi. Her hands immediately began fidgeting with the things on the desk.

'It was on my table this morning,' she said, picking up the little marble idols of Ganesh, Laxmi, the Buddha and Lord Mahavir on Sarla's desk with the pallu of her sari and rearranging them in a straight line.

Sarla opened the envelope and removed the card. It showed a person lying by a waterfront in the dead of night. Face down, naked body half covered by a red sheet, he had ten swords sticking out of his back. The note inside this one too said, 'All good things come to an end.' Radhi heard a quick intake of breath, but other than that Sarla's face betrayed no emotion.

'This is a joke,' she declared, 'some horrid, elaborate prank someone's playing on us, Kiran. Don't bother yourself about it.'

'Prank?' Kiran's eyes widened. 'I don't believe that for a second, Sarla!' She turned to Radhi. 'Would *you* call this a prank?' she asked, then without waiting for an answer she turned back to Sarla. 'This has gone on long enough now! What I don't understand is why you aren't taking it seriously.'

'Who said I'm not?' asked Sarla.

'Well, what are you doing about it? Can we at least visit a tarot card reader and see what these cards mean?!'

'I've asked Hansa to look into it,' said Sarla.

'You have?' Kiran blinked. 'Good.'

Sarla nodded. 'Let's wait to see what she comes up with. In the interim, don't worry about it. It's just a silly distraction.'

Before Kiran could protest, Radhi asked, 'Were your cards different from Sarla Aunty's?'

'Different cards. But same message.' Kiran was now pacing the floor. Just then there was a knock at the door and a young woman entered the room. She looked like Kiran in every way except that she had thicker hair and was wearing a summer dress with very high heels. 'Ma, that Bhavana ben is asking for you again. She's creating a fuss—' She halted mid-sentence, noticing the sombre expressions on Kiran's and Sarla's faces. 'What is it?' she asked, looking from one to the other.

Kiran pointed to the red envelope and the tarot card lying face down on the desk.

'Oh, again?' The young woman snatched it and gasped when she saw the impaled man. 'How ghastly! I am positive this is from that dreadful woman downstairs!'

'Come now, Zarna,' cautioned Sarla, 'let's not make accusations on the fly. Let's think this through.'

'I have thought about this! It makes perfect sense! That woman opens her pseudo matrimonial bureau downstairs and a few months later we start receiving these!' Zarna waved the card and envelope in front of them. 'She's clearly trying to spook us out!'

Sarla shook her head. 'We'll talk about this later. Didn't you want your mother for something?' Then looking at Kiran, who was twirling the end of her sari agitatedly, Sarla said gently, 'Kiran, if you are too upset, I could see to Bhavana ben . . .'

Kiran shook her head as if clearing it. 'No, no,' she said and scurried out of the room, her daughter trailing behind her.

Sarla tucked her hair behind her ear, removed her heavy-looking gold studs and placed them on the desk, gingerly rubbing her earlobes.

'You don't really think it's a joke, do you?' asked Radhi.

Sarla sighed. 'I don't know . . . but I can't tell Kiran that. She can't handle it. She'll just have a meltdown. I can't have her interacting with clients in that frame of mind.'

'What about the police? Can't they help?'

'Good heavens, no! I don't want their help!' Sarla looked horrified. 'Do you know why people come to us, Radhi? It's our reputation. In our business that's everything. I couldn't risk it for this. Besides, don't worry, I'm handling it in my own way.'

She picked up her phone and asked the receptionist to come see her. Then she hastily gathered all the red envelopes and tarot cards lying scattered on her desk and swept them into a drawer before Juhi entered the cabin.

'Juhi, this is Radhika. She's writing about Soul Harmony and what we do here. I would like you to show her around, introduce her to everyone and tell her a little bit about how it all works.'

Young, probably in her early twenties, Juhi was dressed smartly in a knee-length grey skirt and a white, lace-edged sleeveless top. She was a little too thin perhaps, but her black hair was thick and lustrous and her eyes were dark and doe-like, making her face distinctly attractive.

'Yes, ma'am,' she said to Sarla, and then smiling at Radhi, she said, 'let me first show you the desk I've cleared for you.'

As she led Radhi towards one of the desks at the centre of the office, she pointed out the various frosted glass doors lining the corridor. 'That first one on the left belongs to Kiran ben and her daughter, Zarna. The smaller one beside it is Alpa's; she is our wedding planner. Beside her is our utility room. It's got our printer and the filing cupboards and all that. And these,' Juhi stopped at the white desks in the centre of the office, 'are for the people who come in just a few times a week.' A man in a blue shirt with a bulbous nose looked up at them curiously. 'For instance, Girish, our accountant.' Juhi smiled at the man before pointing to the empty desk behind him. 'And that one's for our wedding-card designer, but she usually comes on Mondays and Wednesdays. And this one, right here, is the one you can use.'

Radhi placed her bag and laptop on the empty desk assigned to her before following Juhi past Sarla's large office. 'And this here is where our astrologer, Neetu ben, sits,' Juhi said stopping outside the cabin to Sarla's right. 'And the one next to it is for Hansa ben, who is in charge of our "research".' As she said the last word, she made air quotes with her fingers.

Radhi raised a curious eyebrow and Juhi smirked. 'You'll see,' was all she said. Then pointing to the room with a white door right at the end, she said, 'And that is our pantry. So, who would you like to start with first?'

Before Radhi could answer, a horse-faced woman in a purple salwar-kurta came walking briskly towards them. Her white-streaked, straw-like hair was held together in a loose bun with a golden butterfly clip, and thick spectacles framed an otherwise unadorned face.

'Hansa ben,' Juhi stopped her as she tried to go around them. 'One moment please.'

'I need to go see Sarla ben,' said Hansa as she glanced at Radhi curiously. 'She wanted to talk to me, no?'

'Yes, yes,' said Juhi, 'but I just wanted to quickly introduce you to Radhika Zaveri; she is writing about Soul Harmony. Sarla ben wants all of us to talk to her about the work we do for the bureau.'

Behind her glasses, Hansa had sharp little eyes, which were now flitting up and down as she took in Radhi's finely tailored Jaipuri jacket, the gleaming Bengal tiger on her Sabyasachi belt and the delicate silver peacocks dangling from her ears. It was such a probing glance that Radhi had the distinct feeling that the woman had calculated the cost of everything she was wearing and put a price tag on her.

'Hmph,' Hansa snorted. 'I'm not much of a talker, but you can come along to see how I work if you like. I'm going to be stepping out in some time.'

'That would be great!' Radhi said.

As she watched Hansa make her way to Sarla's cabin, she asked Juhi, 'What exactly does she do?'

'Oh, you'll see soon enough,' said Juhi, grinning at Radhi.

Radhi leaned against a white Hyundai Accent in what she hoped was a discreet spot and looked around furtively before lighting a cigarette. She was waiting below the building for Hansa, who was going to meet her there in a few minutes. As she drew in a deep and satisfying puff, she thought about how she hated sneaking around like this. It took half the joy out of it, but she knew the rules of her close-knit, privileged neighbourhood well enough. The residents of Temple Hill simply did not smoke. That is, not in full view. Not in broad daylight. And certainly not if they were women. Smoking in public led to immediate aspersions being cast upon your character and upbringing. And anyone who didn't fully grasp exactly how one's parents were to blame for one's nicotine addiction had no business being on Temple Hill. Radhi took another deep puff and checked her watch. For her part, she couldn't give a rat's ass about what people thought of her or her values, but she couldn't risk word getting out to her sister. The families in this part of town had lived here for generations. People knew people. And people talked. If her sister found out that Radhi had started smoking again, she would be terribly disappointed. After Radhi's divorce, when she was smoking two packs a day, it was her sister who had begged, bullied and blackmailed her into quitting. For a long time after that Radhi hadn't touched a cigarette. But a year ago, when her relationship with Mackinzey ended abruptly, she had picked up a pack in a weak moment. Now she was terrified of admitting it to her sister. She was halfway through her cigarette when she heard a woman's agitated voice.

'She said the exact same thing again. And the other one won't even deign to meet with me. Best matchmakers, my foot! I wouldn't hire them as maids!'

Surprised at the viciousness of the tone more than the language, Radhi crushed her cigarette with a shoe and came out from her spot behind the car to see who it was. But the woman had just got into a waiting red sedan and all Radhi managed to see was an arm with an orange sleeve and a dozen gold bangles as the car door was pulled shut.

3

Hansa stepped out of the building and stretched out an arm to hail a taxi.

'We can take my car,' said Radhi, pointing to the opposite side of the road where Ramzan bhai, her driver, was waiting. 'Should I call for it?'

Hansa turned around to glance at the blue BMW and, smirking, put out her arm again. 'That won't do,' she said.

When they were inside a cab, Radhi glanced at Hansa. She was scratching her face with one hand and going through the messages on her phone with the other. Clearly, the work that she had stepped out to do wasn't big on presentation. Her bun was even messier than before, and her purple kurta now sported a tea stain.

'So what kind of research do you do?' asked Radhi, making sure not to lean against the damp fabric of the seat cover, which, since December wasn't a monsoon month, could only be wet because the previous passenger had sweated into it. Radhi's jacket, which had seemed chic when she gave herself a once-over before leaving home that morning, was proving to be impractical without the perennial bubble of air conditioning she was used to.

'Research? Is that what they are calling it?' Hansa smirked in her humourless way again. 'Well, I suppose it *is* that in a way. I try to dig up information on the boys and girls whose biodatas we receive.' She glanced at Radhi to see if the younger woman was familiar with the term.

Radhi nodded, then asked, intrigued, 'So you conduct a background check?'

'Exactly. Biodatas are all very well. They give you the basic facts. Age, height, education — that sort of thing. But people are not a neat sum of their degrees and vital stats. They are more complicated than that, you know.'

Radhi nodded. The few biodatas Juhi had shown her earlier that morning were thorough when it came to a person's family lineage and horoscope details but completely lacking in personality.

'Besides,' Hansa continued, 'the question to ask is how accurate that information is in the first place.'

'You mean to say people lie on their biodatas?' asked Radhi, fishing about in her handbag for a tissue paper to wipe the light film of sweat which had begun to form between her nose and her upper lip.

Hansa frowned. 'Not lie so much as stretch the truth. You know how it is . . . anything can be made to look good if you embroider it a bit. Of course, alternatively, they may simply choose not to mention something. Lying by omission.'

'Oh bhaiya,' she said, leaning to address the cab driver, 'go down Moksha and stop once you cross Cotton Green Park.'

One of the oldest and greenest neighbourhoods in the city, Temple Hill comprised four gently undulating slopes, Karma, Moksha, Teertha and Shloka, which led up to the main Temple Hill Road where a 120-year-old Jain temple dedicated to Lord Adishwarnath stood proud and resplendent, its divinity intact despite the trappings of modern life that surrounded it. This was perhaps what Radhi found most remarkable about the neighbourhood she had grown up in. It was steeped in history, with ancient temples nestled between bakeries and boutiques and twelfth-century shrines flanking cafes and art galleries, but the places of worship weren't relegated to being tourist attractions on maps — rather they were a rich and throbbing part of everyday life, holding sway over Temple Hill and its many devout with an effortless confidence.

Radhi tilted her face towards the window, grateful for the slight breeze that was flowing in now that the cab had picked up speed. 'So have you ever caught someone who wasn't, say, "forthright" on their biodata?' she asked after a while.

'Oh, plenty of times! It's the parents really. They either want to gloss things over and make their children sound perfect. Or they're simply not aware of what their children get up to. There was one guy whose biodata said Jain, but his parents had no idea that when they were out, their son would order in chicken kebabs and chicken biryani and whatnot!'

Radhi, who was a Jain herself and knew exactly how passionate her community was about ahimsa, knew that non-vegetarian food was a deal-breaker.

'I don't think Sarla ben has any clients who are ambivalent about *that*,' Hansa said. 'Not only the parents but most of the girls and boys themselves are pretty clear that they want vegetarian partners.'

Radhi nodded. She was a strict vegetarian herself and it had been one of the few things Mackinzey had never really understood about her. For him, food was food, closely connected to sustenance and pleasure. Its ethical and moral complexities, which were woven into the very fabric of her culture, had always been a little lost on him.

'But how do you find such information in the first place?'

'You'll see soon enough,' said Hansa, who was clearly enjoying this interview despite her claims of not being much of a talker. 'I have my ways.'

'Stop here, bhaiya,' she said to the driver, handing him a fifty-rupee note.

The taxi halted outside a lane flanked by a row of shanties covered by tin roofs and blue tarpaulin. Radhi got out and narrowly missed stepping into a heap of cow dung on the ground. Up ahead, tied with a rope to an electric pole was the bovine presumably responsible for it. A pair of plastic chairs had been set up near the entrance of the lane, where a roadside barber was giving a client a shave while another waited his turn.

'This is also Temple Hill, you know,' Hansa said, as Radhi looked dubiously at the flies buzzing over a small pile of wet garbage in one corner. The vegetable peels, eggshells and other rotting items, which she did not dare inspect closely, were emanating a putrid smell into the air.

'This is Kanchi Nagar, isn't it?' Radhi sensed that Hansa was perhaps enjoying her discomfort.

Hansa nodded and took her phone from her purse to make a call.

Radhi knew that a lot of the cooks, drivers and maids who worked for the posh residents of Temple Hill rented or owned rooms in Kanchi Nagar, and that her own housekeeper, Lila, lived here. But Radhi had never come this far to the outskirts of Temple Hill and was appalled at how filthy the surroundings were. She resolved to go home and talk to Lila about it.

A man with tobacco-stained orange lips and a blue and white checked lungi walked up to them, a small cloth bundle tucked under his arm. Hansa fished around in her purse to come up with a two hundred rupee note, which she gave the man, who handed over the bundle in return. Then with the slightest of nods, he walked back into the narrow opening of the lane. The entire exchange had taken place without a single word spoken.

'Come,' Hansa said, turning to Radhi.

They walked past a tiny paan shop, two tailors' outlets specializing in 'alterations' and a repair store for home appliances until they reached a small, low-cost joint for South Indian fare. A poster at the door announced that customers were expected to share a table in case of a rush.

'I didn't get a chance to have breakfast today. Can we sit in there and talk?' asked Hansa.

It was clear that Hansa was expecting her to resist. But Radhi preferred a grimy hole-in-the-wall restaurant to the idea of being thought predictable. She may have had a privileged upbringing steeped in luxury, but she'd be damned if she let it become a disadvantage.

'Of course,' she answered brightly, walking in ahead of Hansa.

The place was bustling and noisy, with rows of steel tables arranged close together in neat lines. Instead of chairs, each table had two steel benches, chosen for their lack of back support to discourage people from getting too comfortable. The faster they moved on, the faster others could take their place. No sooner had the two women taken their seats than a waiter in a grey uniform slapped a laminated menu card on their table. It was a concise list of ten to twelve items, which Radhi appreciated. Regardless of where she was eating, Radhi liked her menus short. She believed it suggested a confident kitchen.

'What would you like?' Hansa turned the menu card to face Radhi. 'I'll have to order idlis. I got a root canal done yesterday and I think I'll be having baby food for the rest of my life!'

'A Mysore sada and a filter coffee please,' said Radhi to the waiter who had reappeared in exactly three minutes as if nobody could possibly take longer than that to make up their mind.

Hansa turned her attention to the cloth bundle lying on the seat next to her. Her fingers worked quickly to unravel the knot and with some relish she removed a crumpled white linen shirt, dark navy khakis, a red Lacoste collared T-shirt and a pair of ripped denims.

'See these clothes? They belong to a client's son. He has recently returned from the US and Sarla ben suggested we . . . what was it you called it, oh yes . . . do a background check.'

'So that man we met, he was their dhobi?' asked Radhi incredulously.

'Exactly. I asked him to show us some of the young man's clothes before he washed them.'

'But why? What can you possibly tell from this white shirt?'

'Come now, think about it for a minute . . . surely there are a few things you can see.'

Radhi picked up the shirt with her index finger and thumb, her nose wrinkled, not because the shirt smelled bad but because the idea of touching someone's unwashed garments was distasteful.

'Well, there's the brand name; it's an Armani shirt and so are those jeans. Clearly, he spends money on his clothes . . .'

Hansa nodded. 'That's a bit obvious. What else?'

A little irritated at Hansa's condescending tone, Radhi sniffed the shirt. 'It smells of smoke . . . so either he was hanging out with a smoker or . . . he's a smoker himself.'

'Good, that's better.' said Hansa. 'What else?'

Radhi turned the shirt around this way and that, wondering what else there was to see.

'The collar,' she said, lifting it so that the underside was visible, 'it is completely frayed . . . and so are the cuffs . . . which means it has been washed a lot and that it's probably an old shirt.'

She picked up the collar of the red Lacoste T-shirt. Its underside was a much deeper red than the T-shirt itself. 'This one's been washed a lot too; its original colour has faded.'

Hansa was smiling now. 'Yes . . . so what does *that* tell us?'

Radhi frowned. 'I don't know . . . that he needs to go shopping? Or that maybe he is a careful spender?'

Hansa was nodding encouragingly. 'And why do you suppose that could be?'

'Come now,' said Radhi, beginning to see the direction Hansa was thinking in, 'you can't possibly conclude that he may have money problems because of a couple of old shirts.'

'True,' said Hansa, putting the clothes away as the waiter approached with their food, 'it may be nothing. But at the very least it has opened up a direction for us in which to dig further.'

While the waiter placed their food and coffee on the table, Radhi went to the steel sink situated in the corner next to the kitchen to wash her hands. There was a damp hand towel hanging from a napkin holder which she looked at doubtfully before wiping her hands on the back of her jeans. Feeling a little icky at having rifled through someone's dirty laundry, she rubbed her hands with a big blob of hand sanitizer from her purse for extra measure. When she returned to the table, Hansa had begun eating. She clearly had no such qualms.

The food was simple and fresh. Radhi's dosa was sprinkled liberally with ghee and gunpowder. It was served with generous dollops of tangy tomato and coconut chutneys and a piping hot bowl of sambhar.

Hansa had ordered Kanchipuram idlis and kesari bhat topped with pineapple and cashews.

After they had enjoyed the first few bites of their food in silence, Hansa said, 'There are a lot of other things you can tell from clothes, you know. Sometimes they smell of perfume and you can tell if it's a nice, expensive one.

Sometimes they've got stains and you can see what they've been eating or drinking. Often I find things in the pockets, bills, receipts, ticket stubs, valet parking tokens, wrappers, soiled tissues, money, which I obviously keep, and all sorts of other knick-knacks.'

Radhi smiled when Hansa said she pocketed the money but quickly realized that the older woman wasn't joking.

'Pockets are a veritable gold mine. Sometimes from a single bill you can tell what restaurant someone's been to, what they ordered, when they went, how much they spent, and if you care to dig deeper, you can even land up at the restaurant and find out who they went with!'

While she spoke Hansa had finished her idlis, pushed her plate aside and started on the halwa. She glanced at Radhi's dosa, which was also almost done, and waved at the waiter to bring their bill.

'This was interesting.' Radhi took one last sip of her filter coffee. 'I'd never thought about how much clothes could give away.'

'Oh, but this is the least of it,' said Hansa clearly flattered. 'Apart from the dhobis, I am also in touch with cooks and maids and drivers and all sorts of other support staff that you people of Temple Hill employ. You'd be surprised at how much they know about you. And even more by how much they're willing to tell!'

She said the last bit with a grim relish, just as the waiter placed a steel plate with the bill and bowls of sweetened saunf and roasted coriander seeds before them. Radhi reached for the bill. 'Let me get this. You've been really generous with your time.'

Hansa took a handful of the saunf and smiled. When the waiter had returned their change and they were making their way out, Radhi noticed that Hansa picked up the bill and slipped it into her purse. It occurred to her that Hansa would probably show it as an expense and claim a reimbursement from the bureau.

'So . . . you are actually a detective,' said Radhi.

They had returned the bundle of clothes to the dhobi and were now in a cab on their way back to Soul Harmony.

'PI.' Hansa gave her a sidelong glance. 'I like to think of myself as a private investigator.'

'But isn't it very time-consuming to do this for all your clients?'

'It is, which is why we don't do it for everyone. There's a special charge for it. And not all clients feel the need. Sometimes, though, we do it of our own accord. Either Sarla ben or Kiran ben may request more information on one of their clients.'

'Oh bhaiya, stop here, one second,' said Hansa suddenly to the cab driver. 'I'll just be back,' she said to Radhi and jumped out of the taxi.

Radhi watched her as she walked up to a paanwala. The sign above the shop had the painting of an impressive black handlebar moustache which bore more than a passing resemblance to the paanwala sitting inside the shop. As she watched Hansa speaking to him, Radhi's phone rang.

'Miloni's sangeet. Day after. You remember, no?' said Madhavi as soon as Radhi had answered the phone.

'Obviously, di,' said Radhi, who had completely forgotten about her cousin's wedding festivities.

'Please, Radhi,' Madhavi brushed off Radhi's lie matter-of-factly. 'So how's it going with Sarla Aunty? Helpful?'

Radhi smiled. She had stopped marvelling at how her sister always knew what she was thinking and simply accepted it as a way of life. 'Yes, very! She's given me access to all her staff and is even going to set up meetings with a few clients.'

'Good. She always comes through, no? Remember how she took us to her Mahabaleshwar bungalow the winter after mom and dad passed away?'

'Yes, and insisted we go strawberry picking with her even though neither of us was in the mood.'

'It couldn't have been easy dealing with us. Me crying constantly and you angry with everything and everyone all the time. But she didn't let up.'

Both women were silent for a few moments.

'That strawberry jam we made with her . . . is the best I've ever had.'

'Me too . . . I don't think we told her that, though,' said Radhi.

'No, we didn't . . .' Madhavi agreed. 'Will you tell her that I was remembering her and that I said hi?'

'I will, di.'

'Let's go, bhaiya,' Hansa got into the cab and instructed the driver, just as Radhi hung up the phone.

'Didn't get yourself a paan?' Radhi noticed Hansa had come back empty-handed. 'No.' Hansa shook her head and proceeded to look outside the window, quiet and preoccupied all the way back.

4

A man was sitting in the waiting area when Radhi and Hansa walked in. He seemed about fifty, with oiled hair and the top three buttons of his faded blue shirt open, revealing a gold chain with a Sai Baba pendant entangled in matted grey chest hair. His general appearance was scruffy and seemed out of place in the posh office. Hansa gave a little start when she saw him but recovered herself quickly.

'Juhi, will you come see me before you leave for the day?' she said, stopping at Juhi's desk. Then without waiting for a reply, she gave the man a nod, indicating that he should follow her.

'Who was that?' Radhi asked once Hansa and the man had disappeared down the corridor.

Juhi shrugged. 'Probably one of her "sources". So? How was it? Useful? Interesting?'

'Both!'

She smiled. 'Who would you like to talk to next?'

'You, actually. Before I meet anyone else, I thought you could give me a little overview of how things work.'

Juhi checked her watch. 'I need to be here at the reception for at least an hour more, then I can take my lunch break and we can chat. Why don't you meet Alpa, our wedding planner?

I know for a fact that she doesn't have any appointments this morning.'

Alpa's cabin, if it could be called such, was a small, windowless room with just enough space for a desk, two chairs and a chest of drawers. However, she had done an excellent job of decorating it so that one hardly noticed the lack of natural light. In one corner, there was a tall plant stand with three shelves, each of which held a tray of little succulents, bamboos and ferns. The chest of drawers was covered with a mustard jute runner on which she had placed scented candles, a ceramic lamp, a teapot and other tasteful little knick-knacks. There were frames on the walls, but instead of photos of couples, these featured quotes and witticisms on marriage and wedded life.

Alpa had appeared annoyed at being interrupted when Juhi had knocked on her door to introduce them.

'Is it a client?'

'No but . . .'

'One of my vendors?'

'No, it's a—'

'Juhi, please, not right now. I'm in the middle of ten things here.'

But once Juhi had explained that Radhi was doing a profile on Soul Harmony, the door had flown wide open, and her entire demeanour had transformed.

'Can I offer you some water? Tea? Coffee? Coke? Is the AC too cold? Will you be needing a picture of me, as well?' she asked Radhi, all in one breath, patting her hair self-consciously at the same time. 'I had no idea I was going to be doing an interview today or else I would've worn something . . . a little more glamorous.' She glanced down at her sophisticated yellow linen tunic and white cutwork palazzos.

She was an attractive woman of average build and seemed in her late twenties. She had short, extremely silky hair which she wore stylishly pinned to one side.

'I'm not taking photographs of anybody right now. You can email me a nice picture of yourself later,' Radhi assured her.

'Let me just tidy the table.' Alpa attempted to clear the catalogues, files and papers from her desk. 'I really wish Sarla ben had told me about this before . . . I'd be more prepared.'

'No, don't,' said Radhi. 'I'd love to see all of this. For instance, is this a themes catalogue?' She pointed to a large binder that was open to what looked like a Rajasthani mahal.

'Yes!' Alpa pulled the binder towards her and ran her hand fondly over the glossy print of the pink stone turrets. 'This is for our royal weddings. We have everything from intimate havelis and heritage forts to majestic palaces with sprawling, landscaped lawns. We customize things depending on the number of guests and the budget you're working with.'

Radhi turned the pages of the catalogue to see pictures of grooms arriving on horses with embroidered red velvet saddles, in vintage Jaguars adorned with lush drapes of roses and jasmine, and even atop elephants, sitting under zari-edged umbrellas studded with semiprecious stones.

'Though if I say so myself, royal weddings are a bit passé now,' Alpa said, then her eyes widened and she put her hand to her mouth as if she'd realized she'd made a mistake. 'Please don't quote me on that, we make our biggest commissions on these Rajasthani weddings. And,' she said, looking even more alarmed now, 'please don't quote me on that either!'

When Radhi had assured her that she wouldn't, Alpa continued, 'What I meant was that these days young people don't want the palaces and beaches. They are looking for unique ideas. For instance, a few months ago we organized a wedding inside a wildlife sanctuary. Accommodation for the guests was in luxury camps and the sangeet had the couple and their friends dancing by a bonfire. We also arranged for guests to take a safari into the national park in their free time. And can you guess what the wedding favours were?' She paused, her eyes twinkling, then without waiting for an answer, she continued, 'Binoculars! Isn't that just apt? The wedding photographer and I had the most fabulous time!'

'Alpa?' The door opened a crack and Hansa poked her head in. 'Oh, sorry,' she said when she saw Radhi sitting with Alpa, 'I didn't realize you were with someone.'

'No problem. How about I come and find you in some time?' Alpa was polite enough, but there was an edge to her voice.

'I'll be in my room.' Hansa nodded and shut the door behind her.

Alpa gave Radhi a bright smile. 'So where were we? Oh, yes!' She leaned across her desk and opened the chest of drawers to pull out a few folders.

'See, these are the menus of some of the caterers we work with. Anything, from any part of the world — Mexican fajitas, Mongolian stir-fries, Cantonese chow mein — if there's a vegetarian version, it's in here.' Alpa thumped one of the heavy files proudly before handing it to Radhi. 'The Gujaratis on Temple Hill are a bit nuts when it comes to one-upmanship over food!'

Radhi smiled in agreement. She knew exactly how integral food was to their culture. For a people who were big on the pursuit of the non-violent way of life, this cut-throatedness over who hosted better dinners always amused Radhi.

'And this, right here, is the magic our florists do,' Alpa continued, waving another folder at Radhi. Then she brought out a slim red file from one of the drawers in her desk. 'Oh, and these are some of my signature décor ideas. I've designed these myself. This is not part of my job at Soul Harmony. It's just something I do in my free time.'

Radhi took the file from her. It had superbly detailed, hand-sketched designs of mandaps. Each mandap, though similar in form, looked completely different from the other. While one was bedecked in pale pink carnations and lemon-green organza drapes, another had the entire canopy made of yellow and orange marigolds and still a third had a resplendent peacock mounted on each of the four pillars, constructed entirely out of blue orchids.

'All of this is so interesting! May I take them to my desk outside and spend some time looking at them?' Radhi looked up from the file.

'Actually, you can sit right here.' Alpa got up from her seat. 'I have a few calls to make, so I'll be right outside in the lobby. You let me know if you need anything else.'

Radhi thanked her as she left the room, then turning her attention to the folders and files in front of her, she brought out her golden polka-dotted diary to make her notes.

'I hope you like Thai.' Radhi held up a food delivery bag in front of Juhi. 'I've taken the liberty of ordering us some lunch.'

It was nearly 1.30 p.m. Radhi had spent almost an hour going over Alpa's folders and then came out to find Juhi.

'I've never had Thai food, it's a little like Chinese food, isn't it?' asked Juhi.

'A bit, I suppose . . .' Radhi smiled.

'Then I'm sure I'll love it!' Juhi picked up her phone and purse from the reception desk and stepped out from behind it. 'You shouldn't have ordered anything, you know, I carry my lunch from home . . . but doesn't matter now, I'll just give my lunch to our peon, Jeevan, he's always eying my food anyways. Let's take this into the lunchroom. Sarla ma'am hates any lingering smell of food in the office.' Juhi led the way down the corridor and stopped outside a plain white door beside Hansa's cabin. The lunchroom was a small, grey room with one window and just enough space for a round glass table, three plastic chairs and a platform with a microwave, a two-burner stove, a coffee machine and a water filter. In a small cupboard above were assorted plates and cutlery. Unlike the rest of the office, which was heavily air-conditioned, this room was hot and stuffy.

'Is that the fastest this can go?' Radhi studied the lethargic ceiling fan. She had begun to sweat. Radhi and Madhavi were like their dad — built for cooler climes, they used to always tell their mother. Radhi took off her jacket and draped it on the back of her chair.

'Let me ask Jeevan to bring you a chilled drink.' Juhi took out her phone to send him a text.

'I am going to switch on the record button on my phone so that we can eat and talk at the same time. Does that work?' asked Radhi as she began opening the various containers and the fragrance of lemongrass filled the small room.

'Sure,' said Juhi eying the food appreciatively.

Radhi served her some jasmine rice topped with a fresh green vegetable curry full of brightly coloured peppers, broccoli and tofu and some pad thai sprinkled liberally with roasted peanuts and coriander.

'So what's your role here?' she asked as she handed Juhi the plate and began serving herself.

'Well, I started out as Sarla ma'am's assistant, and then last year, I began handling the reception desk as well.'

'And how long have you been with her?' asked Radhi.

'Oh more than half my life! My aai used to be her cleaning lady. If not for ma'am, I would've been one as well! Ever since

I was ten or eleven, aai would take me to their home to help her out. She'd ask me to fold clothes or dust, something light like that. But Sarla ma'am would always scold her. "There should be a book in her hands, not a mop," she'd always say.'

Juhi took a few bites of her rice before continuing, 'When I turned sixteen and finished school, my parents wanted me to start working full-time. Sarla ma'am objected. Said she would pay my college fees and buy my books and anything else that I might need, but my father said that the family needed the extra income and I had to work. I had two younger brothers who needed to be put through school. I remember crying so much. That's when Sarla ma'am said that she would hire me, provided they let me go to college. Luckily, my parents agreed. The income was less than what I would've made if I worked full-time but it was safer to send me to someone they knew well rather than have me work at a stranger's house.'

The door opened and Jeevan entered holding a tray with two glasses of Coke.

'Thanks, Jeevan, you can keep that here.' Juhi cleared a spot on the table where he could place the drinks. 'Have you had lunch?'

'Not yet.' The man glanced self-consciously at Radhi. He had a baby face, with chubby cheeks and hardly any facial hair. He looked eighteen or nineteen tops.

'Wait, one minute.' Juhi turned around and retrieved a steel lunch box from her bag, which was hanging behind her chair. 'You're going to love this dudhi ki subzi,' she said, handing the dabba to Jeevan. 'Avoid the chutney, though.'

Jeevan nodded as he made to leave the room.

'Make sure you clean my lunch box properly before you give it back,' Juhi called after him.

The young man smiled and blushed as he shut the door behind him.

'Taking you on like that was really nice of Sarla Aunty,' Radhi said.

Juhi put her fork down and looked at Radhi. 'It was . . . her kindness changed my life.' Then she smiled and picked up her fork. 'This noodle dish . . . it's very good . . . what's it called, again?'

'Pad thai.' Radhi served her another helping of it. 'One of my favourites as well.'

'Paad thaayee,' Juhi repeated it as if trying to memorize it for future meals. 'Anyways, so after college, I'd go to Sarla ma'am's house and help her out with whatever needed to be done . . . like cleaning methi or sorting the cutlery drawer, that sort of thing. But soon Sarla ma'am realized that I could be equally helpful with some of her office work. So then instead of sending me to the kitchen, she began calling me into her study. I would sort the biodatas we received and file them, make phone calls to vendors, write invoices — those days she didn't have such a big office — and her son was still young . . . so she used to bring a lot of the work home. When I finished college, she offered me a full-time job here and I took it!' she said, smiling before taking another big bite of her noodles.

Radhi smiled back; she was enjoying watching Juhi eat. She was putting the food away with a speed and vigour that Radhi found refreshing. Finally, with a satisfied sigh, Juhi pushed her plate aside.

'So how was it with Alpa ma'am? Did she get off her high horse?'

'Yes, she was very helpful in fact. Showed me all her catalogues and folders. Some great stuff in there.'

Juhi wiped her hand with some tissue and stuck it deep into her bag to retrieve a handful of Cadbury Eclairs. 'Dessert?' She offered them to Radhi.

Radhi took one of the hard and chewy toffees with a smile.

'But I don't know why Alpa ma'am was acting all so busy in the first place.' Juhi unwrapped a toffee for herself and threw the golden wrapper in the bin. 'The number of weddings we plan has significantly gone down these days.'

'Oh, why is that?' asked Radhi surprised.

'No idea. I overheard Sarla ma'am and Kiran ma'am talking about it a few weeks ago. But listen,' she added, suddenly remembering why Radhi was here, 'please don't put that in your book.'

'Of course not,' Radhi reassured her, switching off the record button on her phone.

So? How was it at the matrimonial bureau? Feel like getting married, yet?

Radhi's phone pinged, and she smiled at the message from Nishant. Before she could reply, he sent another.

Because if you are . . . I might know a good boy 😊

Radhi and Nishant had begun dating a few months ago. He had been set up with her cousin Prachi but had decided he liked Prachi's cousin more. She knew he had messaged in jest, but some part of her recognized that he cared deeply for her. Far deeper than she currently allowed herself to feel. She hoped that in time this would change. She responded with a smiley and a promise to call him later that night.

A couple of hours later Radhi was at home sitting in her favourite bottle-green winged chair with her feet propped up on the centre table and her laptop on a cushion on her lap. Though she had a quiet study to work from, in the evenings she preferred to write in the living room with its cheerful potted plants, large French windows and her beautiful Raza paintings on the walls.

'How was your day, didi?' Lila, Radhi's housekeeper, asked as she offered Radhi a cup of ginger tea.

'Surprisingly, fun.' Radhi looked up from her notes to smile at Lila. 'It's not easy, this business of setting people up.'

'I wouldn't think so. Finding people their life partners is such a big responsibility.' Lila took her customary seat on the window ledge with a cup of tea. 'I wouldn't do it, you know. Heaven forbid, you fix the wrong people up. What then? They'll curse you for as long as you live. And they would mean it too.' Lila shuddered. 'Can you imagine that on your head? An unhappy marriage? Or worse, a divorce? I wouldn't know how to sleep at night!'

Radhi took a sip of her tea and considered what Lila had just said. Her mind went back to the tarot cards that Sarla and Kiran had received. She wondered if that's what they were. The result of a miserable marriage.

'My neighbour's son works for them, you know,' Lila continued.

'Where? Soul Harmony?'

'I think so. A Sarla Seth runs it, no?'

Radhi nodded.

'His name is Jeevan. He is an office boy there.'

'Oh, I met him today.'

'You did?' Lila put her cup down excitedly. 'Oh, didi, you must put in a good word for him, he is such a sweet boy. My neighbour will be so grateful.'

'I will,' Radhi promised, leaning forward to take a few chips. 'Speaking of neighbours, I wanted to ask you if you would consider moving out of Kanchi Nagar? I was there this morning and I think . . .' Radhi struggled to find the right words which wouldn't offend her proud housekeeper. 'I think you can do better,' she said finally. 'I would, of course, help.'

'You're always helping me, didi.' Lila got up, empty teacup in hand. 'But I'm fine there. We are happy.'

'But think of Shiv.' Radhi handed Lila her own teacup and empty bowl. 'You could get a one-room kitchen, with your own bathroom. Some place quieter, where he could study better?'

A few years ago, Lila had left an abusive marriage and she now lived with her mother and nine-year-old son, Shiv.

Lila shook her head. 'It does sound great, didi, but our relatives and friends live there. Our entire lives revolve around Kanchi Nagar. What would we do all alone in some fancy building? Sure, we would have twenty-four-hour running water, but really how many times a day are we going to bathe?' She gave Radhi a fond smile. 'You're sweet to always think of me, though.'

Radhi! How did it go today? At the matrimonial bureau? Interesting? Exciting? Earth-shattering? Listen, I know you weren't too keen on this arranged-marriage project. But now that you've been there, please tell me you've changed your mind? Honestly, I think you're only resisting it because I'm pushing you for it. And I know, you don't like to be forced. But seriously, what's not to love about this idea? It's relevant. Nuanced. Has the human-interest angle that you always go after. And it's from a culture you're intimately familiar with. Now don't you deny it. You know I'm right. Sometimes I think if I weren't a literary agent, I would've made such a fab therapist. Speaking of, have you found a good one in Mumbai? I know you were going to talk to the one your doc recommended. So did you? Please don't put it off.

I love you.

What? You know I do.

XOXO

George

Radhi stared at George's email in frustration. Picking up her phoenix-shaped lighter from the seat beside her, she walked to the window and lit a cigarette. Below her, the sea was drowsy, exhausted from a day of flinging itself at the rocks. And the sky had turned amethyst. It was a pity, Radhi thought, that the sun never got to see the sky at its most stunning, having disappeared by the time the sky turned jewel-toned.

Again, George hadn't told her what she really wanted to know. George was her agent and a very dear friend. But at the moment, she was annoyed with him. A few months ago, after a terrible dry spell of two years, Radhi had finally written a book. A murder mystery. It was very different from the critically acclaimed literary fiction she had written before, but when she started working on it, it had seemed to flow so naturally that she knew she was onto something. When she sent George the first draft, he had promised to read it quickly.

While my team and I go through it, why don't you get started on something else? You've finally got your mojo back, please don't lose it again Radhi.

Radhi, who had also been terrified of exactly that, had wanted to begin work on another mystery. She already had ideas for the next book in what she hoped would be a series. But George had urged her to work on the book about arranged marriages.

This is commissioned work, Radhi, do this for the publishers, if not for me. Make your publishers happy.

Radhi knew her last interaction with her publishers hadn't been very professional. They had given her an advance for her next book and waited patiently for the manuscript. But after more than two years and at least half a dozen missed deadlines, when she'd had less than a page to show them, they had cancelled her contract. Thanks to George's relationship with them, they hadn't bad-mouthed her in the industry. But word did get out. And now she knew she had to earn the respect and trust of her peers again. Which is why she had agreed to do the arranged-marriage book. But she was annoyed with George for not having read her manuscript. He, more than anyone else, knew how hard it had been for her to start writing again. And he had to know how anxious she would be to hear back. So why hadn't he said anything? Unless . . . unless . . . horrified with the thought that had just occurred to her, Radhi hurried back to her laptop and clicked reply.

5

Wednesday

Radhi opened the door of the old-time elevator with one hand while balancing her laptop and a lunch box and a thermos of tea in the other. Sarla had told her that Jeevan opened the office by 9.30 a.m. to clean it, while the rest of the staff arrived an hour later. Radhi liked to start her day early. She had fixed up a meeting with Neetu, the astrologer, for eleven that morning, followed by another with Kiran at noon. But before that she wanted to go through some of the biodata files Juhi had shown her the previous day.

She could hear the faint sound of music when she got out of the elevator, which got louder as she approached the office of Soul Harmony. Jeevan was mopping the floor in the reception area.

'Is that K-pop?' She stood at the door surprised.

Startled, he turned around.

'Uh, yes . . . no . . . I don't know actually, ma'am. Juhi sent me the song. What's K-pop?' he asked, hitting the pause button on his phone, which was propped up on the reception desk.

'Music from South Korea,' said Radhi, then looking at his blank face she added, 'I think the band you were listening to is called BTS. But hey, please don't stop it on my account, I'll be working inside.'

'Oh, but I haven't cleaned in there yet.'

'That's fine, you can get there at your own pace, I'll just be at my desk.'

'One second, ma'am, hold on.' Jeevan hurried behind the reception desk. 'I'll just switch on the lights in there.'

Radhi smiled at the idea of Jeevan listening to K-pop. How different this new generation of support staff was compared to the cooks and cleaners her family had hired just two decades ago. Her mother's cook would watch Marathi film songs on the TV, which Radhi or Madhavi would have to help set up for him because all the buttons and dials were in 'that *bekaar* English' and too complicated for him. But these youngsters like Jeevan and Juhi had seen the inside of a classroom and that's what had made the difference. They had access to the internet and with that, the world. Slowly but surely, things were changing for them.

Radhi had gone down the red-walled corridor and crossed Sarla's cabin when something on the floor caught her eye. It was a small puddle of maroon in the shape of a shoe. Puzzled, she went closer, bent down to get a better look and gasped at the unmistakable smell of rusted iron. Blood.

It seemed to have seeped out from under the frosted glass door to the left of Sarla's cabin. Quickly, leaving her purse and things on the floor, Radhi walked up to the swinging door and tried to push it open, but it only moved a few inches. There seemed to be something blocking it. Next, she tried to pull the door towards her and it swung open freely. Without thinking, Radhi stepped inside the room and almost tripped. With a cry of shock, she steadied herself and stepped back. There, lying on her stomach, spreadeagled on the floor, her face turned away from Radhi, eyes wide open staring straight ahead to a point under her desk, lay Hansa Patani. Dead.

Gathering herself, Radhi swiftly bent to check her pulse and confirmed what she had already sensed. There was a bruise on the back of Hansa's head where the hair had become matted and stiff, from which blood had trickled down onto the floor and eventually out of the room. Radhi stood up and took a few steps back. She looked around, unsure of what to do first.

This wasn't the first time she had seen violent death up close. The first had been the mangled bodies of her parents when they had both died in the car crash from which she had so miraculously escaped unhurt. And the second had been last year when she had seen someone fall out of a window. Both deaths had been completely different and yet they had both produced a similar response in Radhi, not the urge to turn away but instead to stay, to look closer.

With a shudder, Radhi stepped out of the room and closed the door behind her. She wasn't sure what had horrified her more, the body or her own reaction. She got out her phone and dialled 100 for the police. After she had given them her name and address, she called Sarla and told her what had happened. Sarla had gone completely quiet for a few moments. So silent that Radhi had to check whether she was still there. But once she had recovered from her initial shock, she asked Radhi some quick questions and promised to be there in fifteen minutes. Radhi hung up and looked around. Her purse, laptop and thermos were still on the floor. She picked them up and put them on her desk. She could hear the sound of 'Dynamite' coming to her from the lobby where Jeevan was still cleaning, oblivious to what Radhi had found. She knew she should remain where she was and wait for the police to arrive, but she found she couldn't stay away.

Back in Hansa's room, lying beside her body, face down, exactly like Hansa, was an arm-sized statue of Nataraja, the god of dance. It looked heavy, made of metal and was most certainly what Hansa had been killed with. Kill. What a strange, alien word it was. Especially on quiet Temple Hill. And especially in this bright room flooded with sunlight. Unlike Alpa's cabin, this room was large and airy and had two French windows at eye level with swaying palm trees. But again, unlike Alpa's office, Hansa's room was almost bare, no paintings, picture frames or potted plants, its personality defined by its absolute lack of one. Radhi turned her attention to Hansa's wooden desk. There was a bunch of green files with names of what she assumed were clients written on the spine, a notepad, a phone and a pen holder with thin ball pens of the cheapest variety. There was also a square patch of discoloured wood where she assumed the Nataraja statue must have stood for a long time. The only thing of any interest and almost incongruous to the rest of the room were six delicate glass cats in different colours, arranged equidistant to each other, straight across the upper edge of the desk. Hansa's bag was hanging from an arm of her chair. Careful not to touch anything, Radhi walked over to the other side of the desk. Instead of facing Hansa's chair, the notepad was facing the opposite side. It was blank but a closer look revealed the impression of a floral, heart-shaped doodle and a phone number, which had most likely been written on the previous page. Radhi got out her phone and took a picture of the notepad. Then she took pictures of the desk, Hansa's body and the whole room. It occurred to Radhi that if someone had walked in at that moment and asked her what she was doing, she'd have found it hard to explain.

Bending down, she took a closer look at the wicker wastepaper bin. There was a used tissue paper, a banana peel, a couple of empty sugar sachets, a golden toffee wrapper, the stub of a bus ticket, a crumpled polythene bag and underneath it something shiny and purple that Radhi couldn't see properly. Radhi duck-walked to the other side of the dustbin to see if the purple item could be seen from that angle, but it couldn't. She knew she wasn't supposed to touch anything that would tamper with any fingerprint evidence, but something told her that the purple item wasn't trash. She looked around, wondering what she could use to lift the bag. There was no tissue box in sight and Radhi was not of the handkerchief-carrying generation. She went out and fetched two pens from her bag. Holding them like chopsticks, she gingerly lifted the polythene bag. Underneath was another glass cat, this one purple. Radhi dropped the bag and stood up puzzled, wondering what the animal was doing in the bin. The room didn't show signs of a scuffle. There was no mess or disarray. Whoever had hit Hansa with the statue had done it suddenly and from behind. Hansa had not seen it coming. She hadn't tried to block the blow or protect herself from her killer. How then had the glass animal been swept away into the bin? Radhi wondered who could've wanted the woman dead. And, more importantly, why?

She walked to the window and stood there for a moment looking outside. On the street below, the fruit sellers had just finished setting up their stalls. Artistically arranged pyramids of pears, pomegranates and oranges glistened proudly in the sun. Lycra-clad women in twos and threes were stepping out of a Zumba studio, laughing and chatting. Their good spirits, Radhi suspected, more a result of the endorphins released during the workout rather than genuine bonhomie. The temple-goers were rushing to the temples; the office-goers were rushing to theirs. The world below was bustling as usual. One little death of no consequence in its grand scheme of things.

'How well would you say you knew the victim?' the inspector asked Radhi.

They were sitting in Sarla's cabin and Inspector Gopi Shinde had just finished asking Radhi how she had found the body, what she had done after and why she had come to the office early. A young constable was sitting in a corner behind Shinde, taking notes. With his heavily pockmarked face and impressive pot belly, Inspector Shinde looked like he was in his late fifties though it was entirely possible that he was younger. He spoke broken English with a thick Marathi accent, and even though Radhi spoke in Marathi, he refused to switch to his mother tongue. This, Radhi noticed, was a new development.

They had crossed paths before. A few months ago, when her best friend's father had died by suicide, she had gone to the inspector with her theory that things may not be as straightforward as they seemed. He had scoffed at her then for watching too many police procedurals on Netflix — all in chaste Marathi. She wondered if he recognized her with her hair much longer than before. So far, he hadn't given any indication.

'We just met yesterday. I hardly knew Hansa ben,' said Radhi.

'And how did she seem to you? Did she seem stressed or worried about something?'

'Not really, no. But then again, I'm not the best judge.'

'Is there anything about yesterday you'd like to tell us?'

Radhi thought back to the previous day. She had spent a large part of her morning with Hansa but could think of nothing that was out of the ordinary — except of course Hansa's job profile, but that wasn't what the inspector was asking. Unconnected though, there *was* the nasty business with the tarot cards. But that wasn't her story to tell.

Radhi shook her head. 'I'm sorry, I wish I could be more helpful.'

'And where were you between six and eight last evening?'

'At home.'

'With? Kids? Husband? Parents?'

'I live alone,' Radhi said. 'However, my housekeeper was with me till about seven.'

The inspector jerked his head in a little upward motion and the constable jotted down something in her notebook. 'That's all for now, you're free to leave. Please send in . . .' he consulted a list in his hand, 'Kiran Shah. Also, I hope you're not planning on leaving town for the next few days, we might need to meet you again.'

Radhi nodded, but instead of getting up to leave, she continued sitting in the chair. 'Did you see the purple cat?'

'What?' The inspector frowned.

'The purple glass cat in the wastepaper basket. Did that seem . . . odd to you?'

The inspector's eyes narrowed. 'And why, may I ask, were you poking around in the dustbin?'

'I wasn't. Poking around, that is. It's a bright colour, it would be hard to miss.'

The inspector gave her an appraising look but didn't press the matter further. 'Yes, we are looking into it.'

'It's strange, isn't it?' Radhi pressed. 'Especially because there didn't seem to be any tussle?'

Shinde rolled his eyes heavenward. 'Deva re deva! Here we go again. I wasn't sure it was you at first, but now I am. I urge you, ma'am, with folded hands, to please not start this again. The last time you put all those ideas in your pregnant friend's head about her father's death. And what came of it? Tell me?'

Radhi remained silent, her lips pursed. There had been a murder. More than one, in fact. But as far as the police were concerned, nothing had come of it.

'Your conjectures are not helpful, ma'am. We do things very methodically here. Why has one of the cats fallen into the bin? Good question. But surely you agree that the bigger questions are who murdered that woman and why, and that's what I need to focus on. In any case, like we said, we're going to look into it. Was there anything else?'

Radhi knew from her past interactions with him that pushing the matter further was pointless. Shinde was a man of limited imagination. And besides, to be fair, he probably saw her as just another rich Gujarati woman with plenty of time on her hands. She thanked him and left the room.

The police had come in a couple of hours ago. They had combed through Hansa's office, or the crime scene, as they referred to it among themselves. A doctor had examined Hansa's body before two cops carried it away. Now a team was still working in her room, dusting for fingerprints, while another was searching through the other cabins. Shinde had just begun interviewing the staff, most of whom were huddled in a stunned, incredulous hush in the reception area outside. Sarla had asked Juhi to cancel all appointments for the day. She had given her cabin to the police for questioning and was sitting with Kiran and Zarna in their office. Radhi made her way there.

'Kiran ben, the police would like to see you next,' Radhi said on entering the room.

Kiran looked as if she had been crying. Her eyes were watery, and she was sniffling, a crumpled handkerchief pressed to her nose.

'Why me, first?' She looked anxiously from Sarla to Zarna. 'Shouldn't Sarla be speaking to them before me?'

'You are listed as partners, Mummy. They don't know that Sarla Aunty is the big boss,' Zarna said harshly. 'They'll probably call her next.'

Radhi was surprised at Zarna's tone but Kiran didn't seem to notice.

'Poor woman . . . Such a ghastly way to go.' She left the room, muttering to herself.

Zarna watched her mother's back with a frown. 'Jesus . . . what a thing to happen . . . and what timing!'

'What do you mean?' Radhi took Kiran's empty seat.

'It's a milestone year for us. We'll make a thousand matches! We've planned a party, we've planned . . . things.' Zarna paced the room. 'Now we're going to be in the news for all the wrong reasons!'

Sarla, who had been sitting quietly so far, staring at the floor, lost in thought, looked up. 'We'll figure it out, Zarna. Let's deal with one thing at a time.'

Zarna ignored her and continued to walk up and down the room. 'This is terrible . . . it's . . . aargh!' She shook her head, frustrated.

Radhi watched the restless woman and wondered at how swiftly life overtook death. For all the power dying held in people's imaginations, most went back to thinking about life mere moments after being confronted by death.

She turned her attention to Sarla. 'Will you be telling the police about the tarot cards?'

'No, of course not!' Zarna whirled around, snapping at Radhi before Sarla could answer. 'Isn't this enough of a scandal as is? Why would we add fuel to the fire? I hope you haven't gone and said something!'

'I haven't,' Radhi answered levelly, 'but shouldn't the police know? It may help them with their inquiries.'

'How? Whoever sent the tarot cards had a bone to pick with Mummy and Sarla Aunty. How does Hansa ben fit into it? There's zero connection. Besides, I overheard one of the cops saying that they think it's a robbery.'

'Robbery? But her bag was right there,' said Radhi.

'Yes, but the wallet is empty and her phone is missing,' said Zarna.

'Even the petty cash that she kept in the bottom drawer of her desk is gone,' added Sarla quietly.

Radhi studied Sarla — she seemed drawn and tense.

'Was it a lot? The money in the drawer?' asked Radhi.

'Not really . . . just some five–ten thousand rupees or so. Hansa kept it to pay her sources. When they came forward with the information she had requested, she'd give them a few hundred or thousand rupees depending on how valuable the information was and how difficult it had been to come by. I'd give her some money each month, and at the end of the month, she'd give me an account of how she'd used it,' said Sarla.

'But what if she'd spent it already?'

'Not likely, I gave it to her just two days ago.'

The three women were quiet for a few minutes, each lost in her own thoughts.

'I almost forgot,' Zarna said looking up from her phone, 'I had a meeting with that paper company that wanted to come by and show us samples of wedding cards. I'll just go and cancel that as well.'

Sarla nodded absent-mindedly and Zarna left the room.

'What is it, Aunty?' Radhi asked gently after a few minutes. 'I know it's been a hard day, but you seem preoccupied. Were you close with Hansa ben? Had she been with you for many years?'

Sarla sighed and straightened up. 'Not close. I wouldn't say that. She wasn't very chatty or open about her own life. But she'd worked with me for over ten years, there was a kind of trust there. We understood each other. And she was a good problem-solver. In fact . . .' Sarla glanced at the door to ensure they were really alone. 'In fact, I think she had managed to get to the bottom of this tarot card business.'

Radhi's lips rounded in a silent 'O'.

'She called me last evening saying she had some important information to share.'

'About the tarot cards?'

Sarla shook her head. 'She didn't say. We were going to meet this morning to discuss the other things she was working on; she said she'd tell me then.'

Radhi leaned back as the import of what Sarla was saying dawned on her. 'So Hansa ben's murder could be connected with the tarot cards, after all?'

The older woman looked back at her miserably.

6

'Sarla?' Kiran appeared at the door a few seconds later looking agitated. 'Will you please come with me? The police want to know Hansa's role at Soul Harmony. What exactly it involved. How she did what she did. Who she employed . . . I didn't know how much I should tell them . . . so I've just said that you deal with that side of things.' She studied Sarla's face anxiously. 'That was the right thing to do, wasn't it?'

'Yes, yes, quite right.' Sarla pushed her chair back to get up. Then with a weary glance at Radhi, she accompanied Kiran out of the room.

Something about what Kiran had just said nudged at Radhi's memory, but before she could put a finger on it, a harried-looking Juhi came to the door.

'Is Sarla ma'am or Kiran ma'am around?' She quickly scanned the empty room.

'Why? What's happened?'

'It's Divya, our wedding-card designer, she seems to be having some sort of a breathing problem.'

'What do you mean?' Radhi immediately got up to follow Juhi out of the room.

'She is sweating and breathing very, very fast,' said Juhi as she led Radhi down the corridor.

A small circle of people had gathered around the young woman.

'Just ask one of the police doctors about what we can do,' Alpa was saying as Radhi walked up to them.

'The medical team left with the body. Wait, I'm just googling this!' someone said.

'Excuse me. Excuse me.' Radhi tapped on a couple of shoulders before the ring of people parted to reveal a plump, bespectacled woman rocking back and forth, crying while at the same time breathing heavily.

'Please . . . don't crowd her,' Radhi said to no one in particular. 'Quickly, can anyone get hold of a paper bag?'

Radhi, who had suffered from anxiety ever since her parents' car crash, knew a panic attack when she saw one. She sat on the chair beside the woman and gently began to stroke her back. 'Sshh . . .' she said, 'it's all right . . . it's all right . . .'

The woman looked at Radhi but continued crying silently.

'Listen, what's happening to you is scary, but I promise it's not dangerous,' Radhi said gently. 'You just need to calm down.'

'My . . . chest . . . it's burning,' the woman tried saying in between deep breaths.

'Yes, that can happen . . . don't worry about it . . .' Radhi continued rubbing her back. 'C'mon, can you name three things you see?'

'Wh . . . what?' The woman looked at Radhi as if she was crazy.

'Any three things, c'mon . . . it will help.'

The woman looked around. 'Uhm . . . that magazine?'

Radhi glanced at the *WedMe Happy* magazine on the centre table, which incidentally had Sarla on the cover. The accompanying caption said, 'The Indian Wedding Awards Are Back'.

'Yes, that's good.'

'The carnations . . . and the red wall,' finished the woman.

'Good,' said Radhi. 'Now name any three things you can hear.'

It was a technique her therapist had taught her. Focusing on the physical world outside pulled her away from her spiralling thoughts and feelings and helped her stay in the present moment.

'The buzz of the air conditioner . . .'

'Very good.'

'All the people talking . . .'

'Here you go.' Juhi handed over a paper bag to Radhi.

'Good . . . now, Divya, look, you need to breathe into this. Like this . . . you understand?' Radhi demonstrated, holding the bag open and sticking her face into it. Then she handed the bag to Divya. 'Take a few breaths into the bag and then look up and take a few normal breaths.'

Slowly, as the woman did as she was told, she began to calm down and her breathing returned to normal. On the couch to Radhi's right, the accountant she had seen yesterday was talking intently on his phone, while at its other end, a sari-clad woman with a nest of short, frizzy hair and a saffron tika on her forehead was rolling a string of prayer beads between her thumb and index finger. Her lips were moving in silent prayer, but her sharp little eyes were flitting this way and that, observing everything and everybody. Radhi's eyes met hers for an instant and the woman looked away. But it was enough to send jitters up Radhi's spine. Her gaze was singularly piercing and cold. Radhi looked around for Juhi but could not see her anywhere. At the other end of the reception lobby, Alpa had waylaid one of the cops and was talking to him in an agitated manner. Radhi got up and walked towards her.

'There, you may know more than him!' Alpa exclaimed when she saw Radhi at her elbow. 'I'd like to know what's going on in there. And how long will it all take? But he is refusing to answer any of my questions!'

'Ma'am . . . I'm not at liberty to say anything.' The young constable seemed harried. 'Please have patience. It won't be too long now,' she said before hurrying away.

Alpa turned towards Radhi now. 'It's so frustrating. They won't answer basic questions. All I want to know is when I'll be able to leave. My mum is in the hospital, and I need to take her lunch!'

'They were with Sarla Aunty and Kiran ben. But they should be done by now, I think.'

'You spoke to them, right? What did they want to know?'

'Just some basic things . . . like where I was yesterday, how well I knew Hansa ben, if I could think of anyone who'd wish her harm . . . that sort of thing.'

'Oh I could name a few,' snorted Alpa.

'Really?' Radhi asked.

But Alpa looked like she immediately regretted her remark. 'No, no! I'm just being unkind. I shouldn't have said that.' She craned her neck to see beyond the end of the corridor. 'I'm going to go in and see if anyone will tell me anything.' She hurried away leaving Radhi wondering what she had meant.

Radhi wandered towards the pantry in search of water. She had just reached the door when it flew open and Jeevan stormed out of the room, his eyes wild and his face the colour of ash. He seemed not to notice Radhi, for he walked right past her and let the door close behind him with a loud bang.

Radhi watched his retreating back curiously before opening the door to the pantry. Juhi was standing in the middle of the room, equally pale-faced and upset. She was startled to see Radhi and with a visible effort arranged her features into a weak smile.

'What is it?' asked Radhi, concerned. 'What's happened?'

Juhi shook her head. 'Nothing . . . It's Jeevan . . . I'm just worried about him. The police really grilled him and it's got him really scared. I hope he doesn't go and do something stupid.'

'What do you mean?' Radhi pulled out chairs for both of them and they took a seat.

'He is usually the last to leave the office. He locks up after all of us around seven thirty and comes back in the morning to open the office and clean it before we get here. The police think that Hansa ben died sometime between six and eight last evening. Which means . . . which means . . .' Juhi's voice trailed off.

'That he was probably around when she was killed,' Radhi finished gently.

'Oh didi.' A single tear rolled down Juhi's cheek. 'I'm really scared for him. What if the police think he had something to do with it?'

Radhi clicked her tongue. 'It's not as simple as that. There can be many explanations for how she could've been killed without him being involved.'

'You really think so?' Juhi said eagerly.

'Of course.' Radhi got up to get water from the water cooler. 'The police need proof and motive, just opportunity isn't enough.' She sat down and took a long gulp from her glass, realizing as the chilled water hit her sinuses that she hadn't had a morsel of food that day. Her thermos of tea along with the breakfast of paranthas that Lila had packed lay forgotten on her desk.

'They're saying some money's gone missing.' Juhi looked at Radhi for confirmation.

'Yes, but it's not a big amount.'

'For people like Jeevan and me, they'll believe that's motive enough.' Juhi cradled the glass of water in her hands without taking a sip.

Radhi was silent. The economic disparity between them was so vast that to deny it would be meaningless and unkind. 'What time did you leave yesterday?' she asked, changing the topic.

'Around six thirty. I went to a friend's house so that we could study together.'

'And what about the rest of them? Was anyone around?'

Juhi shook her head. 'I thought everyone had left but I didn't check any of the cabins so I can't be a hundred per cent sure.'

'And what about Jeevan? Did you see him before you left?'

'Yes, he was in the reception area. Watching YouTube videos on his phone.'

Radhi studied Juhi's face. It seemed open enough, but she had hesitated for just a fraction of a second.

'But if the office was empty, why didn't he just lock up and leave?'

Juhi looked embarrassed. 'It's the free Wi-Fi, didi; we don't have Wi-Fi in our homes.'

The difference in how they lived shouldn't have surprised Radhi after all these years, but it did. This was yet another reason for Lila to move out of Kanchi Nagar. She made a mental note to bring it up with her. Her son would need a proper internet connection to pursue higher studies.

'But please don't mention the Wi-Fi to Sarla ma'am,' Juhi said. 'I don't want to get Jeevan in trouble.'

Radhi nodded reassuringly. 'Can you think of anyone who would want to hurt Hansa?' she asked after a few moments, thinking of Alpa's comment.

Juhi frowned. 'Her work did get her involved with all sorts of people . . . but I don't know if anyone was really dangerous like that.'

'Oh!' said Radhi clutching Juhi's arm, as the thought that had escaped her earlier that morning in Kiran's cabin suddenly came back to her. 'Juhi, do you remember that man? The one who came to meet Hansa ben yesterday?'

Juhi's eyes widened. 'Yes! Yes I do. The one with the gold chains.'

Radhi nodded. 'I could swear that she seemed surprised to see him. Uncomfortable, almost. Do you know who he was?'

7

Radhi walked briskly towards Sarla's cabin, where Shinde was talking to Alpa. Juhi had said she had never seen the man before, but he had signed the register in the reception, which meant his name and phone number were probably recorded there. Radhi waited until the inspector finished talking to Alpa. The wedding planner came out looking hot and flustered. 'The way he's going on, it would seem we're nothing more than common criminals,' she hissed at Radhi before scurrying away.

'Are you in a tearing hurry to leave as well?' Shinde asked Radhi when she entered the room. 'I understand you Temple Hill folk are very busy people, but just to put things in perspective, this *is* a murder investigation.'

The inspector's tone chafed at Radhi, but she kept her cool. 'On the contrary, Inspector, I have nowhere to be. I've just remembered something about yesterday that I thought might be of interest to you.'

A muscle in the inspector's jaw tightened. 'Can it wait until I've finished conducting all the interviews?'

Radhi could sense that he was trying his best to rein in his irritation. And it occurred to her that his prejudice against the type of idle, entitled women he thought she represented ran so deep that he wasn't willing to entertain the possibility that she'd actually have something that might help him.

'Actually, just tell me now,' he said, changing his mind.

When Radhi told him about the man who had met Hansa and the entry in the office register, Shinde nodded.

'Is that it?'

'Yes, but, you see, she might've met him for the first time yesterday . . .'

'She met *you* for the first time yesterday as well, madam,' Shinde interrupted Radhi. 'That's hardly a reason to suspect someone of murder.'

'But she seemed surprised . . .' Radhi tried again.

And again Shinde cut her off, 'You have admitted yourself that you hardly knew the victim, how sure are you that your reading of the situation was accurate? In any case, we are making a note of all the entries in the register, both here and the one that the guard in the building maintains. So don't you worry, we will find out who your mystery man is.'

Radhi, who was by now thoroughly annoyed with Shinde's attitude, nodded coolly. 'Great. Thanks so much for your time,' she said before leaving the room.

Outside, she crossed Divya on her way in to speak to Shinde. The young woman seemed more collected than before, and they exchanged smiles. A few seconds later, Radhi's phone rang.

'Hey, you.' It was Nishant. 'I was just calling to confirm the time for our dinner tonight. I'm making a reservation at Nara — this new Thai place everyone's raving about.'

Radhi smacked her forehead. She had completely forgotten about dinner that evening. 'Nishant, I'm so sorry, but I can't do dinner today! It's been quite a morning here.' Quickly she filled him in on how she'd found the dead body and everything that had happened since.

'That's . . . that's terrible,' he said when she had finished.

'It is . . . can we please push our dinner to sometime later this week?'

'Of course. But listen, why don't I come over with some takeaway? I'll get grilled sandwiches from Flavours, and we can watch something on Netflix. I don't like the idea of you eating dinner all alone tonight.'

Radhi paused to consider his offer. It sounded nice and a part of her was tempted to say yes. But another part, the one that had taken more than a year to get over Mackinzey, had almost thrown her career away in the process and knew how hard it was to heal, didn't want to deal with what 'coming over' could end up in. She had promised herself she would take things slow this time and protect her much-bruised heart at all costs.

'I don't know what time we are going to get done here. Let's play it by ear?' She hung up after promising to call him once she got home and made her way to Kiran's office in search of Sarla. She knocked before she entered the room and got the distinct impression that she had stepped into the middle of an argument. There were no raised voices, but Zarna and Kiran were sitting across the desk silently, glowering at each other. The tension in the room was palpable.

Kiran was the first to acknowledge Radhi. 'Yes, Radhi dear, did you need something?'

'Uhm, I was just looking for Sarla Aunty.'

'She's with the accountant I think . . . What's going on out there? Do you know?'

'They're still taking statements of the staff.'

The door opened and Sarla stepped in. 'I just took a look at our pension scheme to check what we owe Hansa. I plan to go and pay my condolences to her sister and hand over the cheque to her tomorrow.' She took a seat on the couch at the back of the room. 'Should we put in a little bit more from our end as well?'

'We could . . . but I think our pension scheme is generous enough, no?' Zarna said. 'We shouldn't set a precedent, that's all,' she quickly added.

'Precedent for what, Zarna? It's not like we need to worry about paying pension to other murdered employees,' Kiran chided.

Zarna glared at her mother but held her tongue.

'It's just that I feel responsible, somehow. Our employee was murdered in our office. If it was elsewhere . . .' Sarla trailed off.

'No, of course, Sarla, let's contribute a lakh each,' Kiran said.

There was a knock at the door and Jeevan entered carrying a tray with cups of tea, chutney and cheese sandwiches and a bowl of spicy peanuts and mint-flavoured chana.

'I told him to serve everyone refreshments,' Kiran said. 'We've all been here for hours and there's no telling when they'll let us go.'

'Hmm . . . that was a good idea,' said Sarla. 'I hope you've offered the food to the cops also?' she asked Jeevan as he laid the tray down on the table.

'Yes, ma'am,' he said in a small voice. His face looked pale and drawn.

'Where is the bowl with the sugar sachets?' Zarna asked.

'Oh!' He studied the tray, flustered. 'I'll just get some.'

'What's the matter with him?' Sarla asked Kiran when the young peon had left the room.

'The police really grilled him,' Radhi volunteered. 'He's scared of somehow getting mixed up in all of this.'

'They've grilled all of us, haven't they?' Kiran said. 'Where were you yesterday? What time did you leave? Who were you with? How well did you know the victim? Do you know anyone who would want to hurt her? What I can't figure out is how would they know if anyone was lying? I was at home watering my plants before Zarna's father got home at eight. But my plants are hardly going to confirm my statement, no? So how do they check this sort of stuff?'

'What about your maid?' Sarla asked. 'Wasn't she home?'

'She's gone to her village. Back next week. And the cook comes around five to make dinner. He'd left by the time I got home.'

'Who lets him in then?' Radhi asked.

'I leave a spare set of keys with my neighbour. Once he finishes cooking, he gives them back to her.'

Radhi was about to tell Kiran that the police would probably speak to her building watchman or neighbours to try to corroborate her story, but Jeevan entered the room with the sugar bowl just then. He placed it on the tray and then carried the tray around the room.

'What time did you leave last evening?' Sarla asked him.

'Wh . . . at, ma'am?' He seemed startled.

'Yesterday. What time did you lock up?'

'Seven thirty, ma'am.'

'And everything looked normal? Exactly as always?'

'Yes, ma'am . . . I switched off the lights from behind the reception desk, like I always do, knocked on the bathrooms to make sure there was no one inside and locked up the office.'

As he held out the tray in front of her, Radhi noticed that his hands were clutching the tray so tightly that his knuckles had turned white.

'Who was the last person to leave?' Radhi took a cup of tea and a sandwich.

'The office, ma'am?' he asked, rather unnecessarily she thought, as he took the tray towards Sarla.

'Yes.'

'I wasn't around. I had gone down to have a vada pav from Kishore's stall below. By the time I came back, the office was empty, and I locked up and left.'

He looked at them anxiously. 'Why, ma'am? Why do you ask?'

Radhi ignored his question. 'Did you speak to anyone while leaving? Like the watchman? Or one of those drivers who wait with the cars below the building? Anyone who could confirm they saw you?'

Jeevan's eyes widened with fear. 'Do the police think I am lying? Have they said anything to you? They asked me so many questions! And they told me not to leave town!' He clutched the empty tray to his chest like a shield. 'I swear on my mother, I had nothing to do with this!'

'No, no, Jeevan, don't worry!' Radhi hastened to reassure him. 'The police have asked *everybody* not to leave town. All of us included. Nobody thinks you are lying. I was only trying to see if you could get someone to confirm your story so that the police would leave you alone.'

Jeevan looked like he didn't believe Radhi. He waited there silently for a few moments to see if they had any more questions for him before leaving the room.

'Poor boy.' Sarla clicked her tongue sympathetically. 'We should ask the police to go easy on him.'

Radhi didn't say anything. She was puzzled. She knew his fear could as easily stem from his innocence as his guilt. There was a deep-rooted distrust that people from his economic class often harboured against the system. And Radhi knew that more often than not it was justified. Jeevan was probably afraid that he would be harassed and questioned and grilled more intensely than the others just because he was poor. He was afraid of being treated unfairly and yet he probably expected it. But Radhi felt that this wasn't the only source of his fear. This nervousness seemed more jittery, more brittle. But it was difficult to explain and she held her tongue.

'You know, we could've avoided this whole drama if we had installed a CCTV system in the office, like I've been saying forever,' Zarna said between bites of her chutney sandwich.

'Zarna . . .' Kiran's voice had a note of warning in it.

'What, Mummy?' Zarna asked exasperatedly. 'You know I'm right. I just don't understand why you can never speak up!'

'Really, Zarna, this is hardly the time—' Kiran began, but Sarla interrupted her.

'No, she is right. I too was thinking about it yesterday when we got those tarot cards. It may not be a bad idea.'

Zarna looked at her mother triumphantly before turning back to Sarla. 'I'm right about the other thing as well. You guys just don't know it yet.'

'Oh, for heaven's sake, girl, will you give it up,' Sarla said wearily. 'A fancy business degree is not the same thing as building a business, you know.'

'And building a business is not the same as growing one, you know!' Zarna retorted.

'Zarna, that's enough now!' Kiran said sharply, but her daughter ignored her.

'It's easy to be a big fish in a small pond, Sarla Aunty. But what happens when you have to swim in the ocean? You're scared you won't be able to do it, aren't you?'

Sarla's eyes flashed angrily. 'Oh, I can't stand this entitlement! I've built this business from scratch, you know. My mother did not hand it to me on a pretty silver platter. So, really, forgive us if we don't take all your brainwaves seriously. In fact—'

'Excuse me?' Inspector Shinde poked his head into the room with a slight knock on the door. He surveyed the people present before entering. 'We're almost done here, and I just wanted to go over some of the things again to make sure we've got the facts right.'

Without waiting for a response, he opened the small rough pad he was holding and began to read from it. 'Sarla

Seth, you came to work at 10.30 a.m. and left at 5.30 p.m.' He glanced up briefly and Sarla confirmed with a nod. He continued, 'Kiran Shah and Zarna Shah arrived together at 10 a.m. and left by 5.30 p.m. And Radhika Zaveri came in at 11 a.m. and left by 4.30 p.m. Have I got this right?'

There was a murmur of yeses.

'According to this then, none of you were around when the murder took place. But there is no sign of breaking and entering. The grilles at the windows are intact. And the door was locked from the outside like it always is — *if* your peon Jeevan is to be believed, that is. Which then means that *someone* who was in the office killed Hansa and left before the office was locked.'

Both Kiran and Sarla responded at the same time.

'But how is that even possible?'

'Surely, someone would've heard something?'

Shinde held up his hand. 'Or that someone came back while the office was open and Hansa was still here.' He paused to look at them before continuing, 'We tried corroborating these times with the register your guard maintains at the entrance lobby, but unfortunately his system is to just note the going-ins and not the exits. Which would have made this a futile exercise except that one of my constables noticed one odd thing.'

Shinde looked at each of their faces carefully before coming to rest on the one face that had become very pale.

8

'Why didn't you tell us that you'd come back to the office last night?' Shinde asked.

Zarna's eyes darted wildly from her mother to Sarla to the inspector. She shook her head and slapped her forehead with her palm. 'Sorry! I completely forgot. It completely slipped my mind. I . . . I . . . It was just for five minutes . . . very brief. It didn't even occur to me to mention it! Yes, yes, I had come to the office around eight fifteen, I think.' She spluttered and came to a halt. Then she swallowed and tried again, 'Actually, I think it was eight or so. I remember now, I went home and watched *Koffee with Karan* at eight thirty, so yes it must've been eight-ish.'

'But what were you doing here?' Kiran asked astonished. 'You didn't say anything to me when I dropped you home!'

'I just needed a few printouts, Mummy. I realized when I got home that I had forgotten to take them from the utility room. They were for that digital marketing course I'm doing; we have a test tonight.'

She reached for her handbag, which was hanging behind her chair, and brought out a few sheets of paper. 'These,' she said, handing them to Shinde. 'You can check with the online university about the test and everything.'

Shinde scanned the sheets before handing them back.

'Anyways, so I had an early dinner and I dropped by the office again for exactly five minutes, took my printouts and went back home.' Zarna ran her fingers through her hair and laughed nervously. 'I am so sorry, I completely forgot to mention it.'

'Was the office locked then?' Shinde asked.

'Yes, I used my key to enter.'

'And you didn't see anything out of the ordinary?'

'Nothing at all! The office was completely dark. I went behind the reception desk to put on one or two lights. Just enough to pop into the utility room and take my printouts.' She frowned and shook her head. 'I feel like such a fool right now.'

'Where is the utility room?' Shinde asked, turning to Sarla.

But Kiran answered instead, 'It's the first room at the beginning of the corridor. So you see she wouldn't need to pass the rest of the office or Hansa's cabin. There was no way she could've known or seen what had happened.'

Shinde didn't reply. He made a note in his diary before turning to Zarna again.

'Is there anyone at home who could confirm how long you were gone for?'

'My husband came home at nine, so not him . . . but yes, my maid could. She saw me leave home for fifteen minutes and come back with a file in my hand.' She relaxed visibly. 'Yes, you can ask Sangeeta.'

Shinde made another note in his diary. 'Not that that's any indication of your innocence. You could've killed Hansa in fifteen minutes and come back with a file in your hand and your maid wouldn't be any wiser.'

'Look here now, Inspector,' Kiran began angrily but Shinde cut her off.

'No, you look here, ma'am. Your daughter was in this office when Hansa was killed and she lied to us. That's a big problem.' He held up his hand to ward off Kiran's protests.

'Is there anything else anyone else has forgotten to tell us?' His voice was laced with sarcasm.

When no one answered, he nodded. 'All right then. We'll be in touch.'

Sarla closed her eyes as the maid massaged her head. She was using a fragrant hair oil, a potent mix of gooseberries, bitter neem, rose petals and almonds, which Sarla had boiled and strained in her kitchen. It usually helped to cool her down and subdue her frequent headaches, but today the throbbing showed no sign of letting up. Sarla opened her eyes and looked at the photograph of her late husband hanging on the wall opposite her. It was a picture of both of them with binoculars around their necks on one of their birding trips, but she always thought of the photo as *his* photo, because somehow when she looked at it, she only saw him.

Theirs had been a remarkable love story. Not in how they met but in how quickly they had become devoted to one another. An arranged marriage at twenty and then four decades of drinking strong adrak chai together on the balcony every evening, listening to Jagjit Singh ghazals and telling the other about their day. A young Sarla had found that she could talk to her husband about anything. A dream she'd had the night before, an argument about pickles with her mother-in-law, her recurring itch to start her own business, a piece of gossip from the neighbour—it didn't matter what it was, if it was on Sarla's mind, her husband wanted to hear it. She wondered what he would have said about the thing on her mind right now. Not Hansa's death. Not the tarot cards. But the terrible feeling that she deserved the trouble she was in.

Left arm, right arm, fold in the middle. Left arm, right arm, fold in the middle. Kiran's hands worked swiftly and precisely as she folded her sari blouses one after another. She was sitting on her bed with the contents of her wardrobe strewn all around her and a growing pile of neatly folded clothes in front of her. *Left arm, right arm, fold in the middle.* With each fold, the cacophony inside her mind seemed to quieten down. Soon she would be able to see why she was really upset. Right now, it was all just an angry red jumble in her mind. Hansa's murder. The tarot cards. The bureau. Sarla's arrogance. Zarna's . . . Zarna, yes, she could see now that it was her daughter who had unleashed this turmoil in her mind. Her rash, over-ambitious daughter and the awful suspicion that Kiran had suddenly had about her. She moved from her blouses to her salwars. *Left leg, right leg, fold in the middle. Left leg, right leg, fold in the middle.*

Kiran's husband stood at the door to their room, observing the scene in front of him for a while before shutting the door softly and stepping away. He knew it was best to leave her alone when she was like this. Eventually, all the repetitive cleaning, sorting, stacking and organizing would wind her down. The frantic activity dulling the jagged edges of her anxiety. She would lie down then, her arms aching, and he would press them gently until she fell asleep.

Back arched, buttocks out and knees bent, Zarna lifted an 80-pound dumbbell in a perfect deadlift and held it for a few excruciating seconds before letting the weight drop to the floor with a loud thud. Droplets of sweat trickled down her face and fell to the floor. Her trainer handed her a napkin, which she ignored. 'Let's do it again,' she said getting into position once more. With a rough grunt she lifted the weight again and admired her form in the mirror. Her gym was the only place in the world where she felt powerful. At home, her lawyer husband launched debates for every little decision and treated every argument like a court case, insisting on winning it regardless of the cost to their relationship. With her mum it was always about control. You couldn't say by looking at them together because Zarna was outspoken and impatient, but her mum usually got her way. Sometimes it was emotional blackmail but for the most part it was persistence. Kiran could obsessively scratch away at Zarna's defences until it wore her down. And at work, there was Sarla.

Zarna's legs quivered and her eyes bulged from the effort of lifting. It was difficult to find a more alpha personality than her mom's partner, she thought. Sarla was always so convinced that she was right, that she knew what was best. Zarna didn't know how her mom could tolerate her. But she had had enough. Things had to change. She snarled from the exertion but continued holding the weight up and her mind turned to Hansa's death and the police's questions. What a damn nightmare. With a growl she let the weight drop to the floor and straightened up.

Radhi! You complete ignoramus. What a ridiculous conclusion to jump to just because it's taken me some time to get back. Have you no faith in yourself? Or your work? Or your sheer effing talent? Wait, don't answer that. I'm the ignoramus for even asking. The reason I haven't said anything about your book is that I haven't read it yet! I know it's unpardonable. But I've been busy taking Mum for her dialysis and doctor appointments, etc. My sister just delivered twin girls, so she can't hold up her half of it like she used to. It's been frantic. We go into the clinic twice a week and stay for 6 hours each *time. But don't worry. My brother-in-law has offered to help out next week, so that's when I plan to get to your book. Okay? OKAY? Will you please take a deep breath and relax now? And smile. Please smile. You know how I love your f***ing gorgeous smile!*

XOXO

George

p.s. Really, your complete lack of confidence when it comes to your own writing continues to astonish me.

p.p.s. They are called Shelly and Claire, by the way. The babies, that is. Shelly looks exactly like me. Lucky girl, no?

Radhi stared at George's email and buried her face in her hands. She stayed like that for a while, taking deep, steadying breaths. She had just manifested her worst fears into reality and discovered that she could stand it. George didn't like her book, but that hadn't shattered her like she had imagined it would. She could deal with it. What she couldn't stand, what made her livid, was being lied to. Years ago, when George and she had just met, he had told her he got most of his reading done while waiting at his mom's dialysis clinic. It was quiet there and they made everyone switch off their phones. *It's better than going to the library, there's no one necking or playing footsie in the last row and distracting you. Plus, the coffee at the clinic? A million times nicer.* Those had been his exact words. George's email could have fooled anyone else, but he hadn't accounted for Radhi's memory.

Radhi wrote him a short and scathing reply and then went and stood by her window, a cigarette in hand. She had returned from Soul Harmony about an hour ago with an urge to be alone. She had sent Lila home early after promising her that she'd heat the methi theplas properly before eating them. Now she was glad she had done that. Or else she'd have had to explain to Lila why her eyes were glistening right now. And Lila wasn't one to be fooled by half-hearted explanations.

The day had begun with her stumbling upon a dead body and ended with a realization that perhaps her book wasn't all that she thought it was. It wasn't the best of days. But if someone had asked her what had disturbed her more, she would've had to admit it wasn't the murder. Throughout, surrounded by the police and all the conversations about the time of death and murder weapon and alibis, she had felt no aversion, just a terrific adrenaline rush. Her mind had whirred, observing, absorbing, processing, and she had not heard the constant hum of the self-flagellating thoughts that routinely underscored her life. She wondered what that said about her. And what Nishant would think if he knew. She had cancelled their dinner date saying she felt drained, but now she wished she hadn't. Her eyes went to her newly purchased mango wood bar cabinet and the line of expensive merlots she had stocked up on. If she opened another bottle today, it would be the third day in a row that she had drunk herself to sleep. It sounded ugly, those words. But no number of scented candles and Frank Sinatra could take away from how she had essentially put herself to bed. She picked up her phone and called Nishant.

'Would you like to come over?' she asked without preamble when he answered.

'Sure.' He sounded surprised but pleased. 'What do you want for dinner? Sandwiches, paneer rolls or something else?'

She paused before answering softly so that there was no mistaking what she meant. 'Something else.'

When she hung up, her heart was beating hard.

Juhi sat in one corner of her home, a textbook on accounting fair practices by Kotler open on her lap. But she found it impossible to concentrate. Not because of the laughter track that punctuated each crass joke on the comedy show that her father was watching on TV, nor the yelps of her younger sister as her mother ran a lice comb through her tangled hair. And certainly not because of the horror of Hansa's murder. No, she'd decided she wasn't going to think about *that* even for a moment. The police, the questions, the blood, it had all been too much. If she let her mind go there, she wouldn't be able to function. She was thinking of the squalor of her surroundings. Her father in his hole-ridden vest and lungi, chewing his tobacco and spitting into a plastic tumbler that he kept by his side because he couldn't be bothered to get up. The lime walls of their 16-foot by 18-foot one-room kholi, a garish shade of blue because a proper coat of white paint always seemed a wasteful luxury. And the permanently damp smell in the room because of the wet towels and clothes draped across the only two chairs in their home. How Juhi hated coming home! Soul Harmony, plush, perfumed and air-conditioned, was her haven. Murder or no murder, that was where she belonged. She shut her textbook and stretched out onto her mat on the floor to sleep. She covered her face with her blanket to keep out the light and sounds, but it was difficult to keep out the thought of what Jeevan had told her. A tight knot of fear throbbed in the pit of her stomach.

A lane away from Juhi's house, in an identical blue-walled, 16-foot by 18-foot kholi, Jeevan refused to eat dinner and yelled at his mother when she asked again. His father, sprawled on a single bed in front of the TV, and already halfway through his bottle of cheap desi liquor, looked at him curiously through half-closed eyes. Usually, the yelling and shouting was *his* terrain. What had happened to his sissy son? Was he finally growing a pair? His younger brother, who had been rocking back and forth memorizing the eight-times table, with index fingers stuck firmly in both ears for concentration, opened his eyes and stared at Jeevan. For an instant there, his elder brother had sounded just like their father when he was in one of his moods and the young boy had felt his stomach drop.

Jeevan saw his mother's crestfallen face as she went back to the stovetop with his solkadhi and rice untouched and felt ashamed of himself. He didn't know how to deal with the situation he found himself in — just that he needed this job desperately. A thousand rupees every month from his salary was what kept his father away from his mother. For the first time in many years his mum was completely free of bruises. For Jeevan, nothing was more important than that. Not even his desperate love for Juhi. And now he had gone and jeopardized everything. From the corner of his eye, he saw his mother looking at him with concern. He felt he couldn't breathe. The walls of the tiny kholi seemed to be closing in on him. Just like a prison. He got up from his stool, phone and earphones in hand, and stepped out of the house.

'Yes, Ma, five minutes more!' Alpa called out to her mother from the kitchen, where she was preparing a simple meal of yellow dal and rice for dinner.

She had brought her mother home from the hospital that evening and had got her settled into her room. It had been a long and tiring day. She couldn't wait for her mother to finish her meal so that she could help her change into a nightgown and put her to bed. Then for a blissful hour or two she could stop playing nursemaid, put her feet up on the sofa and watch her favourite Korean show about an heiress turned martial arts expert.

A small smile lingered on her lips as she sliced tomatoes and grated ginger for the dal. It had nothing to do with the good prognosis the doctors had given her mother, nor the precious free time she was looking forward to, and everything to do with what had happened at Soul Harmony today. That nasty woman was dead. And Alpa found she had much to be grateful for. Despite the sense of foreboding that had crept up on her that morning. Despite the tiny insistent voice in her head that kept saying that she had to be careful. It wasn't over yet.

9

Thursday

If Lila was surprised to see Nishant in his boxers, reading the paper on Radhi's couch the next morning, she didn't show it. There wasn't even a knowing smile thrown Radhi's way. Radhi had to give her housekeeper full marks for playing it perfectly cool.

'What would you like for breakfast this morning?' Lila asked them exactly like she asked Radhi every day.

Radhi waited for Nishant to answer first. 'Uhm . . . some black coffee would be great and other than that a bowl of fruit or some sprout salad, whatever is easier.'

Nishant, who worked out four days a week and swam the remaining three, ate so healthy that his food choices were a constant source of amazement for Radhi.

'And for me, anything but that,' Radhi told Lila, who smiled and bustled away into the kitchen.

'What? Too healthy for you?' Nishant asked Radhi, looking over his paper.

'Unthinkably so,' Radhi agreed, smiling before going back to the Sudoku puzzle she was solving in the *Bombay Times*.

Who would have thought six months ago that she'd be lending a toothbrush to a man so soon again. She had met Nishant in the strangest of situations when Madhavi's mother-in-law had invited him for dinner with the express purpose of setting him up with Radhi and Madhavi's cousin Prachi. Nishant and Prachi had started off with a pre-dinner coffee and conversation, but as the evening progressed, Nishant had felt himself drawn to the quiet woman with the big, brooding eyes and the perpetual hint of mystery in her smile. Or at least that's how *he* liked to tell the story. At first, Radhi had been hesitant. She had just about managed to piece her heart back together. The glue was barely dry, and she hadn't wanted to risk another entanglement. Besides, it would undoubtedly complicate things with the family. Both her sister's mother-in-law and Prachi's mother, Ila Kaki, would be upset at having their plans foiled. She had resisted for a while, but he had been persistent. And now, as she saw him lounging on her couch, his jaw strong and resolute under his well-groomed beard and the cowlick at the back of his crown standing up stubbornly no matter how many times he brushed his hair, she was glad he had. The previous night, their first together, had been a revelation to her. Full of nibbles and tickles, he had made her groan and giggle and gasp and she had woken up with a sense of wonder at how playful lovemaking could be.

Radhi studied the little crinkle of focus on his forehead and marvelled at how different it was dating a younger man. There was a gap of four years between Radhi and Nishant, which was a new experience for her. Especially after Mackinzey, who had been almost twenty years older and infinitely wiser. Mackinzey had understood her far more thoroughly than she had ever understood herself. From the very beginning, he had sensed the excruciating knot of guilt that she carried within her, and almost instinctively, he had known how to unravel it. Slowly, with the utmost care, but also with a firm resoluteness — for she had protested hotly, trying to thwart him at every chance. And every time the knot had come a little undone, he had held her while she wept, not leaving her side until she had emerged from the dark haze, stronger and lighter.

With Nishant, things were less intense. She knew it had just been a few months, but there was an easy lightness between them, which Radhi found refreshing. He was more devoted, more eager to believe the best of her, and when she was with him, she found that she was less inward-looking and far more carefree. They spoke of films and food and travel, there was no hours-long inquiry into the creative life, no agonizing interrogation of her soul. It wasn't that their conversation was superficial, she could tell that he felt deeply about things and that he wanted more than the little piece of her heart that she had allowed him to glimpse. But he was patient, willing to wait. Or at least that is what she hoped.

'Surely, it can't be that hard?' Nishant nodded at the completely empty puzzle grid that Radhi had been staring at absent-mindedly. He was smiling but there was a thoughtful look in his eyes.

Chuckling, Radhi set aside the paper and gave him her full attention, just as Lila brought in their food and plates on a large tray. 'I was actually solving a completely different puzzle.'

'Which is?' Nishant took an appreciative sip of his steaming black coffee.

'Why would any sane person pick *that* over *this*?' Radhi pointed to his bowl of papaya and muskmelon as she took a bite of her ghee-soaked paneer parantha with a stick of carrot pickle.

Grinning, Nishant swiped a piece of parantha from her plate.

Shiv Samaj was a residential area not too distant from Temple Hill but worlds apart in everything else. Unlike the wide and leafy gulmohar-lined streets of Temple Hill, the main arterial road of Shiv Samaj was narrow, congested and ridden with potholes. The usual kerfuffle of cars, scooters and bicycles was further aggravated by men pulling hand carts. These men made short-distance deliveries of fabrics and added to the general cacophony by swearing loudly at the pedestrians in front of them, the honking cars behind them and the relentless sun above them. The footpaths on either side were packed with little shops and stalls selling everything from glass bangles, bindis and gift envelopes to fake watches, mobile phone covers and cheap glass crockery. Even this early in the morning there was a crush of people. Not the polite bustle of the temple-goers, yoga enthusiasts and joggers of Temple Hill who passed each other with smiles of familiarity and gentle excuse-mes. This crowd was more weary, more pressed for time and far less inclined towards niceties.

'I'm glad you've come along,' Sarla said to Radhi as they waited for the cow in front of their car to cross the road.

The two women were on their way to Hansa's home. Sarla had wanted to offer condolences to Hansa's sister and give her the cheque with Hansa's pension, and Radhi had offered to accompany her.

'There was one more reason I wanted to visit Hansa's home.' Sarla smoothed her sari where it had bunched up in her lap.

Radhi sensed that though the older woman was trying to keep a brave face on things, the events of the last couple of days had rattled her more than a little. 'The tarot cards?'

Sarla nodded. 'Hansa usually kept files on the cases she was working on, but I checked the ones on her desk at work and couldn't find anything there.'

'Maybe the police took them?'

'No, they dusted them for fingerprints and returned them to us after making copies of everything. There were her other cases but nothing on the tarot cards.'

'You think you'll find something at her home? Wouldn't the police have searched there as well?'

'I don't know if they'd be able to make sense of it . . . in any case we have to check . . . other than this I don't know what to do. The thought of telling that bumbling idiot, that inspector . . .' Sarla shuddered in horror. 'He will insist on talking to the staff, our clients . . . and he won't be discreet. I can't have Soul Harmony associated with a scandal like that. I've worked too hard and too long to squander our reputation on a stupid, mean-minded prank!'

'How long has it been, Aunty? Twenty-five years?'

'Twenty-nine! I've been matchmaking before Soul Harmony was even called Soul Harmony! Started off in the living room of my apartment. The same one you used to come to with your mother — you remember?'

'Of course! How can I forget Foofoo? You were the only one among all our acquaintances who had a dog!' Radhi said. Her mother would often drop by Sarla's for tea and Radhi would tag along to play with the Seths' golden retriever.

Sarla smiled.

Radhi shifted in her seat to see what was holding them up. The cow had crossed the road but a small procession, carrying a sari-draped idol of a goddess on a cart, had taken over the left lane of the road, forcing all the vehicles to keep to the right one and slowing the traffic down even more. Through their rolled-up windows they could hear the faint strains of a Hindi film song from a speaker attached to the cart. An ode to a woman's unrequited love. Radhi smiled. The connection between gods and Bollywood continued to elude her after all these years.

'What about Kiran ben? Has she been with you since the beginning?'

'No . . . no . . . when I started, I was doing it on my own. But when the business began to really grow, it became difficult to manage everything, and I brought Kiran on as a partner. She's been with me for almost twenty years. Left to my own devices, I tend to fall behind on the paperwork and payments, etc. But Kiran's got a great eye for detail. She's really good at the organizational aspect of it. You know, she used to be my neighbour in my mother's building. We've known each other since we were girls.'

'How did you get started? What was that first match like?'

Sarla gave Radhi an affectionate smile. 'You're like me, I see. Working all the time.'

'No, no Aunty,' Radhi protested, 'this isn't for work. I'm just interested.'

'But, beta, that's how the best work is done! Because someone is genuinely interested in something and doesn't see it as work. At the risk of sounding immodest, I have to say it's what makes *me* so good at what I do — matchmaking isn't just my job, it's who I am! I love setting people up. And I love everything that that involves. Getting to know the young people in question. Their hopes and fears. What keeps them up at night. What gets them out of bed in the mornings. Meeting their families. Learning their backstories. Their interpersonal dynamics. All of that is very fascinating to me. Even today. Even after being at it for so long!'

Radhi smiled. 'Aunty, this passion, it's inspiring.'

Sarla waved off the compliment with a flick of her hand, but her eyes shone. 'You know, sometimes I can just see two people and tell if they'll be good together. I'll be at a wedding, getting introduced to a young woman and the hair on my arms will stand up, because while I'm talking to her, it will suddenly come to me just how perfect so-and-so's son would be for her. It's like a radar I have, a sixth sense, if you want to call it that! Of course, I'm not infallible. I do make mistakes sometimes.' Her face darkened as she said this.

She seemed to deflate. She began to fiddle with her phone and fell quiet.

Radhi was surprised at this transformation. She studied the older woman's face for clues but there were none. She had withdrawn into herself and appeared to be miles away.

'I think this is it.' Sarla stopped outside a crumbling, grey, four-storey building. She double-checked the faded black letters painted on its facade with the address on the paper in her hand before pushing open the gate and stepping inside. Hansa's building was almost a hundred years old and looked it. The paint was peeling off its walls and the tiny lobby area was dingy and unlit, with a dirty, threadbare maroon carpet on the floor and layers of accumulated grime in its corners. They looked around for an elevator, and realizing there wasn't one, they began making their way up a steep flight of stairs, with Sarla leading the way. On the landing of the second floor, they stopped outside a narrow wooden door with the nameplate 'Patani'. Radhi rang the bell.

There was no answer for a couple of minutes, and they were about to ring the bell again when the door opened a crack. Radhi started and almost let out a gasp. Besides her, she felt Sarla draw in her breath. The face in front of them was so much like Hansa's that for a split second both of them were disconcerted.

'Jigna ben?' Sarla asked.

The woman nodded. She looked at them blankly. Her eyes were swollen and listless and her face had a beaten expression.

'I'm Sarla and this is Radhika, we worked with your sister.'

'I know who you are,' she murmured, looking at Sarla, shuffling aside to let them in.

Hansa's living room was a small, desolate space with one window that was blocked almost entirely by a fig tree. A round plastic table with two chairs, presumably the dining area, was pushed up against a wall and looked like it was rarely used. A large cat with a long, fluffy white coat was napping on the table. It barely stirred at the sound of their arrival. The living room was taken up almost entirely by a three-seater sofa with brown upholstery made of synthetic leather and covered in plastic. In one corner was the most incongruous object in the house — a three-tier shelf delicately shaped and made of rich Burmese teak. It was so incompatible with the rest of the space that it jarred despite its obvious beauty. Sarla and Radhi took a seat on the sofa. Opposite them, a small box television from the 1990s was tuned to a Hindi feature film from the 1970s, where Jeetendra and Leena Chandavarkar were playing a game of spirited and choreographed badminton to the tune of an upbeat song. Jigna switched off the TV before taking a seat diagonally across them on a matching brown plastic-covered armchair.

'We just wanted to say how sorry we are for your loss. Your sister was one of my oldest employees and a very good worker,' Sarla began.

'That's kind of you to say.' Jigna's lower lip trembled from an effort not to cry.

'I'm just being honest.' Sarla opened her purse and brought out the cheque. 'Here, this is Hansa's pension. Kiran and I have also added a small amount as a token of our appreciation for the time Hansa spent with us.' Sarla got up to hand the cheque over to Jigna, who took it without glancing at the amount written on it.

'Did you two sisters live alone? Or is there any other family?' Sarla asked going back to her seat.

'We used to live with each other — so we were never alone.' Jigna's voice shook. 'But now I will be.' She stared out into the distance and was quiet for so long that Radhi wondered if she had forgotten that they were still there.

Sarla and Radhi exchanged worried glances.

'Who is that?' Radhi asked finally, pointing to a silver picture frame on the teak shelf.

It was a black-and-white photograph of two little girls with a younger boy at the centre.

Jigna turned around to see what Radhi was referring to. 'That's us with our younger brother.'

'Oh, you have a brother? That's nice,' said Sarla, who had begun to worry about how Jigna would cope. 'Is he in the city? Will he be able to come here to be with you?'

Jigna smiled bitterly. Her eyes lost their listlessness and flashed with anger. 'He is in the city, all right. But he is our brother in name only. The man is a leech. The only time he comes to see us is when he needs something from us. From Hansa, I should say. She was the one who would always help him out with money or something or the other.'

'What about friends? Relatives?'

Jigna shook her head. 'No close relatives . . . but I do have good neighbours I've known my entire life. So don't worry, they take good care of me.'

Sarla was quiet and appeared to be at a loss as to what to say next.

Radhi spoke up, 'Jigna ben, your sister was working on a few things for us at Soul Harmony. There may be files or documents that she may have brought home. Is it possible for us to look at them?'

'There isn't much.' Jigna pushed her chair back and got up. 'But you're welcome to take a look.'

Sarla shot Radhi a grateful look as they followed Jigna to an adjoining room.

With two cupboards and two single beds pushed to opposite sides, the sisters' bedroom was an even smaller space than the living room. But there was a large window through which natural light streamed in, giving it a gentler appearance than the fluorescent glare of the tube lights in the room outside.

Jigna pointed to the bed closest to the window. 'That side was hers. Under that bed you'll find two boxes with some files and paperwork. You can take a look while I make you some tea.'

She shuffled out, closing the door behind her.

Sarla sat on the bed while Radhi kneeled on the floor and pulled out the cardboard boxes. She gave one to Sarla and turned her attention to the other.

At the top of the box in front of her were a bunch of files, each marked by a surname on its spine, along with a year. *Dedhia*, *Shah*, *Mehta*, *Damani*, *Acharya*, *Choksi*, *Dalal*, *P. Mehta*, *K. Shah*. Radhi read the name on each file and opened the first couple of them. Each had a short, handwritten report on what Hansa had dug out and what she'd concluded on the basis of her findings. A couple of the files even had a few photographs. Sitting down cross-legged on the floor, Radhi read the first report. In broken English, Hansa had explained that the Dedhias had taken four trips that year. According to her source, the maid, at least two of these were international holidays. They had also purchased a new car that year. It was a mid-sized sedan, not very expensive, but it was the third car for this family of five. Judging from the shopping bags that Mrs Dedhia left strewn about the house and the fact that there weren't many arguments related to money in the house, Hansa had concluded that the Dedhias were financially stable.

Radhi shut the file and glanced up at Sarla. 'Aunty, this is . . .' She shook her head.

Seeing it all written down like that had discomfited her more than watching Hansa go through someone's unwashed clothes. It didn't make sense, she knew. Laundry was probably more personal than someone's travel calendar. But Radhi couldn't help feeling that this was a terrible invasion of privacy. She didn't know how to say it to the older woman without sounding like she was criticizing her. But something in her tone must have conveyed her discomfort.

'I know, beta, this is my least favourite part of what I do.' Sarla extended her hand for the files. 'But think about why I do it. And what happens if I am not thorough. My clients don't come to me to buy jewellery or clothes. I'm in the business of selling futures. They're trusting me with their children's lives. Do you know what a heavy responsibility that is?' She glanced at the files and frowned. 'These clients are at least a decade old. I wonder why she has their files at home.' Sarla turned the file to read the year on the spine. '2013 . . . Oh, that's right. That's the year the office was under renovation. We'd all had to keep our paperwork home those days.' She kept the files away. 'What else is in there?' She asked Radhi who was rifling through the box again.

'Just some old *Chitralekha* magazines and this diary.' Radhi gave it to Sarla. 'It looks like an old address book.'

Sarla flipped through the address book before handing it back to Radhi. 'You can keep that back in.'

Radhi dusted her hands and wiped them on her jeans before getting up. 'What about your box? Anything in there?'

Sarla put her box away with a sigh. 'I don't know what I had expected to find, but there is nothing in here. Nothing except old photo albums and a box full of news clippings about Amitabh Bachchan.'

'Oh, she was a huge fan of his,' Jigna said as she entered the room carrying tea and biscuits on a tray. 'Positively crazy. Saved money to go see all his movies first day, first show.

Took me along as well. It was probably the only indulgence she allowed herself.' She placed the tray on the bed and handed a cup each to Radhi and Sarla. 'Otherwise, she was always saving money. Saving for her retirement, saving for the pilgrimage we were going to take to Vaishno Devi, saving for . . .' Her voice faltered. Her eyes, which had briefly lit up as she spoke of her sister, turned watery again. The terrible futility of all the planning and saving they had done fast dawning upon her.

Radhi patted her back and gently sat her down on the bed beside Sarla.

Jigna sniffed and wiped her nose with the pallu of her sari. 'Did you find anything useful?' she asked Sarla.

Sarla shook her head and sighed. 'Not really.'

'I thought as much. Hansa didn't believe in bringing her work home. She rarely spoke about what she did all day, I told the others as much.'

'The police?' Sarla took a sip of her tea.

'Yes, the police as well as the other woman who came to see me last night. She was also from your office and needed to see Hansa's papers. Very nice lady. Got me a bag of oranges also.'

'From our office?' Sarla frowned and put her teacup down. 'Who was it? Did she give you a name?'

Jigna frowned. 'Yes . . . yes. It was someone called Neeta. No wait, I think it was Neetu. Yes, Neetu,' she repeated confidently.

10

'Neetu is the astrologer, no? Or are there any other Neetus in the office?' Radhi asked Sarla when they were back in the car.

They had just said their goodbyes to Jigna. Sarla had made her promise that she would call her if she ever needed anything, and now they were on their way to Temple Hill. Radhi would get off midway at a salon because she needed her hair styled for her cousin Miloni's sangeet function that evening and Sarla would head home to Temple Hill.

'Please increase the cooling of the AC.' Sarla leaned forward to instruct her driver before replying to Radhi, 'No, that's the only Neetu at Soul Harmony.'

'Did she and Hansa often work together?'

'Never. They had no reason to.' Sarla frowned. 'I can't think of what in the world Neetu would want from Hansa. The two women, in fact, didn't even like each other very much.' She took a wet tissue from the tissue box at the back of the car and dabbed her face with it. It was past noon and the short walk to the car under the scorching midday sun had turned Sarla's face red. 'I'll ask her when I see her in the office. The police have told me we can resume work from tomorrow.'

'I don't think you should say anything right now.'

'Why not? There was literally no overlap in their work! I would really like to know what she was up to there.'

'But, Aunty,' Radhi paused meaningfully, 'you're assuming she'll tell you the truth.'

'You think . . . you don't think . . . oh . . .' Sarla who had been fanning herself with the pallu of her sari became still. Her eyes widened and she fell quiet.

'Could she be the one sending you the tarot cards?' Radhi spelled it out for her. 'Or could she have something to do with it? Have you or Kiran ben had any kind of disagreements with her? Any reason why she'd do this?'

'No! Nothing! She's worked with us for almost a decade.' Sarla looked distressed. 'We didn't give her an increment last year, but surely that can't have upset her that much?!'

'It seems unlikely,' Radhi admitted. 'Also, she's an astrologer. Sending tarot cards would be kind of obvious.' She frowned. 'Neetu wouldn't want to draw attention to herself like that if she really was behind it.'

'But she doesn't do tarot!' Sarla sat up. 'She makes horoscopes and practises palmistry, but no tarot readings. Looks down on them, in fact. We all know that. Maybe she thought we wouldn't associate her with tarot cards?' She shook her head as if to clear it. 'But the question is why? Why would she do this?'

'I don't know.' Radhi bit her lip. She picked up a Tupperware bottle from the side pocket of the car and took a long, thirsty sip. 'But let's for a second focus on what we do know. *One*. Someone killed Hansa right after she told you she'd found out something about the tarot cards. *Two*. Neetu arrived at Hansa's home before any of us could look through Hansa's paperwork. *Three*. The file on tarot cards, if there ever was one, is missing. So far, so good?'

Sarla nodded.

'Now, bear with me for a moment longer. What if Neetu was sending the tarot cards and Hansa found out and threatened to tell you? Neetu would try to reason with her, but what if Hansa didn't listen? What if in desperation Neetu killed Hansa to protect herself and then proceeded to get rid of the evidence?' Radhi gave Sarla a grim smile. 'I realize how far-fetched that sounds, but please let's not say anything to her or the others until we know more.'

'Okay . . .' Sarla agreed weakly.

'I was going to interview Neetu for my book anyway — let me talk to her and see if I can find out anything else.'

Sarla nodded and turned towards the window.

As the car wove in and out of traffic, the two women fell quiet, each lost in her own thoughts. At a signal, two street children knocked on Sarla's window, a bunch of tube roses in the girl's hand and a fan of women's magazines in her younger brother's. 'Thirties, the new age for love' screamed one of the headlines.

Sarla rolled down the window and gave the girl a fifty-rupee note. 'Share,' she instructed the children. Then rolling the window back up, she turned to Radhi with a faint smile. 'So? Why are you getting all decked up at the salon? I hope it's for the benefit of someone interesting.'

Radhi rolled her eyes and smiled as she hung her purse on her shoulder in anticipation of getting down. 'I'm dressing up for myself, Aunty. For my pleasure alone.'

'I don't believe you for a second.' Sarla's eyes glinted mischievously, her worries momentarily forgotten.

Only the terribly naive would assume a wedding on Temple Hill was just a wedding. Most recognized it for what it was — a diamond-studded, bejewelled and bedazzling opportunity for all kinds of delicate social manoeuvring. It was a chance to rekindle friendships and renew relationships without the awkwardness that comes from not being in touch for many years. It was an opportunity to mend rifts, with both the invitee and the one doing the inviting absolved from making any actual apologies. An occasion to strengthen old partnerships without trying too hard, and to woo new acquaintances without appearing too obvious. And most essentially, it was a way to assert your standing in society. A measure of your success. Or rather, a showcase of it.

As Radhi surveyed the glittering lawns where her cousin's sangeet night was in progress, she admired the cut-crystal chandeliers dangling from the branches of trees and the elaborate floral sculptures and water fountains that had been erected almost overnight across the vast green expanse. The cost of this wedding, with all its pre- and post-wedding festivities, would probably amount to a small country's GDP, and yet mere extravagance would not impress the row of formidable aunts and matriarchs sitting closest to the stage. Resplendent in their crisp, zari-edged organzas and heirloom pearls, they would sit through the night, their eyes and ears on everyone and everything. Their most stringent scrutiny reserved for the bride, her chemistry with her new mother-in-law, and, of course, the food.

'Where are you guys?' Radhi asked Madhavi on the phone, struggling to be heard over the loud music.

Up on the stage, the compere for the evening had made way for the groom's uncles who were dancing to a Bollywood song about how marriage was like a big, sweet laddu. Those who got a taste of it regretted it eventually, but then, so did those who didn't. A loud cheer went up from the audience and Radhi missed Madhavi's reply.

'What did you say?' She covered one ear with her palm.

'Away from the stage, near the buffet counters,' repeated Madhavi. 'Start walking to your left once you enter.'

As Radhi picked her way through the hundreds of guests spread across the lawn in dazzling clusters of emeralds, rubies and diamonds, she smiled at many, waved at others and was forced to stop and chat with some.

'Finally!' she announced, coming to a halt at her sister's table and stooping to give her a hug before kissing her two young nieces and saying hello to the rest of the family.

'Oh, Radhi, we didn't expect to see you all alone today!' sang Ila Kaki, Radhi's Machiavellian sweet-talking aunt, whose presence Radhi only tolerated because she was married to their father's good-natured brother, Pankaj Kaka.

'Ila, leave the girl alone!' chided Vrinda Fia, who had been like a second mother to Radhi and Madhavi after the girls lost their parents. She was their father's sister and their staunchest supporter.

'What?' Ila widened her eyes innocently. 'The speed at which she moved the last time around, I thought she'd have sealed the deal by now!'

'Not everyone's after a "deal", Kaki,' retorted Radhi, the blood rushing to her face in that unique combination of anger and embarrassment that only Ila could elicit. 'We can't all be as calculated as that. Some of us just want to have a little fun.'

'Come now, darling. Surely, you realize that you've crossed the age to just have fun,' said Ila Kaki, her eyes glittering like icicles.

'Oh, I don't know if there's an age for it, Kaki. Some people are fun and some just aren't.' Radhi knew she'd regret her next words, but she said them anyway, 'At least that's what Nishant says.'

Ila gasped at what Radhi had just implied about her daughter. 'My Prachi can be a lot of fun!' she spluttered. 'She . . . she . . . loves to dance and party and she isn't . . . isn't like some . . .'

'Did someone say Nishant?' Madhavi's mother-in-law, Roma Bansal, interrupted them from across the table. 'What about him? What are the two of you talking about?'

Ila whirled towards the old tyrant with unhidden glee. 'Surely, they've told *you*, Roma ben? You know, na?'

'Know what?'

'Why, you remember how you introduced Parul ben's son Nishant to my Prachi, no?'

Roma nodded impatiently. 'Of course, I do. I'm not senile — yet.'

'Well, turns out our Radhi has been going out with him.'

'Going out? But where?' asked Roma Bansal, confused. 'And why has nobody told me about it?'

'Because there's nothing to tell, Mummy,' Madhavi placated her mother-in-law. 'They've just gone out on a few dates. That's all.'

'That's all? But that's hardly all, is it?!' Roma looked around affronted. 'My friend's son and my daughter-in-law's sister, whom *I* introduced, have been stepping out together and no one felt the need to keep me informed? When were you all planning on telling me? When the wedding cards were getting printed!? Or after the honeymoon?'

'It's all my fault, Roma ben.' Vrinda jumped in to soothe Mrs Bansal. If anyone could tackle Madhavi's obnoxious mother-in-law with ease, it was Radhi's formidable aunt. A professor of psychology, Vrinda was as erudite as she was socially connected. A member of a number of charitable boards and women clubs, she regularly lunched with ladies from all the major business families in the city. It was a quality Roma Bansal both admired and coveted.

'*Your* fault? How?' Mrs Bansal looked at Vrinda, astonished.

'Nishant had called me about a book we had discussed when we met at your place, and when he asked me for Radhi's number, I didn't see any reason not to give it. Obviously by then his mother had already informed us that he didn't think Prachi and he were a good fit.'

Vrinda said the last bit looking at Ila, who bristled at the suggestion that any man could possibly reject her rose-like daughter. 'And by the way, Ila, Radhi had decided not to go out with him, thinking perhaps that things would be awkward with you. But *I* insisted that she go. I told her that her Ila Kaki was large-hearted, she would be happy to see her heartbroken niece move on in life. Was I wrong to think that?' asked Vrinda, giving her sister-in-law an opportunity to end this conversation with some grace.

But Ila's envy of Radhi ran deep and could be traced back to Radhi's mother, whose good looks and position within the family she had always been inordinately jealous of. She found it impossible to retract herself from the situation.

'Of course, beta,' said Pankaj coming to his wife's rescue. 'Your aunt always has your best wishes at heart. We are happy if you're happy.'

'Well, I still think someone should have told me,' declared Roma, feeling like she had been left out of the conversation for too long and that they had digressed from the main issue. 'If Parul had called me with questions about Radhika and I didn't have an inkling of the matter, wouldn't I have come across as an ignorant fool?'

'Nobody in their right mind would dare to call you a fool, Mummy,' grinned Anshul, Madhavi's husband, who had just walked up to the table with two plates of samosa chaat topped with a generous sprinkling of sev.

'You ladies are missing that.' He nodded towards the stage, where the bride's aunts had started dancing to a song about the many perils of walking alone through a field of maize at the tender age of seventeen.

As Roma and the rest of her family turned their attention to the dance, Anshul caught Radhi's eye and winked. Radhi smiled back gratefully. Her brother-in-law had an uncanny ability to get her out of trouble.

'I had better get the full HD version of this story,' he said, coming to stand beside her.

'There's no big story, jiju.' Radhi groaned. 'We've just gone on a few dates.'

'Well, there should be.' He took a bite of his samosa chaat before adding, 'Nishant's a nice guy.' He went back to join his wife and mother.

On the stage, the bride's aunts were now heaving their ample bosoms at the thought of the many indiscretions that could happen in the maize field. A crowd of youngsters was cheering them on from the sides with calls of encore. Behind them, the backdrop of the stage was covered with a stunning curtain of yellow marigolds broken only by two life-sized peacocks fashioned out of rare blue orchids. Radhi smiled to herself; these middle-aged aunties were so priggish in real life that not one of them would dream of holding her own husband's hand in public. But up on the stage, every one of them had transformed into a Bollywood siren.

'Fia, shall we get something to eat?' Radhi bent down to speak in her aunt's ear.

'Yes please, before I lose my appetite!' Vrinda pushed her chair back and stood up.

'Come now, Fia, they aren't that bad.'

Vrinda rolled her eyes.

'Well, I think it's nice that they get to have some fun.' Radhi linked her arm with her aunt's and they made their way to the lavish buffet counters that traversed the length and breadth of the globe with placards announcing 'Mexican', 'Italian', 'Chinese', 'Ethiopian' like itinerary stops on a grand world tour.

'Hmm . . . now that's a new one.' Radhi paused at a huge iron grill with colourful vegetables arranged around its circumference in concentric half-circles.

'Mongolian barbeque,' Vrinda read out loud from the placard on the counter. 'Shall we try some of this?'

At a nod from them, the chef behind the counter began to throw in strips of zucchini and carrots, florets of cauliflower and broccoli, and julienned peppers, bamboo shoots and green beans into the centre of the pan. He tossed them together in what looked like a ginger-based golden sauce, a soy-based brown sauce and a bright crimson sauce that looked so unnatural that Radhi knew it couldn't just be red chillies. Next, he added the noodles and cubes of tofu. After serving the stir-fry into two bowls, he topped each one with a handful of peanuts, roasted sesame seeds and green onions.

'Uhmm . . .' Radhi said between crunchy mouthfuls of her stir-fry. 'I have to say Gujju weddings never disappoint when it comes to food! I've yet to come across such a staggering spread anywhere else in the world.'

'True,' agreed her aunt. 'Nor the constant one-upmanship that's responsible for it. That's unique to us as well!'

Radhi laughed. 'Also, true.'

As they made to return to their table, Radhi noticed a familiar figure eating alone next to the Mexican food counter.

'Oh, that's Kiran ben,' said Radhi, pausing to get a better look before changing course. 'I know her from Soul Harmony. Come, Fia, let's say hello.'

'Radhika! Fancy seeing you here,' Kiran greeted Radhi.

'The bride is a distant cousin from my dad's side,' Radhi explained, once she'd introduced Kiran to her aunt. 'And you? Who brings you here? The bride or the groom?'

'Neither. Actually, I should say both! They met through Soul Harmony.' Kiran smiled at them.

'Is Sarla Aunty here as well?'

'No, not today. In fact, it is she who usually attends these things. I rarely ever come. This is far too many people for me,' she said looking around. 'But Sarla wasn't feeling up to it today.'

Having spent the morning with her, Radhi knew this was true.

'Have you planned the wedding, as well?' asked Vrinda. 'If yes, I must compliment you on the caterer.'

'Not this one, I'm afraid. We often plan weddings, but not always.'

'Well, please don't eat alone, come and sit with us,' said Radhi and steered the woman towards their table.

'Everyone, this is Kiran ben,' she said as they took their seats. 'She's one of the partners at Soul Harmony, the matrimonial bureau where I've been collecting the information I need for the new book I'm working on.'

'Oh everyone knows Soul Harmony!' Ila leaned forward excitedly. 'I've been trying to get an appointment with Sarla ben for more than a month now. I didn't know she had a partner!'

'Who did you want to see us about? Son or daughter?' Kiran smiled, absently arranging the bean and cheese canapes on her plate in a straight line.

'For my eldest, Prachi. She's such a wonderful girl!' Ila rifled through her purse and handed over a photograph of Prachi to Kiran.

If Radhi had been on better terms with her kaki, she would have cracked a joke about her carrying Prachi's photograph to a wedding. But seeing as things were, she stuck to exchanging amused glances with her sister.

'She seems lovely.' Kiran glanced at the photo politely before giving it back.

'She's a fashion designer. Studied at NIFT. She supplies to luxury boutiques across the country. And she is only twenty-five,' Ila rattled off Prachi's many selling points as she dug deeper into her bag. 'I should have her biodata in here somewhere, as well.'

'No, no, that's quite all right. We would love to help you. Why don't you drop by the office tomorrow?'

'That would be perfect!' Ila beamed at them all, her sulk from earlier in the evening forgotten in the face of this unexpectedly lucky meeting.

If only today was yesterday.

Radhi's phone lit up with a text from Nishant as she waited outside the sangeet venue for Ramzan bhai to bring her car around. She read it again and blushed at the thought of his hungry kisses from the night before.

Who said it can't be?

She typed back with a smile, which lingered on her lips all the way home.

It was only later that night, when Nishant was lying fast asleep beside her, and Radhi was staring at the gentle rise and fall of his chest, wondering whether it was worth leaving the crook of his arm for one last smoke, that a small detail from the evening floated back to her. Something she had seen on the stage that now puzzled her. Straightening up, she reached for her office bag, brought out her diary and made a note of it.

11

Friday

Radhi reached the office early the next morning hoping to find an answer to the niggling little doubt that had crept up on her.

As she signed her name into the visitor entry book, the security guard followed the movement of her hand closely. He was clearly spooked by the week's events and seemed to be approaching his job with a newfound seriousness.

'I doubt she'll be in any frame of mind to see you,' said a voice behind Radhi.

Radhi turned around to see a middle-aged woman with stylishly short hair and a crisp, white linen dress smiling at her.

'I noticed that you wrote Sarla under "People to meet", but Sarla ben is probably caught up with the recent problems at Soul Harmony.' She extended her hand for Radhi to shake. 'I am Renuka, by the way. I run Pair Perfect, the most transparent matrimonial bureau on Temple Hill.'

Radhi raised her eyebrows at Renuka's declarations, both about Sarla and her own, but didn't comment. Instead, she said, 'I'm very glad we've run into each other. I have been meaning to speak with you.'

'Oh?' Renuka seemed intrigued.

Radhi told her briefly about the arranged-marriage book she was working on and the interviews she was conducting.

'How interesting! And here I thought you were just looking for a husband.' Renuka checked her watch. 'Well, I *am* free for the next one hour. We can talk now if you like?'

'Yes, please,' said Radhi and after Renuka had signed the register they headed for the lift.

Pair Perfect was the exact opposite of Soul Harmony—at least when it came to its interiors. With light-veined veneers, white walls, white couches and lots of reflective glass surfaces, Pair Perfect was modern and minimal in its décor. Unlike the dramatic flower arrangements and gilded picture frames of Soul Harmony, the only pop of colour here was a cerulean herringbone-pattered rug. It looked more like a Finnish design studio than an Indian matrimonial bureau.

Renuka waited for Radhi to take it all in, watching her closely. Radhi knew she was expecting her to comment on the décor — it was the kind of space that elicited a reaction — but she found she couldn't do it. Saying anything nice to Renuka felt too much like a betrayal of Sarla. Renuka seemed disappointed at Radhi's silence, but only for a moment.

'In here,' she said, leading the way through the waiting area into her cabin.

She offered Radhi coffee before pulling out a glass bottle of a thick, green smoothie for herself.

'Spinach, tomatoes and amla,' she took a large sip of the drink and made a face, 'excellent for gut health — supposedly. So tell me, what would you like to know?'

Radhi placed her phone on the table. 'Do you mind?' she asked, pressing the record button.

Renuka shook her head.

Radhi consulted her golden polka-dotted diary, where she had listed her questions. 'Why do you think arranged marriages are still so popular in our country? So many things have changed in the last few decades but why not the way we get married?'

Renuka took another sip of her drink before answering. 'Arranged marriages are still popular because marriage as an institution is still popular. As long as people want companionship, security, children and all the other comforts that a conventional marriage offers, there'll be takers for arranged marriages. And why shouldn't there be? They are such a tried and tested way of doing things in our culture.

'Besides, it's not like arranged marriages haven't evolved. Fifty years ago, you met your intended for coffee — once — with extended families from both sides present. Now the two of you can go out to dinner or a club and meet half a dozen times if you like. It's become quite liberal.'

'But the parents are still very much involved.'

'Yes. The parents are invested,' Renuka smiled. 'They have to be, no? It's not like the western countries, where the children move out at eighteen and then you see them during the holidays. Here grown sons are expected to live with their parents long after they are married and have families of their own. It's essential that everyone gets along and that the parents have some say in the matter, no?'

Renuka put away her smoothie bottle and dabbed her lips with a checked, parrot-green tissue from the tissue box.

'What sets Pair Perfect apart from the other matchmaking services? I mean, you've chosen to set up shop in the same building as Soul Harmony, which is probably the most famous matrimonial bureau on Temple Hill. So why would people choose to come to you? You mentioned you were the most transparent bureau — does that have something to do with it?'

'Absolutely! We are very transparent in the way we work and match people. I don't mean to badmouth Soul Harmony or any other bureau for that matter. But I find there is so much that happens behind the scenes that their clients may not even be aware of! Why X is set up with Y and not Z. Why A is given an appointment, but B is not. The real reason C has rejected D. Not all of it is disclosed to the clients. Whereas I believe they have a right to know. Unlike Sarla ben and team, when we conduct background checks on people, we don't withhold any information to suit our ends. We are very forthright about what we find.'

Renuka seemed to know a lot about how Soul Harmony functioned or at least presumed to. Radhi was about to ask her how when they were interrupted by a knock on the door. A young woman entered the cabin and handed Renuka a slip of paper.

'Oh, would you excuse me for a minute?' Renuka said when she had read the note. 'A client has dropped by without an appointment. I'll just go talk to her.'

Radhi nodded and Renuka slipped out of the room, quickly shutting the door behind her. But not before Radhi had caught a glimpse of a bright pink kaftan and a face she had seen before.

'Hi Juhi, is Sarla ben in yet?' Radhi had wrapped up her interview with Renuka and come to Soul Harmony.

'She is, didi. But she isn't free. The inspector has come back to see her.' Juhi had been doodling furiously and looked troubled.

'Apparently, Hansa ben's visitor entered fake information in the entry register. And now the police are mad at us for not checking ID cards of our visitors. But you tell me, didi, does any office ever adhere to these things so strictly? People come, they sign and they go in to meet whoever they have an appointment with. It's not like we work for some big bank or government agency or something.'

The phone on her desk rang. She picked it up, listened briefly and replaced the receiver. 'Sarla ben's calling me,' she said before hurrying away.

Radhi followed her down the corridor to her own desk. The office was full by now, but the bustle of clients and conversations Radhi had seen on her first day was missing. The mood was sombre and even those who were talking did so in hushed tones as if they had forgotten that it was impossible to disturb the dead. Radhi glanced into the cabins. All the rooms except Hansa's were occupied. What she needed to check would have to wait.

She was to meet Zarna at the Temple Hill Gymkhana for lunch. She hoped she would get to speak to Sarla before that. She had just switched on her laptop and opened the box of watermelon Lila had packed for her when Sarla's door opened and Inspector Shinde strode out, followed by Sarla and Juhi. He glanced around the office, his eyes narrow and probing, like a stern school principal looking to make an example of a wayward student. When his eyes met Radhi's, however, he looked away instantly, clearly averse to getting pulled into a discussion with her.

Radhi smirked and looked down at her computer.

'We'll send the artist this afternoon, latest by four,' Shinde said to Sarla. Then promising to be in touch, he followed Juhi down the corridor.

Radhi waited until they were out of earshot.

'All okay, Aunty?' she asked.

Sarla gave her a slight nod. 'They want to make a police sketch of Hansa's visitor. They'll show it to the paanwala, the drivers, cleaners, the vada pav fellow to see if anyone remembers him. Maybe he bought a cigarette or ate something or spoke to someone.'

Radhi nodded. 'I got a good look at him as well. If Juhi needs help, let me know.'

'Thank you, beta.' Sarla patted Radhi's shoulder.

'And, Aunty?'

'Hmm?'

'I was wondering if I could talk to you for a minute.'

Sarla looked at her curiously. 'Come,' she said, walking back to her office. 'You know, I have this terrible feeling that we haven't seen the worst of it yet.' She sighed wearily as she took her seat. 'First, the tarot cards, then Hansa's death . . . I dread to think of what's next.' She turned over some files and papers on her desk absent-mindedly before shaking her head as if trying to clear it. 'Anyways, tell me, what was it you wanted to talk about?'

'I went to Pair Perfect just now. And I—'

Sarla frowned. 'What were you doing at Renuka's bureau?'

'Well, I wanted to interview her for my book. But I also remembered Zarna saying that the tarot cards started coming after she opened her bureau, and I thought it would be a good opportunity to just poke around, ask her a few questions and see if she knew anything.'

'And? Does she know anything? About tarot or about matchmaking, for that matter?'

'She *did* seem to know a lot about how Soul Harmony functioned.'

'Well, she was our client once. She had registered her son with us. She would know how we work.'

'Oh! She didn't tell me that.' Radhi was surprised. 'Did it not go well?'

'Never you mind all that. How was her office? Has she tried to copy us?'

Radhi shook her head. 'In fact, she takes great pride in being different. Called her bureau the most transparent in town.'

Sarla snorted. 'Transparent? What rubbish! This is matchmaking! We don't have the luxury of being transparent! We're dealing with anxious mothers here. There's literally no human subsect on earth more demanding or insecure. Some of these women have only one goal in life — to get their offspring married. Try telling one of them that her son was rejected because the girl he was set up with didn't like his nose!' Sarla held up her hand to ward off Radhi's protestations. 'It's happened. Much stranger things have happened! Now you tell me, what good will honesty do in a situation like that?' Sarla shook her head. 'We are dealing with people's feelings and their futures and their fragile, fragile egos. We have to be tactful. And gentle. People don't always need the truth. Sometimes they need to be protected from it. And it's our job to know what to say when. Honestly, it's hard enough for young people to put themselves out there. Especially with all the parental pressure they have to deal with. So with all due respect to Renuka, transparency, my foot! They don't need a cold, hard mirror to show them a clear picture. They need a cushion to soften their bumps and falls.' Sarla took a large swig of water.

'Whoa, Aunty, that was quite a speech,' Radhi said, impressed, once again, by Sarla's passion for her business.

Sarla took another large gulp of her water and reached out for her phone. 'Juhi, can you ask Jeevan to bring in two cups of tea please.'

Then she turned her attention to Radhi. 'Thank you. I think I needed that. I've been asking myself of late why I do this.'

Juhi entered with a slight knock, carrying a tray with two teacups and a plate of khari biscuits. Made from plain flour and butter, the soft and flaky calorie-ridden biscuits were such a contrast to Renuka's spinach smoothie that Radhi couldn't help but smile.

'Why did *you* bring this? Where's Jeevan?' Sarla asked.

'He isn't well, ma'am, and hasn't come in today.'

'Why, what's happened to him?'

Juhi hesitated. 'I think it's all this police business, ma'am, it's really got to him.'

'It's got to all of us,' Sarla muttered. 'And you? Are you okay? You seem very pale too. Did the police trouble you too much, as well?'

Juhi gave a strained smile. 'Not too much. But I'll be glad to see the back of that Shinde.'

'Me too, beta, me too,' Sarla said absently. 'Remind me to speak to Jeevan tomorrow. He should tell me if they're troubling him unnecessarily.'

'Yes, ma'am,' said Juhi and she was turning to go when Radhi stopped her.

'Juhi, what did Hansa ben want to talk to you about?'

Juhi stared at her. 'Me? When?'

'That day, when she and I returned from our "outing", she asked you to come and see her, no?'

Juhi's face cleared. 'Oh that. Yes, I did knock on her door; in fact, it was immediately after that man left, but she was busy on the phone and asked me to come back later, and then I completely forgot.'

'How did she seem?' Radhi asked eagerly.

'Meaning, didi?'

'She'd just finished her meeting with that man . . . did she seem upset or angry?'

Juhi frowned. 'I had poked my head in only for a second, so it's difficult to say. I supposed she seemed serious . . . but she always seemed like that,' she looked at Sarla for confirmation, 'right, na, ma'am?'

Sarla nodded. 'Yes. More or less.'

When Juhi left, Sarla took a sip of her tea with closed eyes, savouring it. 'Sorry, we got completely derailed. Tell me, what did you want to speak to me about?'

'So on my first day here, I saw a heavy-set woman in an orange kaftan waiting in the reception area. I remember well because she seemed very upset about something. Then this morning I saw her at Pair Perfect and Renuka ben referred to her as a client. But Juhi has told me that you have an exclusivity policy with your clients. So it got me wondering what she was doing there.'

Sarla frowned. 'Yes, yes, we do. When we take on clients, they aren't allowed to sign up with any other bureau for the one year that they are with us. But maybe she wasn't a client? Maybe she came for an initial appointment and didn't sign up? Wait . . . we can easily find out.' She reached for the phone. 'I'll just ask Juhi to bring her register.'

'I think her name was Bhavana ben,' said Radhi. 'That's how Juhi addressed her. It stuck with me because of her odd behaviour, I think.'

Sarla put the phone away. 'Bhavana. Of course.'

After a moment's pause, she said, 'Bhavana's daughter, Khushi, has had a broken engagement. We had set up the couple. But a few months into the engagement the boy broke it off saying he wasn't ready to settle down yet. So Bhavana is angry with us.'

'But it's hardly your fault!' said Radhi, surprised.

'No, but human nature is such that it helps to have someone to blame. Besides, it *was* our responsibility to ensure that the boy was ready to get married before we introduced him to any of our clients. That's a big part of why we insist on meeting the candidates ourselves. We want to gauge where they are at. To see if they are only doing it to appease their parents or if they are really invested in the process themselves.'

'And there were no red flags in your initial meeting with him?'

'That's the thing, *I* didn't meet with him, so I can't be sure.' Sarla took another sip of her tea. 'Yug was Kiran's client.

But she insists that he was amiable and seemed completely invested. In fact, this was the other thing Hansa was working on. I had asked her to find out if there was anything that could've led to a change of heart. Say, an old girlfriend who had suddenly resurfaced. It would've helped our case with Bhavana.'

Sarla dunked a khari in her tea, managing to extricate it at exactly the right moment. A second longer and it would have softened too much, plonking right into the cup. 'Anyways,' Sarla continued after she had eaten her biscuit and wiped her hands with a tissue, 'I'll have to have a word with Bhavana. It is one thing to sit sulking in our reception and quite another to sign up with a competitor! She lives nearby. I'll check if I can drop by after work one of these days.'

'May I come with you?' Radhi asked.

Sarla raised her eyebrows.

'The tarot cards. When did they start coming?'

Sarla realized what the younger woman was getting at. 'Well, let's see.' She flipped the calendar pages back and forth before looking up at Radhi gravely. 'They began a week after.'

'A week after the broken engagement?'

Sarla nodded and the two women exchanged a grim look.

12

The Temple Hill Gymkhana or the THG was where the residents of Temple Hill came to play. Sprawled lazily by the sea, it was a lavish four-acre stretch of squash courts, badminton courts, swimming pools, gymnasiums and all sorts of other sports facilities. But the pursuit of fitness was only its second most important goal. For, as anyone who had ever sipped a protein shake at one of its juice bars knew, its raison d'etre was to offer its privileged members regular access — to each other. Here new friendships were forged during yoga classes and Zumba workouts, deals struck amid tennis matches and soccer games, and alliances cemented over gin and tonics at the bar. Cliquish to an extreme, the THG guarded its exclusivity with exorbitant fees and antiquated rules, which meant that apart from the members' children who grew up and became members in their own right, no new memberships had been given to outsiders in almost a decade.

Zarna had promised to give Radhi 'a young people's perspective on matchmaking'. As Radhi waited for her at the THG's Italian restaurant, she looked around and marvelled at how everything could change so completely and yet stay exactly the same. The grey and white décor with its exposed brick walls and lacquer finish floors was new, so were the waiters' sharp uniforms and the elegant menu cards peppered with words like 'pastiera napoletana' and 'tartuffo', but the chatter of the middle-aged ladies digging into their tiramisus while discussing their new diets was still the same. This time of day was entirely their own. Their husbands were at work. Their children were no longer children. And they had passed on the reins of their households to their daughters-in-law. No longer responsible for running busy kitchens and managing large retinues of cooks, maids and nannies, they were free to keep their salon and spa appointments, visit exhibitions to check out the latest designer clothes or simply meet their friends for lunch and talk candidly about how ably or terribly their daughters-in-law were managing in their absence.

'Sorry!' said Zarna as she slipped into the chair across Radhi in a bustle of scarf, bags, keys and phone. She removed her sunglasses, placed them on the table and flashed Radhi an apologetic smile. 'Sorry, this Hansa ben episode has thrown my whole schedule out of whack!'

'That's perfectly understandable,' said Radhi shutting her diary and pen. 'Did you work with her often?'

Zarna shook her head. 'No, she was more of Sarla Aunty's creature, and in any case, I really didn't like her whole vibe . . . know what I mean? But I had to cancel a few appointments on the day she . . . uh . . . died, so now I'm trying to reschedule everything.'

Zarna picked up the menu and flipped through it. 'What are you having?'

The last time she had seen Zarna, the woman had seemed frazzled by Shinde's interrogation. Now the interaction seemed behind her. A momentary blip in an otherwise smooth and privileged existence.

Once they had ordered their food, Zarna nodded towards Radhi's diary. 'I'm very excited about this piece you are writing on Soul Harmony. I hope you're saying only good things!'

Radhi smiled. 'Of course. It's such a success. You should be proud of what Sarla Aunty and your mum have achieved!' She placed her phone on the table with the record button switched on. 'Okay with this?'

Zarna nodded.

'So tell me, how long have you worked here?'

'More than three years now.'

'And what do you think makes Soul Harmony so successful?'

Zarna twirled a lock of hair, thoughtfully. 'I think the whole enterprise is very genuine. We aren't here to find you a match; we want to find you the "right" match. Sarla Aunty and my mum are truly invested in the longevity of the marriage. I've seen them discard easy matches because they don't "feel" right about them. Of course, when I say "they" I mean Sarla Aunty. She's a big one for "going by the gut".'

Radhi wondered if Zarna was being sarcastic, but then Zarna continued, 'Of course, there have been times when I haven't agreed with them. Thought they were being overscrupulous. But all in all, whatever they are doing seems to clearly work for them.'

The waiter cleared their bread basket and laid out their lunch order. Between them, they had ordered a pink sauce risotto with peppers and zucchini, a watermelon and feta salad with pine nuts and a light drizzle of Balsamic vinegar and a small but heavy three-layered bean and cheese lasagne.

'Uhm, this is good!' said Radhi after taking a bite of her risotto.

'You sound surprised.'

Radhi took another bite before replying, 'You know how it is with Italian? So many places just use the standard bottled sauces. But this is fresh, I could smell the basil and the rosemary even before I tasted them.'

Zarna shrugged. 'I wouldn't know. I personally have no interest in food. Neither in eating it nor in cooking it.' She had a spoonful of her salad. 'For too long I feel women in our culture have been forced to care about food, you know. I mean regardless of how privileged we are, how much help we have at home or how flourishing our own careers may be, when it comes to the kitchen it is our responsibility. But what if we don't want to do it? What if we want to never enter our kitchens? Our men get away with it, no? Then why can't we?'

Radhi nodded thoughtfully. 'I enjoy cooking and tinkering about in the kitchen every now and then. So I haven't really thought about this much. But I suppose the onus of that lies on Indian parents. If they trained their sons better and expected more from them, they wouldn't be so dependent on the women. And then the women could be at liberty to pursue their own plans.'

'Exactly!' Zarna waved her fork in the air for emphasis. 'That's exactly it. I have great plans of my own which don't include the kitchen!' She laughed.

Radhi laughed with her and took another helping of the lasagne. 'Do they include Soul Harmony, though?'

'Oh absolutely! I think there is just so much potential that we haven't yet explored!'

Radhi waited for her to elaborate.

'I think what the place needs is a new perspective. For so many years Sarla Aunty and Mummy have been doing the same thing in the same way that they don't realize how things could be different. How efficient we could be. How quickly we could grow!'

'How so?' Radhi wiped her fingers with a tissue and picked up her pen to make some notes.

Zarna put her fork down and pushed her plate away. The topic on hand was clearly more delicious than the food on her plate.

'It's simple. The business should be moved online! So much of what we currently do happens in person. But it shouldn't have to. The biodatas and the onboarding interviews could easily be done over Zoom calls. We would be able to save so much time!'

'But isn't that the speciality of Soul Harmony? The personal touch? Sarla Aunty says that she either knows the families she works with or she gets to know them. She understands their lifestyles, their priorities and what the young man or woman in question expects from a potential partner. And only then does she recommend one family to another.'

'Phssh!' Zarna was dismissive. 'Yes, yes. All that's true. And it has worked for them in the past. But is it right for the future? There is such an opportunity here to scale up! Just imagine if Soul Harmony existed online. Gujaratis from across the country, across the world, could sign up! Do you know that there are more than fifteen lakh Gujaratis in the US alone? And I haven't even looked at the UK or South Africa numbers.' She shook her head, her eyes shining. 'We could be so big!'

'What about Sarla Aunty and your mum, do they agree?' Radhi asked.

Zarna smiled confidently. 'They'll come around. Sarla Aunty is the main hurdle. But I have a plan. Once I have convinced her, Mum won't be so hard. Mum, in any case, agrees with me. Or at least she sees how much more money it could mean. She just doesn't like to contradict Sarla Aunty openly.'

They were quiet for a while as they focused on their food. Then Radhi switched off the recording button on her phone.

'What about Hansa's death? Do you really believe it was a robbery?'

Zarna shrugged. 'I have no reason to believe otherwise. I was worried about it initially. About how it would appear and what people would say, but one thing I've realized is that it is all about perception management. If we don't make a big deal about it, then nor will anyone else.'

'What about the tarot cards? Why did you seem to think Renuka ben was sending them?'

Zarna made a face. 'This is off the record, okay?'

Radhi nodded.

'There is some bad blood between Sarla Aunty and Renuka ben. I have no idea what or why. This was before my time, more than a decade ago. Even Mom doesn't know the full story. Just that Renuka ben was a client of Soul Harmony and then one day she wasn't.'

'But why suddenly start sending tarot cards after all this time?'

'Why suddenly start a bureau in the same building as ours?' Zarna countered. 'She could have set it up anywhere. Why here? Doesn't it seem spiteful? Like she has an agenda?'

The waiter had begun clearing their plates and handed them the dessert menu, but they ignored it.

Radhi was quiet, going over her interaction with the founder of Pair Perfect. It did seem that the bureau had been set up to be everything Soul Harmony wasn't. But wasn't that just clever positioning? A good marketing ploy? She hadn't thought that it had been done out of spite. But now she wasn't so sure.

'What about you?' Radhi asked Zarna after they had called for the bill. 'Did you meet your husband through Soul Harmony?'

Zarna smirked. 'No, no, that sort of thing is not for me.'

Radhi waited for her to add something, but when she didn't, Radhi asked, 'You mean arranged marriage?'

Zarna nodded. 'Yeah. I could never do it. I could never get married to a stranger.' Then she gave Radhi a broad smile as if remembering who she was talking to. 'But that certainly doesn't mean other people shouldn't do it. The system works splendidly. We already know that, right?'

Radhi smiled back. Her parents had had an arranged marriage and they had always seemed happy and wonderfully suited to each other. But like Zarna, she didn't think she could do it. She supposed she would always cling to the picture of romance she had found in the books she had grown up with. Her idea of a love story was still the Elizabeth and Darcy kind.

Zarna's phone rang. She mouthed a silent 'excuse me', pushed her chair back and walked a few paces away to take the call.

Radhi studied the woman with her poker-straight hair, pencil pants and angular features. She was sharp and ambitious, no doubt. But Radhi thought her vision was blinkered. There was an unwillingness to see that which didn't suit her ideas for the future. She wondered how far the woman was prepared to go to realize her ambitions.

---

*OK FINE. YOU WERE RIGHT. I don't know how you knew but you should know it's annoying. People don't like people who call them out. Which is not to say that I don't like you. I f***ing adore you. But I'm not most people. So don't make a habit of this 'calling people liars' business. Okay I'll get to the point. I wasn't being completely honest with you. But it was only because I had your best interests at heart.*

I read your mystery as soon as you sent it to me, and I enjoyed it thoroughly. I thought it was taut, brimming with tension and excellently constructed. I absolutely loved the world you've set it in. All the twists and turns. The superb pacing. And the characters. I f-ing adored the characters (is that aunt in your book for real? You must introduce us!). But I did have one problem. I didn't want to say anything about it to you until I wasn't completely sure myself. So I've asked a couple of people on my team to read it. Once they get back to me, I plan to write to you with consolidated feedback. I know that sounds worrying, but please, please believe me when I say it's nothing a writer with your kind of experience can't handle.

XOXOXO

George

p.s. Please don't be mad at me. I can't stand it!

Radhi blew out angry rings of smoke into the air. She had returned from her lunch with Zarna and had been standing below the office of Soul Harmony, enjoying a post-lunch cigarette when George's email had soured her mood. She could tell he was telling the truth this time, but she was furious at him for still keeping her on the edge. Why couldn't he have just told her what the bloody problem was! She went back and read the email a second time and groaned silently in frustration. For the life of her, she couldn't guess what it could be. Not because she thought her first draft was perfect. But she hadn't anticipated any problems so huge that George was scared to bring them up with her without getting a second opinion. Radhi lit up another cigarette and was contemplating her response when a street child selling strings of white jasmine gajras walked up to her urging her to buy one. Radhi smiled at her and pointed to her loose hair. 'How will I wear it?'

The girl smiled back. 'Please?' she persisted.

Radhi looked around and saw the vada pav vendor at the corner of the street. 'Hungry?' she asked.

The girl followed her gaze and nodded eagerly.

'Come,' said Radhi.

In a surprisingly loud voice, the girl called out to the other street children playing on the pavement with a deflated beach ball and asked them to follow her.

'Bhaiya, give all these children a vada pav each,' Radhi said to the vendor when they reached him.

'Can I have two?' asked one of the children.

'Me too, I want for my sister!' said another.

'My granny is unwell. Could I take one for her?' asked a third.

In a flurry of *yesses* and *one at a time, one at a time*, Radhi handed the vada pavs to each kid as fast as the vendor could make them, watching with pleasure as they wolfed down the food and eyed her shyly for seconds. When all the children had had their fill and taken little parcels for their sisters, grannies and anyone else they could think of, Radhi brought out her wallet to pay the vendor.

'I'm done for the day,' he said happily to Radhi as he accepted her cash. 'I can shut my stall and go home now.'

'I'm glad.' Radhi smiled back at him.

'I think my good luck is on. Even two–three days ago, some college students came and polished off all the food!' He counted the change before giving it to Radhi.

'Good for you!' Radhi pocketed the money and began making her way back to Soul Harmony. The young girl with the gajras came running to her. 'Here, didi,' she said, holding a gajra in her outstretched arm, 'gift for you! Sprinkle water on the flowers and place them near a fan, your whole room will smell nice!'

'Thank you!' Radhi accepted her gift with pleasure and placed it gently on top of her handbag. She was a few minutes late for her meeting with Neetu and she hurried into the building.

Renuka, who had been observing Radhi from behind the white blinds at her window, returned to her desk once Radhi had entered the building. She took a tiny nibble of her date and walnut cookie, suppressed the urge to take another and began pacing the room. She was agitated, her mind whirring with possibilities and plans. She knew she could use Radhi to push her schemes further. But it would require stooping lower than she had so far allowed herself to go. She glanced at the *WedMe Happy* magazine on her desk with Sarla's smiling face on the cover and felt her chest burn. Anger. Not red hot or urgent but a deep amber, the kind that had been simmering for a long, long time. She had a moment of clarity then and she made up her mind.

Unlike the rest of the office, which was lit up by bright, yellow LEDs, a lone lamp illuminated Neetu's small, windowless room. There was a strong fragrance of camphor and sandalwood in the air, accompanied by a thin haze of smoke. A large photo of Sai Baba stood on a corner stool and in front of it was an oil lamp and two incense sticks. A soft chant of the Gayatri Mantra played on loop from a speaker placed next to the photo.

'Thank you for taking the time to see me, especially with everything that's been going on,' Radhi said as she pulled out a chair for herself and rifled through her bag for her diary and pens.

'It's not like I had much of a choice.' Neetu pointed a remote towards the speaker and the music stopped. 'Juhi told me that Sarla ben would like me to talk to you, so let's talk.'

Radhi looked up to find the older woman's face expressionless. 'Don't worry, we'll keep it short.' She pressed the record button on her phone. 'I hope this is fine?'

Neetu shrugged.

There was a slight knock at the door and Juhi came in bearing a tray with many cups of tea and coffee. She placed one in front of Neetu and turned to Radhi with a questioning look. 'Didi?'

'Tea, please. Thank you,' Radhi said, and when Juhi had left the room, she turned to Neetu and continued, 'This afternoon cup is so essential, no? I find myself slipping into a slump if I skip it.'

Neetu remained silent.

'Did you know that in the West, they sometimes read tea dregs to tell the future?' Radhi tried again and this time got a reaction.

'Please!' Neetu said sharply. 'Tea leaves, crystal balls, all that is bakwaas! It's entertainment at fairs. Please don't confuse it with what I do here.'

'No, no, of course not. I know that astrology is a science. I only meant—'

'I can see what you mean on your face,' Neetu interrupted. 'You have no faith in all of this. Tell me if I'm wrong?'

She wasn't wrong. Radhi didn't believe in horoscopes or astrology or in the ability of any one person to predict another person's future. Ever since her parents died, she'd had trouble believing in God, let alone in stars and planets affecting one's fate. As far as she was concerned, a world that could take away her beautiful, vital, generous parents in one cruel moment could not possibly be governed by any kind of sensible laws, planetary or otherwise.

Neetu continued to stare at her challengingly, but Radhi remained silent. Maybe it was because Radhi had chosen not to lie or because she'd seen something else on Radhi's face that Neetu thawed slightly. 'Astrology is a science. It involves maths and precision. And I'm a bit sick of people around here treating it as some kind of joke.'

'I'm sure that's not t—'

'Do you know how many calculations are required to draw up a horoscope?'

Radhi shook her head.

'We use a person's time, place and date of birth to map the exact position of the planets and stars under which the person was born. The exact degree to which a planet is inclined, ascendant or descendant, all of that is taken into account.'

'And when you're matching two horoscopes? I'm guessing you need to do further calculations then?'

'Exactly!' Neetu put down her cup of tea emphatically, spilling some on the table. 'Satyanash . . .' she cursed under her breath before fishing out a checked, parrot-green tissue paper from her purse and dabbing the puddle of tea with it.

'So how does it all work? Can you tell me a little bit about your process?' Radhi asked when Neetu had cleaned her table to her satisfaction.

'Well, when Sarla ben or Kiran ben come to me with two candidates they are planning to introduce to each other, I draw up their horoscopes and compare them to see if they'd make a good match. Mainly we want to see if the union will be sexually and intellectually compatible and financially prosperous. We study the nature, temperament and tendencies of both individuals to see if the marriage will be harmonious. And most importantly, we determine the health of the family resulting from such a union. Will reproduction be easy, how many children will they have, will they get along with their progeny, that sort of thing.'

Radhi raised her eyebrows but didn't say anything. She hadn't known that the analysis was so detailed. She jotted down a few follow-up questions.

Neetu continued, 'There's a score given to each of the aspects that we compare. If the score is below eighteen, we advise against the match. And if it is above twenty-six it is considered a stellar match.'

'This is fascinating.'

'Yes, it is. But you still don't believe in it, do you?'

'I don't know,' said Radhi honestly.

Neetu studied Radhi's face. Then she asked, 'How many divorces have you had?'

Startled, Radhi answered, 'One.'

Neetu nodded. 'So that's one divorce and at least one major failed relationship, am I right?'

Radhi stared at her wordlessly and Neetu nodded again. 'It says so, right here.' She touched her forehead and then pointed to the two mounds on Radhi's forehead. 'Multiple failed relationships in your youth. Of course, you may settle down eventually. But I can tell by the curve of your nose that there's still time for that. If I had your horoscope in front of me, I would probably be able to tell you exactly when you'll settle. But with face reading, I can't be that precise.' She got up to pour more oil into the lamp in front of the photo of Sai Baba. Then without turning she said, 'Of course, with a rational mind like yours, you're probably thinking that I've got this information from someone or somewhere and now your brain is trying to figure out where.' She turned around to face Radhi, who couldn't hide her surprise. 'You can't accept any of this at face value, can you?'

'It's not that,' Radhi started but then thought better of it. 'Well, it is hard for me to digest this, yes. But that's not to say that what you're doing is not genuine. I just don't know enough.'

Neetu nodded thoughtfully as she came back to her desk, 'Well, at least you have the humility to admit you don't know better. It is the other kind of people here that I have a problem with. The ones who show no respect.'

'Come now, Neetu ben, I'm sure you're well-regarded here,' Radhi said. 'Juhi tells me you've been here almost since the beginning. And that they never suggest a match without your blessing.'

Neetu scowled. 'Oh, you think I don't know why Sarla ben keeps me around? It's only because her clients ask for their horoscopes to be matched! Not because she has any real faith in what I do.'

Radhi started to protest, but Neetu cut her off, 'Left to her own, our dear founder would much rather trust the findings of that two-bit PI than someone learned like me. So often I've advised them to go ahead with a match because the horoscopes were well-suited but then that Hansa has whispered something in Sarla ben's ear and—foosh!—it's like I had never spoken!'

'Did you two often have to work together?' Radhi asked even though she knew the answer.

'Hansa and me? Never. I couldn't stand that woman. She was so full of herself.' Neetu glanced at the photo of Sai Baba, murmured a quick prayer and shook her head. 'I shouldn't speak ill of the dead. Everyone will get their just reward in the end.'

She swivelled around in her chair, got up and selected a slim volume called *Kundali: Matching Horoscopes the Indian Way* from an overhead shelf on the wall behind her.

'Read this, it will give you a better understanding.'

Radhi took the book from her and flipped through it before putting it in her bag. On the shelf she could see books on palmistry, numerology, gemology and all sorts of astrology-related subjects.

'Was there anything else?' Neetu asked.

'Would you happen to have a simple book like this on tarot as well?' Radhi asked.

Neetu made a face. 'Again the same nonsense? I told you I'm not an entertainer. Tarot is a trick for parties. There's no science in that. You focus on that.' She pointed to Radhi's bag where Radhi had kept her book.

When Radhi left, Neetu brought out her jaapmaala from a drawer in her desk and began to roll the prayer beads gently, absent-mindedly. It was a habit that had lost its religious significance long ago, right about the time that it had become sacred to her. An all-important emotional crutch, helping to calm her down or lift her up depending on the day, the beads a talisman to protect her against her own thoughts. And she needed the protecting, even her birth chart said so. Or else she tended to go to a dark place, finding it hard then to step back into the sun.

For the longest time, the thing that had eaten her from inside, pecking away relentlessly at her sense of self and feasting on her crumbling confidence, was her overwhelming need to be respected. Nobody took her job seriously. She had done courses on numerology and Vedic astrology, studied tomes on palmistry and astronomy and trained under Sri Surishankar for face-reading, and yet, at best, her work was treated as a frivolous science.

At home, her husband just humoured her. A computer engineer by profession, he was a man who thought in a box girded by bits and binaries. He was unable to process her world, the syntax of ascendant houses and planetary positions too obscure for his taste. Sure, he would wear the moonstone ring she suggested for his health or delay signing a new contract if she told him the stars weren't favourably aligned. But she knew it was more to keep the peace in their marriage than any kind of faith in her work. Even her children didn't think of it as a real profession. As kids they had been awed by it, but now that they were older, she suspected they were embarrassed. If you asked them, they would deny it of course, but in school forms they always wrote 'housewife' under 'Mother's Occupation'. And not once had they asked her to come to their class on career day, preferring always to take their father.

But it wasn't them that she was really angry at. They may not understand her work, but they tried not to hurt her feelings. Her children loved her, and in his own limited way, so did her husband. What made her livid was the attitude of the people she worked with. Kiran wasn't so bad. She was a believer in her own jittery way. But Sarla's arrogance really got to her. It wasn't in anything that her employer said, rather it was her casual disregard of Neetu's advice when it didn't suit her. Almost as if she considered the salary she paid Neetu a substitute for respect. Neetu had often observed that Sarla tended to trust her own instincts more, and when in doubt, she turned to Hansa for additional information, rather than ask for Neetu's advice. The PI's shady findings were clearly more valuable to her than the knowledge that Neetu had amassed after years of study.

Neetu stopped rolling the beads and touched the cool sandalwood jaapmaala to her forehead before putting it back in the drawer. She had a small smile on her face at the thought of Hansa and how accurate her prediction had been. There were other things which she knew she was right about as well. Things she'd seen in her own chart. And Sarla's. And the future of Soul Harmony or rather the lack of it.

13

Radhi, promise me you won't freak out. I know we were just about to become friends again, but I'd be a terrible agent if I didn't suggest this. Just try not to react please until you've read the entire email. Okay?

So I finally got around to reading the Word doc you sent me with your initial notes and descriptions of Soul Harmony, the matchmakers, the wedding planner, the PI — and I have to say, I can't get over it. It all sounds so fascinating! I honestly believe we have a cracker of a book on our hands! But it got me thinking that as a reader what I would also like to see is what it's like to go through the whole process yourself. Yes, of course, I want a bird's eye view of how it all runs and how a match is made and all of the deliciously juicy trivia that you've thrown in, but what I also want are a few personal stories of what it's like for people who are set up on that date. How do they process the whole experience? Yes, I know you're planning on talking to some of the young people who are signed up at these bureaus — but that will still be a third person account for us — something that you will hear from them and then recount for us. But what if — and this brings me to my idea — what if you were to go on an arranged date yourself?

Now, Radhi, just remember, you promised me no knee-jerk reactions. Can you just for a minute consider it? I want to know how it feels to be getting ready for that date, why you wear what you wear, why you order what you order, what the two of you talk about, how awkward it is, how different it is from going on a Tinder date, for instance — I want to know it all. Can you imagine how much richer it would make your book if you could put all of that in and filter it through the lens of a writer?

That's it. I rest my case. You know I'm right so there's no point in saying otherwise. Now the question remains how quickly you'll be able to see it yourself.

Toodle-oo! I love you too! J

George

'Damn! Damn! Damn!' Radhi threw her head back and covered her face with a cushion, muffling the sound of her own cursing. She was on the couch in her living room, steadily working her way through some notes and a bottle of a brawny merlot she had opened for the evening. Lila had given her a plate of steamed dudhi muthiyas flecked with sesame seeds before leaving for the day. But so far, Radhi had ignored the snack.

Radhi lowered the cushion from her face and crushed it to her chest, staring frustratedly at the laptop in front of her. Now she had two reasons to be mad at George. One, he still hadn't written to her about her previous book, and two, because of what she had instantly recognized — as much as she abhorred the idea, as much as the very thought of being set up horrified her — he was most likely right about this one. Radhi picked up her cigarettes and went to stand by the window, too agitated to light up. She wasn't a very social person at the best of times, but to sit across a stranger with the express purpose of considering marriage didn't bear thinking about. And yet . . . and yet she couldn't deny that he had a point. Zarna had announced that arranged marriages were not for her. Radhi felt much the same way. But if she went on a couple of arranged dates, she realized, she'd be able to say so with so much more authority. It would give her writing a whole new dimension. Cursing George again, she reached for her laptop.

Okay, Georgie boy, here's the deal. You tell me what the problem with my mystery is. Now. Not a month later. Not a week later. Now. I know you said you liked it. But what is the problem with it? No circumventing. No beating around the bush. Just give it to me straight. And in return for your honesty, I will go on an arranged date. (Yes, for real.) But if you try to bullshit me, I promise you, I will see through it and I will stop writing this book.

If you think this is an empty threat, do you even know me? J

Love you too

Radhi

Radhi tilted the bottle of wine over her glass and cursed as only a thin trickle flowed out. She had finished the whole bottle in the course of the two hours that she had been home. Lila would be upset with her for not having eaten the muthiyas but she would deal with that later. Right now, she was beginning to feel drowsy, and sleep was far more elusive and therefore a priority. For years now, Radhi had suffered from anxiety. She found it difficult to fall asleep, and even when she did, she often woke up in the middle of the night with her stomach clenched and chest tight, unable to breathe. It had started when her parents died, getting better for a few years before resurfacing during times of high stress—like her divorce and then again when Mackinzey disappeared. When in the US, at the behest of her sister and aunt, she had consulted a psychiatrist who had prescribed sleeping pills while helping her work through her emotions.

But back in India, she had resisted therapy — the prospect of drudging up the past all over again seemed excruciating and she was reluctant to put herself through it. But no psychiatrist meant no sleeping pills. Which had been a problem until she discovered that a few glasses of wine made her nice and mellow and helped her, on most nights, to fall asleep.

Saturday

BIODATA

Name:
Age:
Weight:
Height:
Date of Birth:
Place of Birth:
Time of Birth:
Education:
Occupation:
Interests:
Looking for:
Address:
Father:
Occupation & Office Address:
Mother:
Occupation & Office Address:
Sibling:
Grandfather:
Maternal Grandfather:
References:
1)
2)

Radhi scanned the empty form in front of her and frowned at Juhi. 'All of this?' They were in the utility room together and Juhi was helping Radhi create her biodata.

Juhi gave her a sympathetic smile. 'It will help us figure out who to set you up with. Sarla ben already has a few ideas, but we'll have to share your biodata with the parents of the boy before you meet. So you need to make one, regardless.'

Radhi glanced at the sheet again. 'What does "references" mean?'

'Family friends. People who aren't related but know you well enough to vouch for you.'

Radhi rolled her eyes. 'Jesus, are we hunting for a job or a life partner?'

Juhi handed her a pen. 'C'mon, didi, it's not that bad. Most of these are just one-word answers.'

As Radhi worked her way through the form, Juhi busied herself making them elaichi chai. When the tea was done, she opened a pack of Marie biscuits and arranged them on the plate, like fallen dominoes.

'May I see?' she asked, handing Radhi her tea and taking a seat. She gave the sheet of paper a once-over before handing it back to Radhi. 'See, this is why I have my job.'

Radhi took a sip of her tea and waited for her to elaborate.

'Occupation: Writer. Interests: Books, films and music.' She read out loud from Radhi's form. 'How does this give anyone a flavour of anything? For instance, what kind of films do you like? Documentaries about spiders? Salman Khan blockbusters? Children's cartoons?'

Radhi laughed. 'Okay, okay, I get the drift.' She took the sheet back from Juhi. 'But if I describe myself so thoroughly here, what am I going to talk about when we meet?'

'Oh, you'll find things, didi! I don't know why, but most people are so reluctant to talk about themselves. Earlier I used to think that they are just lazy. But then since last year when I started sitting in on these interviews, I realized that people are just shy and need to be coaxed a little.'

Radhi took a bite of a biscuit before replying, 'So now you help new clients with their biodatas?'

Juhi shook her head. 'Not all. Sarla ben has her own process. It's something else altogether, the way she talks to the boys and girls. She gets them to prattle about all sorts of things. But yes, with Kiran ben, she asks for me each time she signs on a new client.'

There was a knock at the door. It was Jeevan, holding a parcel.

'Oh, sorry,' he said when he saw Radhi and hovered at the door.

'We are almost done in here,' Radhi said. 'Please go ahead with whatever you came in for.'

Jeevan entered the room and showed Juhi the box. 'The cartridges and the stationary that Kiran ben ordered. Should I put them in the utility room?'

'No, that's fine, just give them to me.' Juhi took the parcel from him.

'I hope the police haven't troubled you again?' Radhi asked.

Jeevan started. 'Uh . . . no, it's been okay.'

Avoiding Radhi's eyes, he looked at a spot above her head.

'Can I get you something? Tea? Coffee?' He asked unmindful of the steaming mugs of tea on the table.

When Radhi shook her head, he left the room as quickly as he had come.

'If only these had come sooner,' Juhi muttered as she opened the box of cartridges, 'I would've got the printer guy to insert these in when he came to fix the printer yesterday. Now I'll have to figure this out myself.'

Radhi looked up from her form and stared at Juhi.

'What is it, didi?' Juhi looked at her surprised.

'No, nothing.' With an effort, Radhi shook her head. 'I just remembered I had to send out an email. I'll complete this form at my desk,' she said gathering her things as Juhi stared at her curiously.

Radhi went to her seat, dropped her things on the desk and stared blankly at the form in front of her. Her mind worked furiously, weighing the pros and cons of the action she was considering. When she came to a decision, she bent down to hurriedly complete her biodata. Then she walked down the corridor and knocked firmly on Kiran's door.

'Yes, beta? Are you done with your biodata? Sarla has asked me to set you up with the handsomest candidate in our files.' Kiran smiled at Radhi.

'Yes, Juhi helped me with it.' Radhi handed her the biodata and sat down while Kiran scanned the page.

Like Sarla, even Kiran appeared strained. There were dark circles under her eyes and her smile when she looked up seemed tired. The events of the last few days had clearly taken their toll on her. 'Seems perfect. We should be able to set something up for you right away.'

'I actually wanted to check something else with you, Aunty,' Radhi said carefully.

'Yes?' Kiran put the biodata away and looked at Radhi expectantly.

'It's about Zarna. I was just wondering if it is possible that she has misremembered.'

'Sorry?'

'About that night when Hansa ben died, Zarna said that she came back for printouts. Is it possible she is mistaken?'

Kiran's eyes widened. 'Why? What makes you ask that?'

'On my first day here, I heard Sarla Aunty ask Juhi if the printer had been fixed.' Radhi pretended to hesitate. She was about to make an accusation, but she wanted to make sure it didn't sound like one.

'Go on, beta,' Kiran urged anxiously.

'Juhi said it hadn't, that the repair fellow would be coming the following day. This was the night that Hansa ben was killed, and Zarna said she came back to take a few printouts. But if the printer wasn't working, she couldn't have taken those prints, no?'

Kiran looked confused. She had begun to sweat despite the heavy air conditioning. 'I will ask Zarna. There must be some explanation for this. Just let me talk to her and sort it out.'

'Let's talk to her together. I thought I'd call Sarla Aunty also, but I didn't want to trouble her without understanding the situation properly myself. Besides, I'm sure there's a reasonable explanation for this.'

'Yes, exactly! You were right not to involve Sarla in this. I mean she has got enough on her plate as is. The last thing I want to do is add to her troubles!' Kiran reached for her phone and dialled Zarna's number.

'Where are you?' she asked without preamble. She listened briefly and then said, 'Okay, come straight up. I need to speak to you.' She cut the line and gave Radhi a smile which looked more like a grimace. 'She will be reaching the office in five minutes or so.'

Kiran picked up a magazine and fanned herself with it. It was the *WedMe Happy* issue with Sarla on the cover. 'Is this air conditioner even working?' She put the magazine down and began to fiddle with the AC remote.

Radhi looked around the cabin Zarna shared with her mother. Radhi had first been here the day she'd discovered the body but then the place had been crawling with police. Now she noticed how long the room was and how impeccably neat. Both Zarna's and Kiran's desks didn't have a single paper out of place. They were so clean that it was hard to believe that anyone got any work done on it. The four cushions on the sofa opposite the desks were just so. Even the row of plants by the window seemed to have grown symmetrically. Arranged in a straight line on the yellow wall above the couch were six square wooden frames with quotes on successful marriages and love. One caught her attention: '*A happy marriage is the union of two good forgivers.*' *Ruth Bell Graham*. How incredibly simple and true it was. When she looked back at her marriage, she felt that Bedi and she hadn't had more arguments than the average couple, but their fights had gone on longer. Their marriage had been fraught with the weight of their expectations. And when those expectations hadn't been met, they had hardened into little knots of resentment and lodged in their hearts. Ready to be launched at each other like little cannonballs when an occasion arose. Between them, they'd had far too many pointed fingers and not enough apologies.

'What happened, Mummy?' Zarna asked as she entered the room. Registering Radhi in the visitor's chair she said, 'Is it those dreadful tarot cards again?'

'No, no.' Kiran shook her head impatiently and motioned towards the empty chair beside Radhi. 'Sit here for a minute.'

Zarna put her bag and things on the couch before taking a seat across from her mother.

Kiran continued, 'That night when Hansa ben was ki . . . uh when she died,' she stumbled over the violent words, 'you said you came back to the office that night for some printouts. Is it possible you came back for something else? That y—'

'What? Wh—' Zarna began to protest, but Kiran raised her voice to speak over her.

'Could it be that you came back for something else, Zarna? Because Radhi here just pointed out that the printer was not working then and has only just been repaired yesterday.'

'I . . .' Zarna started and stopped and then began again in a shrill tone, 'I didn't say I *took* the prints that night, I said I *came back* for them! I had shot the prints a couple of days earlier, when the course material came in, but had completely forgotten to collect them from the utility room. And that evening, I realized I needed them for my exam, so I came back to the office.'

Kiran turned to Radhi looking relieved. 'See, I told you there was a perfectly simple explanation for this.'

'I knew there would be, Aunty.' Radhi smiled at the older woman. 'And luckily for Zarna, she can easily prove this.'

'How's that?'

'The police have taken the computers, no? They can easily check the printing history of Zarna's machine. It will have both the date and time that Zarna printed the documents.'

'Oh that's good, then!' Kiran said, her smile faltering as she looked at her daughter who'd turned pale. 'That's good, no, Zarna?'

'Of course it is, Mummy,' Zarna snapped back.

14

*Okay darling, listen up. You've written a cracking good detective story. The mystery is intricately plotted. The clues are cleverly planted. And the world-building is fantastic. But where the f*** is the detective? YOU solved the whole thing in real life, so where are you? Yes, I see the young woman flitting about competently from the neighbour's house to the broker's office, etc., piecing the whole puzzle together. But we know NOTHING about her. Nothing of note, that is. She likes her tea and the colour green, and she is close to her sister. Got it. But what else? We know nothing of her insecurities, of whether she sleeps well at night or if she's ever had her heart broken. Look, darling, I know you are an intensely private person and that to give the world at large a glimpse into your head and heart might be unthinkable for you. But in that case, you need to fabricate an interior life for your detective. And you need to do it without worrying that it'll hit too close to home. Because I know that's what you've been doing. There are places in the story where I caught your protagonist thinking a real thought, a thought that Radhi might've had, but you immediately brushed it aside. You distracted the reader with a red herring or the Bombay monsoons or the gorgeous food. All of which is fascinating no doubt but can't possibly stand in for a person's* *feelings. Every time things get uncomfortably real for the detective, she can't just remove a rabbit from the hat, say voila and draw us away.*

You don't have to respond right away, Radhi. Think about what I've said. And when you're done hurling abuses at me, could you please go back and fix it?

XOXOXO

George

p.s. You owe me an arranged date, now. Don't worry, it can't possibly be as scary as me having to write this email.

Radhi stared at George's email and then she read it again. And again. On each reading the sinking feeling in the pit of her stomach intensified. George had caught her out. She hadn't realized it before but what he said was true. Her book was authentic in everything but in the portrayal of her protagonist. While she had explored the motivations and inner workings of all her ancillary characters, she had shied away from the turbulence of her detective's soul. Choosing to describe her dark circles instead of focusing on why she hadn't been sleeping well. Or talking about how she was friends with her ex-husband instead of delving into why she had got divorced in the first place. Radhi could see it now, how she had tried to hide, how she had tried to keep things light and easy. Groaning, she covered her face, silently cursing George for being right and herself for the embarrassing shortcut she had tried to take, and then George again for pretty much everything. She looked up at the sound of the waiter clearing his throat.

'May I?' he asked before placing a plate of spicy kimchi rice in front of her, along with a bowl of edamame and carrots stir-fried in a bubbly ginger and soy sauce.

Radhi was at an Asian restaurant that had just opened at the bottom of Moksha. She had come to grab a quick bite while she waited for Sarla to return to the office from a meeting. She had come down hungry, puzzling over her conversation with Zarna and Kiran and keen on making notes about the biodata she had filled out that morning. But now she looked at the food unhappily. Her appetite had vanished after reading George's email. Her stomach full with large helpings of anxiety and fear. Reluctantly, she put her notebook and papers away and served herself a spoonful of rice and vegetables. She had learned from experience that eating her meals at regular times was the only way to keep her recurring acidity at bay. As she took a bite of her food, her eyes widened with pleasure. The kimchi rice was packed with flavour, and the vegetables had a nice, juicy crunch.

She checked out the richly done-up restaurant with its ruby-red velvet sofas and black Marquina marble on the floor. What a pity, she thought, that this too would go. And what a wonder that something new would manage to come in its place. Everyone on Temple Hill knew that this space was jinxed. That no business had ever prospered under this roof. Just about two months ago, it had been a cafe called White with bright Van Gogh prints on snow-white walls. And the year before that, it was a laundromat. Over the years, if the stories were to be believed, it had also been an ice cream parlour, a popcorn place, a video-cassette library and an art gallery. But nothing had ever lasted for more than a couple of years. It was a wonder to Radhi and to most Temple Hill folk how its owner always managed to find takers despite its ill-fated reputation.

She took a few more bites of her food before summoning the waiter with a scribble in the air.

'Check please,' she said when he came closer. 'And could you please pack this to go?'

As Radhi's car inched up the steep Moksha slope to the main Temple Hill Road, she kept an eye out for the little girl who had gifted her the gajra the other day. She knew the child would appreciate the leftover food. But there was no sign of her or any of the street children who usually loitered on the footpaths taking care of their younger siblings and their meagre belongings while their parents were away trying to earn a few rupees. When her car crossed the vada pav vendor, she asked Ramzan bhai to pull over for a minute.

'Bhaiya, do you know where the children are this morning?' she asked, walking up to the man.

He smiled at her in recognition. 'There is an alms distribution at one of the temples today so they're probably all standing in line there.' He held up an open white bun. 'One vada pav for you, didi?'

'No, no, but thank you,' Radhi replied.

'That day, I had no supplies left to offer you one. But today I can.' He opened the rectangular wooden box with glass sides, which served the dual purpose of workstation and storage, and reached for one of the deep-fried potato vadas inside it. 'Should I make it? My treat.'

'I've just had lunch. I'm very full.' Radhi smiled at the man. 'Not today. But maybe next time?' She held up the paper bag with the leftover food. 'Would you please give this bag to the little girl with the gajras?'

Radhi was walking back to her car when she remembered something that made her stop and turn.

'Could it be?' she whispered to herself as she hurried back to the vada pav vendor.

'Ma'am, Kiran ben asked me to give you this.' Juhi handed Radhi a sheet of paper as soon as she entered the office.

'This is the biodata of the guy we think will be a good fit for you.'

Radhi was surprised. 'Oh, that was very quick. I thought it would take you all at least a couple of days or so.'

Juhi grinned. 'It does usually, but we thought in this instance we should make it happen quickly — before you change your mind.'

Radhi smiled, reluctantly scanning the biodata.

'We've already checked — he's free to meet tonight. If his profile seems fine, Kiran ben can fix a meeting for the two of you.'

The profile was of a thirty-four-year-old chartered accountant who worked with an international consulting firm. The man had large white teeth, bushy eyebrows and a clean-shaven, intelligent-looking face. Nothing that Radhi could object to at a moment's notice. She handed the sheet of paper back to Juhi. 'This seems fine.'

'He's more than fine, ma'am.' Juhi's eyes were twinkling. 'I was there when Kiran ben interviewed him. Very nice.'

Radhi smiled but ignored the comment. 'By the way, do you know where Jeevan is?'

Radhi found Jeevan in the pantry, his back to the door, washing the used plates and bowls from lunch.

'Jeevan,' she called gently, trying not to startle him, 'can we speak for a minute?'

It didn't help. Jeevan jumped and turned at the sound of her voice and the glass bowl in his soapy hands slipped to the floor.

Dismayed, he looked from her to the shattered bowl, seeming unsure of what he was more upset about — the ticking off he would no doubt receive from Kiran or the fact that Radhi wanted to talk to him.

'I am sorry.' Radhi squatted beside him to help pick up the pieces.

'It's okay, ma'am. I can clear it up later.' He took the pieces from her hand, flustered. 'You . . . you wanted to talk to me?'

Radhi wiped her hands on her pants and straightened up. 'Yes. Can we sit here for a minute.' She pointed to one of the chairs before taking a seat herself.

'I can stand, ma'am,' Jeevan said, clearly unused to receiving invitations to sit at the same table.

'Very well.' Radhi stood up and leaned against the wall with crossed arms. 'Now tell me, on the day that Hansa ben died, you said you were in the office for the most part of the evening except when you went to get a vada pav, am I right?'

'Ye . . . yes, ma'am . . . why? What happened?'

'Around what time was this?'

'Must be . . . seven thirty or so. Why, ma'am?'

'Are you sure? Because the vada pav fellow told me he left early that day.'

'Oh, is it? Could've been seven then. I can't be sure. I didn't check the time. I went when I got hungry.' Jeevan wiped the beads of perspiration that had appeared on his forehead with the back of his sleeve.

'He went off at three o'clock, Jeevan. He remembers clearly because he ran out of stock.'

Jeevan looked terrified. He glanced at the door as if contemplating fleeing but then seemed to decide against it. He opened his mouth to speak, shut it and then tried again. 'I . . . I must be mistaken. I . . . uh I probably ate a sandwich that day. There's a guy who sits across the road from our building.'

'Jeevan, there's no point in lying, you know that, right? It's easy enough for me to go and ask the sandwich fellow.'

'But how could he possibly remember?' Jeevan asked desperately. 'Dozens of people must come to him each day. He probably must've already forgotten.'

'It's possible,' Radhi agreed. 'The vada pav fellow *did* forget. He told the police you bought a vada pav from him that evening like you always do. But he didn't remember he had left early that day.'

'But I ate a sandwich,' Jeevan protested weakly.

Radhi frowned. 'Jeevan, when I tell the police this, they are going to dig further, ask more questions. They are not going to let this be. Why don't you just tell me the truth?'

Jeevan took a desperate step towards her. 'Ma'am . . . no, no! Please don't tell the police! I swear I haven't done anything wrong!'

Radhi changed tack. 'I don't want to. I hear you are a good son, that you support your family.'

Jeevan nodded frantically. 'Yes, ma'am, my mother depends on me. I swear on her life that I had nothing to do with Hansa ben's death. Please don't go to the police!'

'I won't. Not yet. But you need to tell me why you lied.' Radhi's voice was gentler now. 'You don't have to answer right away, Jeevan. Take till the end of the day tomorrow, but come and tell me the truth.'

When Radhi left the room, Jeevan looked at the drops of blood on the floor and then at the cut he had made in his palm by clutching the glass shards of the bowl too tightly.

15

Radhi left the pantry and walked towards her desk, feeling sorry for the young man, but she believed this was the kindest thing she could do for him. She had given him an opportunity to come clean without getting the police involved. To her, his behaviour seemed guilty, but guilty of what? She couldn't quite picture him as a murderer. Or for that matter, as the sender of those tarot cards. Unless . . . unless . . . he was working at the behest of someone else. Radhi's pulse quickened at this new idea, which not only seemed entirely probable but fit in much better with the impression she had formed of the young man. He could easily be the one delivering the tarot cards. He came in to work earlier than anyone else. It would be a simple matter for him to leave the tarot cards on Sarla's and Kiran's desks when he cleaned their cabins.

Movie today? 6 p.m. at INOX. The Lost Daughter. Nishant's message snapped Radhi out of her deliberations and made her smile. *It's got two strong female characters talking about their FEELINGS for two whole hours. You're going to LURVE it!*

That sounds tempting! I would've loved to but I can't! Am supposed to be working this evening. 😊 Radhi typed back.

She was meant to accompany Sarla ben to Bhavana's house that evening. Sarla would have gone on without her, but the part of Radhi that was irresistibly drawn into other people's problems wanted to go too.

Oh and I almost forgot. I'm going on an arranged date!

Huh? Nishant typed back.

For work. I'm going to meet a guy the arranged way so that I can write more authentically about it.

Radhi could see the three dots that indicated that Nishant was typing, but when the reply didn't come for several minutes, she wondered if she should call and explain. She was about to dial his number when her phone pinged again.

How about meeting tomorrow then, for dinner? Also, on Monday a friend has come down from the US and a bunch of us are meeting for drinks. I would love for you to join.

He had chosen not to comment on her arranged date, which could either mean that he didn't think it was a big deal or that it had bothered him, but he didn't want to escalate it. But Radhi didn't have the chance to clarify — his message had thrown her into another quandary. She wasn't ready to meet his friends or get involved in his life in any serious way. She had said so to him on their very first dinner date. Already things between them had got more intense in the last few days. But that was as far as she was willing to go. She didn't have the courage yet to stake more than she already had.

C'mon Radhi, it's just a few drinks. It doesn't mean anything. Nishant messaged again guessing correctly why Radhi was taking time to reply.

Okay. Radhi typed back taking a deep breath. *Tomorrow then.*

In the car on their way to Bhavana's place, Radhi decided not to say anything about Jeevan to Sarla just yet. She wanted to give him a chance to explain himself before putting doubts in the mind of his employer. Even if she was mistaken about him, it would still take him a long time to win back Sarla's trust. It was unfair, she knew, but it was the way it was between their two sections of society. Instead, she decided to tell Sarla about her conversation with Zarna.

'Do you trust Zarna?' Radhi asked at the end. 'I mean, I know she is Kiran ben's daughter but . . . what do you make of her on her own?'

Sarla sighed. 'I've known that girl since she was two. As long as I have known you, in fact! She's clever . . . in the bookish sort of way. And she is ambitious. But she can be . . . brash. You know?'

Radhi nodded. Sarla hadn't answered her question, but Radhi decided not to push the matter further. There were things people sensed but didn't always allow themselves to think, let alone admit aloud.

Bhavana opened the door to her house. She was dressed in a bright blue kaftan with a peacock feather print and her hair was tied up in a high bun.

'Please come in,' she smiled at them stiffly. Her current discontent with them was clearly in conflict with years of conditioned hospitality. 'Will you give me a minute? I just need to light a diya in the prayer room.'

'Of course,' said Sarla.

'Please make yourselves comfortable.' Bhavana pointed to a wide three-seater sofa.

Radhi and Sarla exchanged glances. It was going to be an uphill conversation. A young maid came out of the kitchen carrying a tray with two glasses of water. Radhi accepted one gratefully. The previous night, she had overdone the wine. Finished the whole bottle instead of her regular two or three glasses, and as a result she had struggled with a dry and woolly mouth the whole day. She took a sip of her water and looked around the sprawling living room. It struck her just how much the space was an extension of how Bhavana dressed. The cushions with their fluorescent yellow parrots, the rug with its bold floral motifs and the curtains in the tie-dye shades of pink, all clamoured for attention.

Photo frames on the wall and on the corner table beside them showed Bhavana, her husband and their two children, one boy and one girl, holidaying in various parts of the world. Radhi took a closer look at Khushi; with her broad forehead and deep-set eyes, she seemed to have taken after her father.

'What will you have? Tea? Coffee? Something cold?' asked Bhavana as she entered the room again, the maid trailing behind her.

'I've just had tea,' said Sarla, 'so something cold for me please.'

'Me too,' said Radhi.

'Of course.' Bhavana gave the maid a small nod before settling on the sofa across them. 'So tell me, how can I help you?'

'Khushi is such a beautiful girl.' Sarla ignored the question, choosing instead to pick up a photo frame from one of the corner tables. She studied the picture for a few seconds before putting it back down.

'Well, apparently not enough for some,' Bhavana crossed her arms and leaned back on her sofa, refusing to acknowledge the compliment and set a pleasant tone to the conversation like Sarla had hoped for.

'This is Radhika Zaveri, by the way,' Sarla said without missing a beat. 'She's a writer, currently working on a piece about matrimonial bureaus. She's been talking to all of us at Soul Harmony. And some of our clients. And I wanted her to talk with you as well.'

'Me?' Bhavana frowned. 'I'm not a big fan of Soul Harmony currently, I hope you know that.'

Sarla raised her hands placatingly. 'I *do* know. Which is why it's important we hear your side of the story as well.'

Whatever Bhavana had been expecting from this morning's conversation, it was clearly not this. She said heatedly, 'First of all, it's not a story. It is my daughter's life we are talking about. Do you know what a terrible tag "a broken engagement" is? Especially for the girl? Actually, *only* for the girl. Should the boy break the engagement — there must be something wrong with the girl. But heaven forbid, should the girl break the engagement — what sort of a girl does that? Clearly, there's something wrong with the girl! It's like there's no way to come out on top of it.'

'I understand, but—' Sarla began but Bhavana cut her off angrily.

'But how could you? Do you have a daughter? Let alone a daughter with a broken engagement? No. Then how could you possibly get it? It's not like you've taken the trouble to talk to me before this!'

Bhavana paused when the maid entered the living room again. She was carrying a tray with bowls of banana chips and spicy sev, along with two chilled glasses of thandai with delicate slivers of pistachios floating on top. As Radhi picked up her glass and took a sip, she couldn't help but smile at the irony of Temple Hill. So what if they were in the middle of an unpleasant conversation. That was no reason for the snacks offered and the hospitality extended to be anything but perfect.

'Bhavana ben, Kiran has been taking care of you. Which is why I haven't reached out.' Sarla used the small pause in Bhavana's rant to quickly say what she wanted to say. 'But you'll be amiss in thinking that I don't care. We had in fact asked one of our staff members to look into this. To see if there was another girl involved . . .'

'There was, wasn't there?' Bhavana thumped the seat of the sofa. 'I knew it! Was it his previous girlfriend? He told my Khushi that was over and done with!'

'No, no, please don't jump to conclusions!' Sarla put her glass of thandai down, concerned that this was going in the wrong direction. 'We don't know for sure yet, and now we've had a terrible tragedy at the office, so it may be a while before we can find out. But honestly, that's not important. The point is, from what Kiran tells me, Khushi is a lovely girl and there will be no difficulty in finding her a suitable match.'

'But it *is* important, don't you see? We need a reason — something we can tell the world, something that will deflect this fiasco away from Khushi!'

Radhi who had been quiet so far, knew first-hand just how much harder these things were on women. Girls on Temple Hill were as well educated as the boys, but while the boys were judged on how well they did at work, the girls' careers were ancillary. The primary yardstick that society still used to measure their success in life was how well they married. Yet for Sarla's sake, Radhi felt compelled to try to calm down Bhavana.

'Aunty,' she said, 'you're worrying too much. In a few months, people won't even remember — look at me, forget engagement, I've had a broken *marriage* — do you think people remem—'

'Oh yes! Yes they do,' Bhavana said triumphantly. 'You're Sameer Zaveri's daughter, aren't you? I didn't recognize you by face, but when Sarla ben introduced you, your name rang a bell. Didn't you run off and get married to some Punjabi guy in the US? We heard all about how quickly you got divorced! If no one says anything to you about it, it's not because they don't remember! It's because they are being nice!'

'Look here, Bhavana ben,' Sarla said, 'I understand you're upset but—'

'It's been three months since the broken engagement, she's not met anyone new since! The only meeting Kiran ben was able to set up was with a divorcee. Now you tell me, is my daughter damaged goods that she should marry a divorcee?'

Radhi stared at her, amazed at how thoughtless people could be. For long, she had just ignored people and their slights, preferring to continue living in the US after her divorce so she didn't have to deal with the busybodies of Temple Hill. But ever since she came back, she had called people out on it. It was all part of 'valuing herself', as her therapist put it.

'You were right, Bhavana ben, when you said that people don't forget, but as time goes on, they don't care. Take yourself, for example. Did you care that I'm divorced and that I'm sitting right here?' Radhi let the question hang there for a moment before continuing, 'But damaged goods or not, Sarla ben here has been able to set me up with a rather successful and good-looking chartered accountant. Who I'm meeting tonight, in fact. So just have faith in her.'

Bhavana stared at Radhi, then she blinked and licked her dry lips. 'Look, I don't mean any disrespect to you. But you have to understand, I had people congratulating me on Khushi's engagement for days *after* it had been called off, because they hadn't still heard. It was awful . . . just awful to watch those congratulatory smiles turn to pity. I could see the speculation going on in their heads, even as they offered their sympathies.'

Sarla brought out a slim file from her handbag and slid it across the centre table to Bhavana. 'These are two biodatas that I think are a good fit for Khushi. But you'll have to be patient, Bhavana ben. Give it some time. Let people find something else to distract them. And then, I promise, we will find Khushi the wonderful husband she deserves.'

Bhavana picked up the file and put it beside her without opening it. 'We'll see.' She picked up the remote and raised it towards the air conditioner mounted above the window to switch it off.

Sarla took it as their cue to leave. She dabbed her mouth with a tissue paper, got up and straightened her sari. But Radhi hadn't moved. She was staring at Bhavana's arm where the sleeve had fallen back when she raised it, revealing a set of slim golden bangles.

16

'She seems really angry,' Radhi said once they were in Radhi's car and had asked Ramzan bhai to take them back to the office.

The car, which had been parked under the sun this past hour, was like a furnace. As they waited for the cooling of the AC to kick in, Sarla fanned herself with the pallu of her sari. 'Honestly, I get where she is coming from. These things are indeed harder on a girl's reputation. I think this meeting helped, though. Don't you think she seemed a bit calmer once she'd had a chance to vent?'

'I don't know,' Radhi said. She proceeded to tell Sarla about the conversation she had overheard while smoking behind a car on her first day at Soul Harmony, and the golden-bangle-clad arm she had caught a fleeting glimpse of.

Sarla was silent for a moment but then she shook her head. 'Yes, she sounds angry no doubt, but she seems like one of those people who bark louder than they bite. Harmless, I should think, for the most part.'

Radhi remained silent. That may have been true for Bhavana on her own, but she had seen her in Renuka's office. Was Renuka also harmless? What if Renuka had got into her head?

Radhi didn't tell Sarla what she was thinking. She didn't want to add to her troubles. Instead, she said, 'Why didn't you tell her to stay away from Renuka?'

'Why would I do that?' Sarla shook her head. 'That would send her running to Renuka even faster. It's just human nature. Don't worry, I am sure all of this will be forgotten as soon as we find Khushi a good match.'

'Well, find one quickly, then!'

'That inspector is here to see you, ma'am,' Juhi said as soon as Sarla and Radhi entered the office.

Sarla nodded at Shinde who was sitting in the waiting area with a constable. 'Give me two minutes,' she said.

'What do you think he wants now?' Radhi asked softly as she followed Sarla down the corridor.

'I think they just want to return some of the things they took from the office that day. Come and sit in on our meeting.' Sarla switched on the lights and air conditioning and put her bag away in a drawer.

They had just settled themselves when the door opened and Shinde and the constable walked in, the latter carrying a brown cardboard box. Shinde nodded at Sarla and ignored Radhi, even as he took a seat beside her.

'This is the victim's purse and the office registers and some of the other things we'd taken,' he said, motioning the constable to come forward and place the box she was carrying on Sarla's table.

'Thank you,' said Sarla. 'Hansa's sister will be happy to have her purse. What about our computers? Have you brought those along?'

Shinde shook his head. 'Our IT department has them still. I think you can get them back next week.'

'How is the investigation going, Inspector? And what about that man . . . the sketch your artist drew?'

Shinde nodded. 'We've made some progress. We now know that he came on a grey scooter; one of the security guards in your building saw the sketch and remembered arguing with him about parking or something. Anyways, we've managed to pull the licence plate from the footage we got from a camera at one of the signals at the street corner.'

'Oh? That's a good thing, no?' Sarla asked hopefully.

The inspector nodded. 'We should have the registration details by the end of today.'

'And then?'

'And then we'll bring him in for questioning.'

Jeevan knocked on the door and entered with a tray, carrying cups of tea and a plate of cream and sugar biscuits. He looked pale and blanched even further when he saw Radhi sitting with the police. Radhi tried to catch his eye to reassure him that this wasn't about him, but he refused to look at her.

'Were there any fingerprints? In Hansa ben's room?' Radhi, who had been quiet so far, asked the inspector when Jeevan had left the room.

Shinde had just picked up a biscuit and was about to take a bite, but he paused. 'None. Nothing on the Nataraja statue nor on the desk, everything had been wiped clean.'

'What about the doorknob?' Radhi asked.

Again, the biscuit hovered mid-air. With a long-suffering sigh, the inspector turned to Radhi. 'Far too many fingerprints on that. Including your own.'

'What about the purple cat in the dustbin?' Radhi asked undeterred by the man's obvious reluctance to engage with her. In fact, she was enjoying the interrogation.

Shinde put back the uneaten biscuit, bristling. 'What about it, ma'am?'

'Did you have it checked for fingerprints?'

'Of course, we did.' He wiped his hands on the pants of his uniform, oblivious to the tissue paper box on the desk. 'No other fingerprints except the victim's own.' He pushed his chair back and rose. 'Now if there's nothing else, I'll take your leave, ma'am. We will be in touch,' he said to Sarla, then turning to Radhi he added, 'And you, ma'am, all you need to do is to trust us a little.'

'Of course,' Radhi smiled sweetly.

She lifted the plate of biscuits and offered it to Shinde, who looked for a moment as if he was going to refuse but picked up two anyway before making a brisk exit from the room.

'I can take Hansa ben's purse to Jigna ben,' Radhi offered.

'Oh, would you?' Sarla looked relieved. 'I can't face her right now. Not when we have no answers to offer.'

Radhi took the purse out of the cardboard box on Sarla's desk. 'You are sure you don't want to tell him about the tarot cards, Aunty?'

'No, please! Not now or he will have our heads for why we didn't say anything sooner. Besides, if this guy really is involved and the murder is solved, the police can be out of our hair, and we can be left to solve this tarot thing on our own.'

Zarna watched the inspector leave with a growing sense of trepidation. She wanted to go to Sarla's cabin and find out what the inspector had told her, but at the same time, she wanted to avoid Radhi. Their conversation that morning had left her rattled. That woman was beginning to get on Zarna's nerves, and Zarna would be glad when her interviews were done and they could finally be rid of her.

Alpa watched the inspector leave without the brown cardboard box and felt her heart plummet. There was something in it that she wanted to get her hands on. Had the inspector found it? Had that oaf understood its significance? Sarla and Radhi were probably opening the box right now. Was there any way she could go into the office and stop them before it was too late? She was thinking furiously about what she would say, what excuse she could give, when the door opened, and Radhi came out of the room holding the very thing Alpa was after.

As Kiran watched the inspector leave, she felt a familiar surge of irritation. Why hadn't anyone told her he was coming? Why hadn't Sarla called her to join their meeting? And what now? After the meeting was over? Would anyone bother informing her what the man had said? Or would she have to go knocking on Sarla's cabin, as usual late to the party? She counted the pens in the pen holder on her desk, once, twice, thrice. Each time the number added up to a reassuring ten. And slowly, she felt herself calm down.

Juhi watched the inspector wolf down his biscuits as he waited for the elevator. She wanted to know what had happened to the sketch she had helped with. Had they been able to find the man? She wondered if she could just ask him outright. But what if he wanted to know why? What if he began asking other questions? No, no, that wouldn't do. She didn't want to go down that path again. She shivered, the goosebumps on her arms had nothing to do with the air conditioning. And everything to do with a conversation she'd had earlier that day. She would find a way to ask Sarla ben or better still, Radhi.

From between the blinds in her window, Renuka watched the inspector leave the building and knew that he had been to the office of Soul Harmony. She felt a thrill of excitement run down her spine. Every now and then, things had a way of working out even better than one had hoped. Now if only she could get through that writer and persuade her to see things from her perspective.

Jeevan watched as the inspector got into the police Jeep. He was leaning against the trunk of the amaltas tree as he furiously smoked a bidi. A part of him wanted to stop him and come clean. Then he'd go home to his mother, lay his head on her lap and ask her to make chicken biryani for him as a special treat. But he knew it couldn't possibly be that simple. They would never let him off that easily. They'd ask him a thousand questions. And when he'd say he didn't know — they wouldn't believe him. What if they locked him up in a cell? Or worse, what if they told Sarla? Would she still let him have his job? He couldn't afford to lose his income. It was the best thing that had happened to him. Hell, it was the best thing that had happened to his family. No, no, no. It wouldn't do to speak up. But if he didn't say anything that woman, that writer, Radhika was bound to say something. And where would that leave him then? Would they be able to guess the other thing as well? He wiped the sweat from his forehead feeling caught. Trapped.

Radhi waited for the steady flow of traffic to slow down so she could cross the road to where Ramzan bhai was waiting with her car. She had just left Soul Harmony and was now headed home to get ready for her arranged meeting that night. It was the middle of December and the sun had begun to set early. At just 7 p.m., the sky was a slab of black granite. As she waited at the intersection with other pedestrians, Radhi started toying with her phone. Suddenly she sensed a presence close behind her and the skin on the nape of her neck prickled. She was about to turn around when she felt a tug on her dress, and she looked down into the smiling face of the flower girl.

'Didi the food you left for me was just delicious!' The girl made a smacking sound with her lips. Radhi smiled distractedly and turned but there was nothing and nobody behind. She looked around to see if there were any familiar faces or silhouettes, but there was no one she recognized. She said goodbye to the flower girl, crossed the road and got into the car, but all the while, she couldn't shake the feeling that she had been in danger.

17

'I can't believe I'm doing this,' Radhi muttered as she gave her clothes one last look in the mirror. She was wearing a crisp, white linen shift dress with a deep neckline and a broad red belt with a Bengal tiger buckle. She had put her hair up in a sort of messy bun, and two silver clusters of red chillies dangled from her ears. Her long clutch bag matched the red of the chillies and the belt perfectly. She liked how the outfit had come together, especially given how quickly she had gone about it.

'What's not to believe, didi?' Lila said from her spot on the window ledge, where she had parked herself as Radhi got ready. 'You are a single young woman going out to meet a single young man. It's a tale as old as time itself.'

Radhi rolled her eyes at her in the mirror as she applied her rouge. 'Don't you have any work to do?'

'None at all.' Lila grinned and flicked an imaginary speck of dust from her sari.

'I think you're just sitting here to ensure I actually go for the meeting and don't chicken out at the last minute.' Radhi chose a dark maroon lipstick that made her full lips appear even fuller.

Lila shrugged. 'So what if I am? After the way you went on and on about how awkward it's going to be. About how you are going to hate every minute of it. You can't blame me if I think you might not end up going.'

Radhi turned around exasperated. 'And would that be so bad? It's not like I don't have a life. You did see Nishant here last week, no?'

Lila grinned. 'But what's the fun with just one, didi? You have to play the field a little.'

'Lila, this is just research for my work. You know that, right?'

'I do. But does he?'

Radhi frowned. She had been feeling guilty about lying to her date but didn't see a way around it. 'No. George, my agent, thought the experience wouldn't be authentic then.'

'This George seems clever.'

'So is that what you're doing with your driver? Playing the field?' Radhi changed the subject. For a few months now, Lila had been going out with one of the drivers in the building, and from the little gifts of jasmine gajras and parcels of sweet, white burri that regularly arrived at their doorstep, he seemed quite into it.

'Exactly,' she retorted. 'He's already talking about marriage, but I am in no mood to wash another man's underpants again. I'm just having fun!'

'Okay, now tell me how I look.' Radhi put her hand on her waist and posed for Lila. At 5'8" with three-inch red stilettoes, Radhi was tall and lithe. She had a flat tummy and long, slender limbs, and the white of the dress stood out in contrast to the golden honey complexion of her skin.

Lila pressed her index finger and thumb together in the universal sign of appreciation. 'He will be floored. You will have to splash water on his face to bring him to his senses. He won't believe his luck!'

'*I* can't believe my luck!' Radhi rolled her eyes at Lila's exaggerated compliments. 'An arranged-marriage meeting of all things. Who'd have thought?! But listen,' Radhi said more seriously, 'I wanted to talk to you about Jeevan.'

Radhi told Lila about how she thought the young man was lying and how she felt that he may be involved in some way in the events that had unfolded at Soul Harmony.

'Oh, but he is such a good boy! I can't believe he would get himself involved in anything shady like this . . . Unless, unless it was for . . .' Lila stopped.

'What is it?'

Lila shook her head. 'It's just that they do need the extra money. His younger brother recently had an appendix operation. And I know it was a stretch for the family. You please don't say anything to the police, didi! I will speak to him and ask him to come clean.'

Radhi nodded. 'Would you please call Ramzan bhai and ask him to bring the car around?'

Radhi looked at herself in the mirror. The last time she had worn this dress she had been getting ready to watch *Wicked* on Broadway with Mackinzey. He had surprised her with tickets and afterwards they had gone to a little Ethiopian restaurant where they had eaten . . .

Radhi shook herself. She really needed to go shopping. All her current clothes had so many memories sewn into the seams that they had become heavy to wear.

Radhi entered the Love Song Café and scanned the imaginatively done up space with interest. There were oversized Japanese fans in shades of fuchsia and emerald-green on the exposed brick walls, while jute planters, cane lamps and wooden swings with thick white ropes and bright silk cushions hung mid-air at varying heights, suspended from a high ceiling made almost entirely of glass.

'Interesting décor, no?' A dark-skinned man with broad, athletic shoulders had walked up behind her.

Radhi turned around.

He grinned and extended a hand towards her. 'Pranav. And I believe you're Radhika?'

'Yes.' Radhi blushed as she shook his hand.

They had received pictures of each other along with the biodatas, but Radhi was struck, and not for the first time, by how often photographs did a disservice to their subjects. Unlike the serious-looking, bushy-eyebrowed chartered accountant in the picture, the man before her had a ready, impish smile, which crinkled the corner of his eyes and made his eyebrows seem irrelevant. Not to mention, the arms of a professional volleyball player.

'Have you been here before?' he asked once they had taken their seats.

'No, it's my first time.' Radhi put her clutch and phone on the table, immediately missing the reassuring feeling of a pen or a cigarette in her hand. 'I just moved back to Bombay earlier this year and haven't had a chance to venture out much.'

'You were in the US, right?'

Radhi nodded.

'I'd love to know what that was like. How long you were there. Why you decided to come back? All of that. But before that, it might be best to get this out of the way.' Pranav smiled as he handed her the menu. 'We'll have fewer interruptions once we place our orders.'

Radhi scanned the menu half-heartedly. Her stomach had been tied up in knots all day at the prospect of this arranged date and she was finding it hard to muster up an appetite.

'They've got excellent grilled veggie fajitas and water-chestnut canapes. They sauté the chestnuts in clarified butter with all kinds of spices before covering them in cheese. They're really worth a try. Oh, and the jalapeno and mushroom quesadillas are delicious as well!'

Radhi smiled. 'I'll go with whatever you recommend. Seems like you really know your way around here.'

'I should. I come here several times a month.' Pranav raised his hand to beckon the waiter.

'I hope it's not an arranged date each time,' Radhi joked.

Pranav grinned sheepishly. 'More often than not it is. I figure if I don't enjoy the date at least I'll be sure to enjoy the food.'

Radhi laughed, her initial awkwardness slipping away in the face of his candour.

Pranav shrugged and smiled. 'Laugh all you want. But when you've been doing this as long as I have, you need something to keep you motivated.'

'Why? How long has it been?'

Pranav shook his head. 'I lost count somewhere after the first forty meetings or so.'

Radhi's eyes widened in surprise.

'Judging by your reaction, I guess you're still fairly new at this?' Pranav asked.

'Brand new,' Radhi smiled, emphasizing the 'brand'.

Now it was Pranav's turn to be surprised. He leaned back and rubbed his hands together with relish. 'Oh, then please allow me to show you how it's done.'

Did you go? What did you wear? It was today, wasn't it? What was it like? Did he ask you if you can cook? Does he live with his parents? Are you guys getting married already?

Radhi grinned at George's dramatic email. She had come back from her date and changed into a pair of shorts and a tank top. Lila had left for the day and the apartment was quiet and restful. She had asked Google to play Ankur Tiwari's newest song about the fickle vagaries of love and had settled into her favourite winged armchair with its delicate mockingbirds and rich bottle-green tapestry. She had traded her customary glass of wine for a glass of warm saffron-infused milk. She had added crushed cardamom and nutmeg to it, along with slivers of almonds and pistachios. It was just like the milk their mum used to make on winter nights. The nutmeg in the milk was supposed to be wonderful for sleep, she used to say. Radhi didn't want to investigate or dig deeper into why she didn't feel like having wine today. It had just been that sort of an evening.

I did. I went on an arranged date like you asked. It was awkward as hell — at least to begin with. But once I'd gotten past why I was there, it was actually very nice. The clarity of intent was refreshing, you know. Unlike with Tinder, there wasn't any ambiguity as to why the other person was here. Did they just want to hook up? Were they going to disappear on you? Were they serial killers? You know, all the second-guessing that accompanies a blind date? That was absent. Sure, sometimes, the not knowing is part of the fun. But if you go on enough of them — I assume it gets old fast. Obviously, being set up by an aunt is still not my idea of romance. But I can see why the system works.

Radhi was in bed, reading, when her phone pinged again. She was in the middle of one of Agatha Christie's lesser-known novels, *Sparkling Cyanide*, marvelling for the nth time at the writer's plotting technique and amazed at how her cliffhangers and red herrings were remarkable even on rereading. Radhi had always been passionate about mysteries. They were her go-to genre for sick days and rainy days and any and every kind of holiday, in fact. But ever since she had attempted writing a mystery of her own, her reading of them had changed. She still loved solving the story's puzzle along with the detective, but the writing part of her brain was now actively observing the mystery's shape and structure. She had thought that reading a book like that would take away from her enjoyment of the story, but on the contrary, she found herself all the more intrigued by Christie's ingenuity. Immersed in the story, it took her a few moments to step out of it and reach for her phone. It was George again.

> *F**k the process. I don't want a treatise on arranged marriages. I will wait for your book on that. Just tell me, how was the guy? How was his game? Assuming he did have some? What did you talk about?*

Chuckling, Radhi put away the phone. She didn't want to risk losing the gentle drowsiness that had begun to envelop her by replying to George right away. She would write to him in the morning.

Sunday

Radhi brought out the envelope from her purse and peered inside, considering its contents thoughtfully. She was on her way to Vrinda's house for lunch, where her aunt was going to introduce her to her neighbour Paras Mehta, a well-known tarot reader. Radhi wanted to show her the tarot cards Sarla had received and see if she could shed any light on them.

Vrinda lived in one of the city's most exquisite Art Deco buildings at the foot of Temple Hill. A four-storeyed pastel yellow structure with cobalt blue ziggurat-shaped bands running across its length and white windows behind iron grilles with intricate nautical motifs.

When she rang the doorbell, a maid ushered her in.

'Hello, darling.' Vrinda beamed at her niece as she got up from her usual perch on the wooden swing by the window to give Radhi a kiss on her cheek. Dressed in a maroon kalamkari kurta, with her tortoiseshell glasses pushed above her short, silver hair and a thick book in her hand, she looked every bit the psychology professor she was.

'*When Being Perfect Isn't Good Enough*,' Radhi read out the title of the book as she gave her a hug. 'Sounds interesting.'

'Oh it is — an interesting take on cognitive behavioural therapy and obsessive-compulsive behaviours.' Vrinda handed the book to Radhi. 'You can borrow it if you like — I just got done reading.'

'Thanks, I will,' said Radhi, who enjoyed her aunt's eclectic taste in reading, putting the hardback in her bag. Their shared love for books was another reason Radhi felt so connected to her aunt. That and the fact that, like her, Vrinda had also always been an outlier. Unmarried and childless, at a time when most Indian women of her generation wouldn't dream of a life like that, Vrinda had chosen to immerse herself in academia and surround herself with books and ideas. Radhi had always admired how her aunt didn't ever let other people's opinions dictate how she led her life.

A maid came out of the kitchen carrying tall glasses of chilled buttermilk. Radhi accepted the drink and took an appreciative sip before announcing, 'In other news, you should know I went on an arranged date last evening.'

Vrinda raised an eyebrow. 'Really? Was this Sarla's doing? I knew she was good, but if she's convinced you, she must be very good!'

'I went of my own accord, thank you very much,' said Radhi with a mock sniff.

'Can't be. I refuse to buy it,' Vrinda dismissed the notion with a wave of her hand. 'C'mon, what aren't you telling me?'

'Okay, fine.' Radhi rolled her eyes. 'It was George's idea. He thought it would be good for the book.'

'That's more like it.' Vrinda laughed. 'So how was it?'

'Surprisingly pleasant, actually. But what about you, Fia? I've never asked you this before, but how come you never got married? Was it something you ever considered?'

Vrinda was quiet for a moment before replying, 'I did. My mother, your dadi, was so keen to see me settle down. I went on quite a few arranged dates actually. But the more men I met — and those days we used to meet with our families — the more convinced I became that conventional marriage wasn't for me. I just couldn't see myself living with in-laws, running a kitchen, managing servants, catering to the various needs of a busy household. No—' Vrinda shuddered. 'I would have been miserable. And I'd have made some poor sod miserable as well.'

'What did Dadi have to say about it?'

'Oh, Mum was very disappointed. Didn't speak to me for months. Called me stubborn and selfish, which, let's face it, I was being — but better stubborn than sorry, no? From the very beginning my interests were always academic. I like, no I *need*, long hours of uninterrupted time to read, write, think. Luckily, at some level, my dad got it. For all his socializing, your grandfather was an intuitive man. He's the one who encouraged me to pursue higher studies at Oxford. And thank God he did! Can you imagine me hosting my mother-in-law's satsangs, like your sister does? Or running around kids and setting up play dates?'

Radhi smiled at the thought of her aunt playing the quintessential Gujarati housewife. 'Well, you made a splendid mum for didi and me.'

Vrinda smiled back. 'I think your mum was the splendid mum, I just tried very desperately to fill her very large shoes. But enough about me. How is Sarla holding up? This business with the death of her employee sounds nasty.'

The doorbell rang just then, and the maid opened the door to a tall, slim woman in a sari. With her grey hair pulled into a high, tight bun, she seemed to be in her mid-sixties, and Radhi was struck by how bare her neck and arms and ears were. Devoid of a single diamond earring, bangle or nose pin, the plainness of her appearance was a rare sight for a woman on Temple Hill.

'Paras, so good of you to agree to lunch at such short notice. I appreciate it!' Vrinda greeted her neighbour before introducing her to Radhi. 'And this is my niece, Radhika. Like I told you on the phone, she's dealing with a strange situation.'

Paras accepted a glass of buttermilk from the maid before she turned to Radhi and smiled. The smile a minor event of sorts because of the transformation it brought about on her face — the severity of her appearance instantly dissolved into deep dimples and clefts.

'Shall we eat first? Then we can dive into this at length,' Vrinda suggested.

'Don't look at me,' Paras said. 'You know I am not going to say no.' To Radhi she said, 'I love your aunt's cook. I've been trying to poach him for years.'

'She's the reason I need to give the man multiple salary hikes a year!' Vrinda complained as she led the women to the dining area.

On the table was an elaborate South Indian spread. A Kerala stew with florets of cauliflower and disc-shaped carrots floating about in creamy coconut milk by the side of a bowl of unpolished red rice. There were uttapams topped with finely chopped tomatoes, onions and green chillies, alongside a tangy sambhar; mini masala paniyarams tossed in gunpowder; and to balance the spice, a traditional salad made of yellow lentils, cucumber and thickly grated coconut.

'Everything looks wonderful, Fia!' Radhi said as they took their seats around the table.

'And smells good too!' Paras looked appreciatively at the bowl of stew Vrinda had served her. She dipped an uttapam in the sambhar and took a few bites before adding, 'Try all you want, Vrinda, one of these days your cook will be mine.'

Vrinda rolled her eyes and smiled.

'I'm not saying it, the cards are,' Paras joked.

'Good thing I don't much believe in your cards then, isn't it?' Vrinda chuckled as she served her friend a dollop of chutney.

'You are too cerebral,' Paras chided. 'You give too much importance to what's going on up here.' She knocked her own forehead with her index finger. 'Everything in this world cannot be processed by the brain.' Paras turned to Radhi. 'What about you? Do you believe in what I do? Or are you like her?'

Caught off guard, Radhi didn't get the chance to be diplomatic. She smiled apologetically. 'A bit like her, I suppose.'

'Never you mind.' Paras helped herself to a few paniyarams and smiled as Vrinda served her more sambhar. 'Someday, you'll both change your minds.'

Once lunch was done, they moved to the living room with bowls of rich and milky payasam in their hands.

'How did you get interested in tarot, Aunty?' Radhi asked as they took their seats on the couch.

Paras's face took on a sombre expression, but she spoke without self-pity. 'When my son was seven, we learnt he had cancer. That same year, my husband's business failed, and he suffered from a stroke which left his right side paralysed.

Don't worry,' she added when she saw Radhi's stricken expression, 'they're both fine now. But meditating on the tarot helped me cope with the uncertainty of those years. It offered me hope. Does that make sense?'

Radhi nodded uncertainly and Paras smiled.

'Now before you tell me your problem, may I see what I can decipher on my own? It's just that I don't want my judgement to be coloured by anything I hear.'

Without waiting for an answer, she brought out a small bundle wrapped in red velvet from a batwa tucked into the waist of her sari. Unwrapping it with swift, practised movements, she brought out a deck of tarot cards, identical to the ones Radhi was carrying with her, and spread them on the red velvet cloth on the centre table between them. 'Shall we?'

Radhi nodded. She hadn't really wanted this to be about her, but she didn't see the problem in humouring the tarot reader.

'Please pick five cards,' Paras instructed her.

Radhi put down her bowl of payasam and complied.

Paras took the five cards Radhi handed her and spread them on the cloth in the shape of a cross. She made a steeple out of her hands and began to study the cards. Her expression, which had been neutral, turned grim. She looked at Radhi curiously before turning her attention to the cards.

'I think we should try this again,' she said after a silence of a few moments. 'Let me do another spread for you.'

'Why?' Radhi leaned forward. 'What's wrong with this one?'

'Nothing's wrong, it's just . . .' She frowned. 'It's strange, let me just try again.'

'Paras, why don't you just tell us what you see. You know our interest in this right now is purely academic, right?' Vrinda said.

Paras bit her lip and turned to look at the spread again. 'It's just that . . . I see you very closely involved in some kind of . . . death.'

Radhi nodded, not surprised. 'Yes, that's partly why I am here. A few days ago, I found the body of—'

Paras interrupted. 'Not in the past. This card has to do with the future.' She paused to study the spread again. 'In other circumstances, I would've said that a situation is coming to an end, but this spread . . .' She waved her hand over it. 'It's all about people. There's a death in the near future.' She looked at Radhi distressed. 'And you seem to be involved.'

18

'What exactly are you saying, Paras?' Vrinda frowned. 'What do you mean involved?'

Paras shook her head thoughtfully. 'I can't be sure, but do you see the Three of Swords?'

Radhi and Vrinda looked at the red heart stabbed with three swords that Paras was pointing at. 'That card speaks about some kind of betrayal. It could also mean some sort of loss or sorrow, but look at the card that follows it. The Tower card is a major arcana and signifies major life changes. At its best, it's chaos. Or some sort of collapse. But in this case . . .' Paras frowned. 'In this case, seeing how it's positioned and the sorrowful Five of Cups that has opened beside it, it could only mean an end. A death of something. Or someone.' She looked up gravely. 'Please just let me do another spread for you?'

Radhi nodded, curious now, despite her initial reservations. Paras picked up her cards, shuffled them and held them out for Radhi to pick from again. When Radhi had chosen five cards, she laid them out in a different pattern this time. One card then a horizontal line of three cards above it and then another card in the same line as the first one. Again, she made a steeple of her hands and was silent while she studied the cards. She pointed to the Five of Cups which had opened up again. 'The card of grief and regret — again. And this time with the Death card in the position of *influences*.' Paras looked up at Radhi. 'I can't tell whether this regret is yours or someone else's. This person who died, were you close?'

'No, in fact I barely knew her,' said Radhi.

Paras nodded grimly. 'Another reason why I believe this has to do with a . . . situation in the future.'

Radhi had an inherent distrust of anything or anyone who claimed to predict how her life would turn out, and yet there was an earnestness about Paras that she found hard to brush off.

'Is Radhi in any kind of danger?' Vrinda asked.

Paras didn't answer immediately, and Radhi, who suddenly remembered the strange feeling she'd had while crossing the road the previous evening, felt a slight shiver run down her spine.

'I can't be sure,' Paras admitted after a while. 'But I don't think so. Or else the Death card and the Tower card in the earlier spread would have been in different positions.'

She pointed to another card with the picture of a yellow moon and a howling dog and wolf. 'See this card?' she asked Radhi. '*That's* the card about the querent, which means you. The Moon can suggest that you're dealing with illusions and secrets. May not be anything too dramatic,' she added when she saw the sceptical expression on Radhi's face. 'For instance, had you come to me for career advice and drawn the Moon card, I would've said, you need to check the terms of a new job or a new contract you may be about to sign or something as basic as that. But look at the other cards in this spread. I would take it as a warning that a situation or a person in your life right now is not what it appears to be.'

Radhi looked at Vrinda with a small smile. 'Gosh, this got very serious, very quickly.' To Paras, she said, 'And how will I know who or what?'

'The Moon card is the card of intuition as well. And because of this Strength card that's opened up in the end, I believe you *are* in touch with your intuition. The cards seem to be asking you to just trust your instincts.'

'Well, that she can do, can't you, Radhi?' Vrinda patted Radhi's shoulder affectionately.

Paras smiled at Radhi, folded her cards back into the deck and put them away. 'Please don't stress. Tarot is never a prediction; it is just a possibility of the way things are headed. You can always course correct.' She picked up her untouched bowl of payasam. 'Okay, now your turn. You can ask me what you need to.'

'I ordered a merlot for you.' Nishant rose from his seat to give Radhi a peck on the cheek as she slipped into the chair across from him.

Radhi had spent the afternoon at her aunt's house before heading home in the evening to get ready for her date with Nishant at a new Lebanese restaurant in town.

'Perfect.' Radhi took an appreciative sip of her drink.

'I thought a little alcohol wouldn't be remiss after the travails of yesterday.' Nishant smiled before adding, 'You look stunning, by the way.'

Radhi was in a bottle-green silk blouse and skirt. The blouse was short, tied at the midriff with a bow, with a deep V-neck and long bell sleeves. She had last worn it for Mackinzey's birthday and he had said the exact same thing.

'What is it?' Nishant asked, watching Radhi's eyebrows furrow.

'Nothing. I was just thinking about how I need new clothes.' She scooped some hummus with a piece of pita from the bread basket and took a bite. 'Umm . . . this is good.'

'So? How did it go yesterday? Was it as terrible as you thought arranged dates are?'

'Not at all! I mean it began awkwardly enough, but when we were past that, the conversation was really pleasant.'

'I told you it wouldn't be too bad. So what does the guy do?' Nishant asked taking a sip of his Scotch and soda.

'He's a chartered accountant. Has his own practice. Divorced. Like me. Studied and lived in the US. Like me.'

'Yeah, must've been easy once you found common ground.' Nishant nodded.

'It was more than easy. We spoke for over three hours.'

'What about?' Nishant looked surprised. 'Let me guess, books?'

Radhi smiled and took another bite of her pita. 'Excuse me, but I've got other varied interests, I'll have you know.'

Nishant leaned forward to wipe a little smudge of hummus from the corner of her mouth. 'No, but seriously, what in the world did you guys talk about? I've gone on a dozen arranged dates myself and never had one that lasted that long!'

'That's what he said as well. Come to think of it, we spoke about all sorts of things.'

Nishant looked at her expectantly, so she elaborated.

'The gazillion arranged dates he's been on, how he had a hot air balloon accident in Turkey, my stolen luggage in Mexico and yeah Indian classical music. He plays the tabla and we chatted about how much we both loved that Prime show *Bandish Bandits*,' said Radhi, then when Nishant looked blank, she added, 'It's about a complicated musical family in Rajasthan.'

The waiter arrived with their food and placed a couscous salad with pomegranate and almonds in front of Radhi and a larger dish of falafels in front of Nishant.

Radhi looked on amused as Nishant swapped their plates once the waiter had left.

'I don't know how you can eat salads for dinner,' Radhi said before taking a bite of her falafel.

'You should really try this.' She pushed her plate towards Nishant.

He took a bite of her falafel and made an appreciative sound.

'I didn't know you were into Indian classical music,' said Nishant after a while.

'But there's a lot you don't know about me,' Radhi teased him.

'I would if you spent more time with me.' Nishant was smiling, but his eyes were serious.

'Well, I'm here now. Ask me what you want to know.'

'Classical music. How did you get into that?'

'Oh, I used to be really into it as a kid. I've studied Hindustani music for eight years. My dad introduced me to it. He used to play the sitar and I would sing. It used to be our Sunday thing. Of course, all that's in the past. I don't sing now.'

'Why not?'

'Just,' said Radhi averting her eyes before drinking deeply from her glass of wine. 'Got busy with other things. Could you ask them to refill this?'

Nishant didn't seem satisfied with her answer, but he let the subject drop and waved his hand at a waiter. 'Well, I feel a little bad for the bugger, your accountant. He didn't know you were there just for research.'

'No, no, I told him. I was feeling terrible about it. Especially since we were having a good time talking. So about an hour into it, I just told him why I had come. I apologized and said we could call it a night if he wanted to. But he said he was enjoying himself too much to leave the conversation halfway like that. So we continued to sit there and chat. In fact, he said he'd like to meet again.'

Nishant stared at Radhi, his expression inscrutable.

'What?' She smiled and put her hand on his arm. 'I'm obviously not going to.'

When Nishant didn't respond, she teased, 'Are you jealous?'

Nishant smiled at that. 'Insanely. I suddenly don't like accountants.' He handed Radhi the menu. 'Now can we forget about them and get dessert?'

He had said it as a joke, yet he was so quiet for the rest of the evening that Radhi realized that her arranged date had bothered him more than he had let on.

Radhi was in bed going over George's comments on her manuscript and making notes on some of the changes she planned on making when she received a message from Sarla, checking if she was awake.

'Sorry, beta, to bother you so late in the night,' Sarla apologized when Radhi called her. 'But I couldn't sleep, and I was wondering if you managed to visit that tarot reader you had mentioned?'

Radhi felt a pang of pity for her mother's friend and wished she could do more to help. 'I did, Aunty, but I didn't learn anything concrete. The tarot reader couldn't see any pattern in the cards that were sent. Nor any deeper meaning to the notes accompanying them. She in fact thought that the person sending them either knew nothing about tarot or was pretending not to.'

Sarla was silent for a few seconds before she said, 'And what about the timing of it?'

'Meaning?'

'They've been coming every Tuesday. I remember because I go to Siddhivinayak that day,' Sarla said, referring to the famous Ganesh temple thousands of people thronged to on Tuesdays. 'I wonder if Tuesday is significant to tarot in any way?'

Radhi thought back to her first day at Soul Harmony and realized that that had been a Tuesday as well. Sarla had asked her to come in by eleven because she would be late to work that day. A thought occurred to her. 'Aunty, what if Tuesday has nothing to do with tarot but with the fact that you aren't in office that morning? So far, you've assumed that the red envelopes are coming to you by post. But what if someone is just leaving the envelopes on your desk with the rest of your mail? And Tuesday is just a convenient day to do it?'

'But Kiran receives the cards too. And she's very much in the office on Tuesday mornings.' Radhi realized Sarla was right. But she felt there was something in her theory about Jeevan. She could feel it in her bones that Jeevan was involved somehow. Once again, she contemplated telling Sarla about it, and once again, decided against it. She would wait to see what Jeevan had to say for himself. They hung up after chatting about Radhi's arranged date, with Sarla expressing great surprise at how long it had gone for. 'I knew you'd be a good match!' she had exclaimed, and Radhi had to tell her that she was dating Nishant, just so that the matchmaker wouldn't get any ideas.

Monday

'Didi, I spoke to Jeevan's mother.' Lila put a steaming mug of tea in front of Radhi before squatting on the window ledge with her own cup of tea in hand.

Radhi was just finishing a quick breakfast of vegetable upma before she headed to Soul Harmony. She looked up from the newspaper she was reading.

'Jeevan's mother said that he's been upset and very unlike himself these last few days. She was worried about him, but she had assumed it was a girl problem that he didn't want to share with her. When I told her about the murder at Soul Harmony, she was shocked. She panicked and began to swear that her son couldn't have done anything wrong. Kept insisting that he was a very good boy.' Lila frowned. 'Now I feel I shouldn't have said anything. That poor woman will just worry, and I don't know if any good will come of it.'

Radhi nodded. 'You may be right, but I still think it was worth a shot. Who knows, she may dig further, and if there's anything, she may be able to force him to come clean to us.'

She checked her watch and got up. She wanted to drop by Hansa's house and hand over her purse to her sister before heading to the matrimonial bureau. As Lila watched, Radhi retrieved Hansa's bag, a misshapen and discoloured brown carry-all made of faux leather, and emptied its contents on the dining table.

'Belonged to the woman who died,' she explained to Lila. 'A woman's purse, Lila, can tell you more about her than any biodata ever can.'

Radhi's own bag carried an assorted jumble of a great many things, and she believed it was an accurate reflection of all the convoluted complications coursing through her mind.

'What about those of us who don't carry big handbags? Does it mean we don't have much on our minds?' Lila, who carried only a small purse to work, joked.

'Your cupboard or drawer at home then. Basically, any space that you consider entirely your own.' Radhi grinned but stuck to her theory.

Lila began to clear the table of all the breakfast things as Radhi rifled through Hansa's belongings, which, considering the size of the bag, were sparse. There was a striped maroon canvas wallet, a comb, a plastic spectacle case beside bus ticket stubs, crumpled tissues and a bundle of old bills. The only things of note were two slim files and one of those old-fashioned alphabetical phone diaries. Radhi opened one of the files. Inside was a one-page document about the case Hansa was working on then. Hansa suspected that Yug Desai, the boy who had broken the engagement with Bhavana ben's daughter, was seeing someone else and had been spotted in her company a couple of times. The boy's parents seemed to be in the dark about his relationship because of which Hansa had concluded that they hadn't knowingly withheld information from Soul Harmony. An important thing for the bureau to know because parents were often repeat clients who came back with their younger children. In the file, Hansa had mentioned Yug's car number and attached a recent photograph. Radhi clicked a picture of all the contents of the file before putting it aside. Next, she picked up the phone diary and flipped through the pages to see if any of the names seemed familiar or jumped out. It was organized strangely, according to the names of buildings rather than people. And under each building name Hansa had listed a few names, numbers and titles. Under Sea Palace Apartments there was a number for Kashi — the dhobhi's wife; and Sunil — the night watchman. Under Arabian Dreams Coop. Society, Hansa had scrawled Sooraj — sweeper; and Shekhawat — cook. Radhi considered taking a picture of all the pages, but there were too many, and she decided she would ask Jigna ben if she could keep the diary. She then turned her attention to the second file, which had just a single sheet of paper with three columns. One, with half a dozen dates, the second with seven- or eight-digit numbers and a third, narrower column with five- or six-digit numbers. She turned the paper around but it was blank. She took a picture of the sheet and made a mental note to ask Sarla about it.

'Anything?' Lila came to stand beside Radhi, picking up Hansa's discarded bag and peering inside.

'Not that I can tell.' Radhi shrugged and turned her attention to Hansa's wallet, which had more old bills and receipts and a single twenty-rupee note. Radhi wondered why the person who had taken all of Hansa's money had left the twenty rupees. Did he or she not see it? Or had they left it out of concern for how Hansa would get home? But why bother about that when Hansa was already dead . . . Unless . . .

'Didi, see.' Lila had noticed a bulge in the lining of the bag and followed it to discover a large hole in one of its chained pockets. She stuck two fingers deep into the hole and emerged with a pen and a few moments later with a visiting card. She handed them to Radhi and stuck her fingers back in to see if she had missed anything.

When Radhi flipped the card, she stared at the name on it in surprise.

19

Pair Perfect
Matrimonial services by Renuka Damani
501 Eden Garden, Temple Hill, Mumbai 400026

A series of questions rushed through Radhi's mind. How did Hansa and Renuka know each other? Had Renuka tried to poach Hansa? Or did Hansa suspect that Renuka had been sending Sarla and Kiran the tarot cards? Was that why she had gone to meet the woman and was that how she had got the card? And lastly, where had she seen the surname Damani before?

Radhi stared at her laptop screen. She was at Soul Harmony and was supposed to be working on notes recounting her first arranged meeting and how her perception of the system had shifted since her own first-hand experience, but she could not concentrate. Her mind kept going back to the new Renuka connection and she wondered if Sarla's rival had been paying Jeevan to deliver the tarot cards. Radhi had come into the office determined to extract a few answers from the young peon today, but he had been out running errands for Zarna. Radhi rested her chin on her palm as she mused about Kiran's daughter. She felt that the younger woman had been avoiding her ever since their conversation the week before. Just that morning, Radhi had seen her pacing below the office building, one finger stuck in an ear, talking on her phone. Instead of acknowledging Radhi, she had pretended she hadn't seen her and done an about-turn. Radhi could understand the younger woman's awkwardness around her, but she found it odd that Zarna was having a phone conversation in the heat, amid all the traffic and roadside noises, when she could easily have been sitting in her own private, air-conditioned office. Unless, Radhi wondered, it wasn't private enough. Unless it was something she didn't want her mother to overhear. But what? Radhi got up with a frustrated sigh and stretched her back with a few twists. The morning so far had proven to be most unproductive. Even her visit to Jigna ben had been for nothing because she hadn't been home. A neighbour had told her that she was at the temple and would most likely be there for an hour at least. Radhi had left a message with them for Jigna, that she would be back in a few hours. Radhi frowned at the document in front of her. She shut her laptop and opened her golden polka-dotted diary to a fresh page and began jotting down all the possible people who might have reason to send Sarla and Kiran the tarot cards and kill Hansa.

Bhavana — angry with the bureau for her daughter's broken engagement
Renuka — competition & some past history with Sarla
Neetu? — angry with the bureau for . . . lack of respect?
Mystery man — mystery motive
Zarna — clashes with Sarla over the future of the bureau

It seemed to Radhi that while many people had reason to be angry with Soul Harmony, none of these reasons seemed a strong enough motive for murder. She knew the police had checked Neetu's and Zarna's alibis along with everyone else's at the bureau. But not Renuka's or Bhavana's, because Sarla hadn't given their names to Shinde. She saw no way of knowing where they had been that evening unless she asked them. Assuming, of course, that they would tell her the truth. Radhi went over the names again. She hadn't really planned on putting Zarna's name on this list, but now that it was there, it seemed entirely plausible to Radhi that the woman would send her own mother threatening tarot cards. Whatever little Radhi had observed of them, there didn't seem much love lost between mother and daughter, and Zarna not only seemed terribly ambitious but also appeared rash enough to take such a step. Radhi was still chewing on her pen when it occurred to her that there was one more person at the bureau who needed further looking into.

'Hello,' said Radhi, knocking on Alpa's door before poking her head in. 'Got a minute?'

The stylish wedding planner looked up from a magazine she had been cutting and smiled. 'Of course. Come right in.'

As Radhi took a seat, Alpa waved her hand at her table which had a stack of magazines on one side and scattered cut-outs on the other. 'Excuse the mess. I always save interesting wedding theme pictures from magazines, they come in very handy when I need to create a mood board for my clients. So tell me, how's the book coming along?'

'I'm still in research mode, so the actual writing of it will take a while. But I'm really happy with all the various facets of arranged marriages I've been able to delve into. In fact, that's the reason I'm here. I wanted to see that folder again. The one with all your hand-drawn designs.'

'Of course!' Alpa beamed as she bent down to retrieve the folder from the bottom-most drawer. 'They're really unique, aren't they? But listen, we can't put them in your book because someone may just copy them, you know.'

'Don't worry,' Radhi assured her. 'I'll just describe some of the designs in words. I really want to give the reader an idea of the kind of variety that's possible.'

After flipping through the pages for a few minutes and making some notes, she handed it back to Alpa, who had been cutting more pages from the magazines. 'Thanks, this was very helpful. By the way, I got the photos you emailed me, they were great!'

Alpa beamed. 'Thank you. I got them clicked professionally, you know. Especially for your book!'

'Well, you look lovely!'

As Alpa patted her hair and giggled self-consciously, Radhi said without preamble, 'You know, I've been meaning to ask you what you meant that day — when you said plenty of people would've liked to see Hansa dead?'

Alpa appeared startled. 'When? Did I really say that?'

Radhi nodded.

'Gosh!' Alpa laughed nervously. 'That's such a nasty thing to say. I obviously didn't mean it. It must've been the shock of that day.'

Radhi remained quiet, looking at her expectantly.

Alpa answered reluctantly, 'It was just that Hansa ben was not a very pleasant person to work with. One shouldn't speak ill of the dead but that's just the way it was. You can ask Neetu ben also.'

'Did you have to work with Hansa ben often?'

'No not really,' she admitted with a frown. 'But you know how it is. This is a small office. And she was always around.

Always poking her nose in your business. One just didn't feel comfortable around her.'

'I get it.' Radhi closed her diary and began to gather her things, then very casually, as if she had just thought of it, she asked, 'What did she want to see you about?'

'What's that?'

'That day when we first met, she'd come to your office, but you were busy with me and you told her you would see her later . . . what did she want?'

Alpa blinked rapidly before answering, 'Oh that wasn't related to work. We were in charge of entertainment for Soul Harmony's 25th anniversary party, and she wanted to speak to me about that.'

'Aah!' Radhi smiled and got up. 'Well, thanks once again for everything.'

'I would appreciate it if you didn't mention it to anybody,' Alpa said softly when Radhi was at the door. 'My comment, that is.' Radhi turned around and Alpa continued, 'It wasn't very nice of me. I am embarrassed about it now.'

'I understand.' Radhi nodded before leaving the room.

Alone inside, Alpa's heart pounded hard as she fingered the edge of the scissors in her hand, pressing her thumb hard into its tip, until a pinpoint of blood appeared, and she dropped the scissors with a gasp. She couldn't believe how incomprehensibly stupid she had been.

Radhi stood outside Alpa's cabin for a few moments, her heart pounding. She had confirmed a doubt about Alpa that she'd had since the day she attended her cousin's sangeet. Alpa was moonlighting and planning weddings on the sly. She had double-checked Alpa's catalogue of original drawings and found an identical design of orchid peacocks which she had seen at her cousin's function that night. Alpa seemed to be taking on Soul Harmony's clients without the knowledge of its owners. But that wasn't why Radhi was walking briskly to her desk now. A much more terrible doubt had just occurred to her. She sat at her seat and opened her polka-dotted diary to the page she had been working on and added Alpa's name to it. Along with a reason.

Bhavana — angry with the bureau for her daughter's broken engagement
Renuka — competition & some past history with Sarla
Neetu? — angry with the bureau for . . . lack of respect?
Mystery man — mystery motive
Zarna — clashes with Sarla over the future of the bureau
Alpa — did Hansa find out she was cheating the bureau and threaten to tell Sarla? Is that why Alpa killed her?

Radhi stared at the latest addition to her list of names. The wedding planner did not look like a cold-blooded killer from any angle. But what if it had been a mistake? What if they'd had an argument and Alpa had hit Hansa in the heat of the moment?

Radhi was doodling little stick figures in her diary when the wedding-card designer she had helped on the day Hansa's body was found walked up to the adjoining desk.

'I didn't get a chance to thank you the other day,' she said, smiling at Radhi as she took her seat and pulled out her laptop from her bag. 'I am Divya, by the way,' she extended her arm.

'Radhika Zaveri, you can call me Radhi,' Radhi said taking her hand.

'It's never happened to me before. At least, not as an adult. My mother tells me as a child I once had a panic attack when my kid brother slipped off the swing because I pushed him too hard and he had to get stitches. But I have only the vaguest memory of it.'

'Well, it's happened to me plenty of times and I know how awful it is. I'm only glad I could help.'

'I have been thinking back to that day and do you know what had really affected me? It wasn't so much the death — I didn't know Hansa ben well at all — but it was because of how spooky it was.'

'Spooky? What do you mean?' Radhi shut her diary to give Divya her full attention.

'Just last month at the Diwali party in the office, Neetu ben predicted that Hansa ben's life was in danger.' Divya pulled her chair closer to Radhi's and dropped her voice down by a notch.

'So Neetu ben was doing a little bit of palmistry for some of us at the party and Hansa ben, who had been observing the whole thing, called astrology a party trick and said that she had no faith in it. As you can imagine, Neetu ben got very irritated. She said she could prove that it was a legit science. She asked Hansa ben to show her palm, but when she had studied it for a few moments, she said she didn't want to make any predictions. At which point Hansa ben mocked her. I don't know if you knew Hansa ben at all?' She paused to look at Radhi curiously.

Radhi shook her head. 'Barely.'

Nodding, Divya continued, 'She could be quite, uhm, how should I say it, dismissive. Yes, that's the word. She didn't have much respect for authorities and boundaries and didn't care much for what people here thought of her. Except maybe Sarla ben.'

Radhi nodded. The description fit in well with what she had gathered in the time she had spent with Hansa and the impression she had formed of the PI.

Divya said, 'She mocked Neetu ben, who as you can imagine was furious. That's when she announced that Hansa ben's life would be cut short in the most unexpected way.' Divya paused to see if the full import of her words had registered.

'What happened then?' Radhi's eyes were wide as she processed this new information. 'What did Hansa ben say to that?'

'Believe it or not, she laughed. She asked Jeevan to bring her another bowl of malpua, saying that she might as well indulge since she wasn't going to live too long anyway.'

'I see now why you were so affected that day.' Radhi rubbed at the goosebumps that had formed on her arms.

'Yes! I was horrified. Juhi was there as well, you can ask her.' Divya inclined her head towards the receptionist who was passing by with a bunch of files in her hands.

'What's that?' Juhi paused hearing her name.

'I was just telling Radhika about that fight between Neetu ben and Hansa ben at the office Diwali party.'

Juhi's face assumed a solemn expression. 'Yes, I had almost forgotten about that!'

'Are you kidding me? That was the only thing I could think about when we heard that Hansa ben had been murdered!'

Juhi nodded. 'Yes, it was freakish what happened. I was right there when they went at it. Neetu ben was reading my hand!'

'Oh yes, I remember!' Divya suddenly smiled. 'What did she tell you? Something about how you were like honey to bees when it came to men?'

Juhi blushed and teased back. 'And didn't she tell you you'd have four children?'

'Three! She said three children!' Divya countered.

As the two of them discussed the other predictions Neetu had made that day, Radhi wondered about Neetu and exactly how offended she must have been. To Radhi that day she had come across as someone who took herself seriously. Herself and her work. She was sensitive about how people perceived astrology, and Radhi could imagine she would be quick to take offence. She'd be mad at Hansa for ridiculing her work in front of the whole office; in any case, she felt insecure, but surely she wasn't angry enough to go that far to prove her point? Radhi opened her diary and crossed out the question mark beside Neetu's name. Neetu seemed like she had a solid motive after all. She wondered if the time had come to ask her directly what she had been doing at Hansa's house the day after her death.

'There, that's the one you wanted, no?' Jigna placed the box with Hansa's old files on the table in front of Radhi.

'Yes, thank you.' Radhi smiled and pulled the box towards her.

She had dropped in to see Jigna once again.

'Hansa's purse,' Jigna had whispered at the sight of her sister's brown, misshapen bag and hugged it to her chest for a moment before accepting the large paper bag of snacks that Radhi had brought for her.

'Oh, this is too much!' she had said repeatedly when she peered inside the bag and saw the multiple packs of crisp chakris, banana chips, spicy methi puris and the cashew and almond chikkis.

She went to the kitchen to make Radhi a cup of tea, and Radhi turned her attention to the box and brought out the stack of files she had been thinking about since that morning. Turning them horizontal, so that their spines were clearly visible, she kept each file aside until she came across the name she had hoped to find: Damani.

'Aah, that's it! I knew I had read it somewhere!' She congratulated herself before opening the file and reading its contents. It was a short paragraph, and when she was done reading, she shut the file with more questions than she had started out with. Questions which would be best answered by the founder of Soul Harmony, Sarla Seth.

As Radhi's car approached Eden Garden, she saw a crowd gathered under the amaltas tree that guarded its gate. She asked Ramzan bhai to drop her there instead of taking it inside the building like he usually did.

'What happened?' she asked, walking up to one of the security guards she recognized.

'It's that peon from Soul Harmony, he is lying unconscious on the footpath.'

'Jeevan?' Radhi asked, shocked. 'Why, what happened to him?'

The security guard shook his head. 'Not sure. I think it was some kind of fit. They've called the ambulance. It should be here any moment.'

As if on cue, Radhi heard a siren in the distance. Quickly, she made her way to the front of the crowd and saw Jeevan sprawled on the pavement; he had frothed at the mouth and some of the yellow drool had trickled down to his chin. Someone had thought to tuck a rolled-up dupatta under his head. Zarna was squatting beside him, red in the face, perspiring furiously.

'Zarna, are you okay? What has happened to Jeevan?'

'Oh thank God, you are here, Radhi,' said Zarna standing up. 'I've been trying to reach Sarla Aunty and Mom but neither of them is picking up their phones! We don't know what's wrong with him. One of the drivers mentioned that he was leaning against the tree, complaining of dizziness. He rushed to get him one of the guards' chairs, but by the time he came back, Jeevan had dropped to the ground!'

The sound of the ambulance grew louder. Within a few moments it had stopped beside them and the medics were rushing out. Once they had carried Jeevan into the ambulance, Zarna and Radhi followed the ambulance to the hospital in Radhi's car.

20

Will fetch you by 9 p.m. Stay ready. You're going to love my friends.

Radhi read Nishant's message and bit her lip. In between her visits to Jigna ben's place and the rush to the hospital, she had completely forgotten that she was to meet his friends that night. She checked her watch. It was already five o'clock. Too late to cancel, especially when he had gone through the trouble of coordinating with his friends. Radhi sighed and looked out of the window. She was in her car, on her way back to the bureau from the hospital. Zarna had got down on the way to run some errands for Soul Harmony's upcoming anniversary party and now, finally alone with her thoughts, Radhi allowed her mind to go to a dangerous place.

The doctors had said that Jeevan had had a severe allergic reaction to some food which had contained peanuts. They had tried to flush some of it out of him, but his condition remained critical. In the hospital his mother had wept and wept, baffled at what her son could possibly have eaten. 'He was always so careful of what he put in his mouth. I can't believe he'd make such a mistake!' she had told the doctor repeatedly. Now, afraid of going there but knowing she had no choice, Radhi allowed herself to wonder what if it wasn't a mistake. What if Jeevan had eaten something on purpose? What if he had felt cornered by Radhi's questions and tried to harm himself? The tarot reader had said Radhi would be involved in a death. Could it be that Jeevan had tried to commit suicide because of her? The thought made Radhi's chest hurt and she found it difficult to breathe. She opened the topmost button of her white shirt and lowered the car window. The sudden rush of air did nothing for her warm, flushed face.

'Didi, is Jeevan going to be okay?' Juhi stood up from behind her desk as soon as Radhi entered the office.

'We don't know yet, Juhi. The doctors are trying their best.'

'But what are they saying? What happened to him suddenly?'

'It's some sort of an allergy. An extreme reaction to peanuts. They've pumped most of it out of his system now. But he is still in danger.'

Juhi shook her head, distressed. 'His poor mother! If something happens to him, I don't know what she'll do! His father is a big, fat good-for-nothing! Jeevan is her only support.'

Radhi felt the tightness in her chest intensify. As if a hard fist had squeezed her heart. The possibility that she could be responsible for the fate of an entire family was too frightening for her to consider.

She pressed Juhi's hand. A gesture to comfort herself as much as the younger woman.

'Don't worry, Juhi. Luckily, we got him to the hospital in time. Another ten minutes and it would have been too late to do anything.'

The receptionist smiled weakly but didn't look convinced.

'Please make sure the servers are all in uniform.' Radhi and Juhi turned to see Kiran approaching the reception area, seeing off a middle-aged man in a checked shirt. 'And no whites please. Your idea of white is very different from mine. They should all be in black shirts and trousers.'

'Yes, ma'am.'

'And white gloves. Half of them forgot their gloves last time.'

'Don't worry, ma'am, I'll personally check this time.' The man removed a small diary from his trouser pocket and made a note.

'Have them get here at least three hours before the event starts. That way they have enough time to make mistakes and rectify them. And no excess oil please.'

'Our food is never oily, ma'am. All of Temple Hill knows that about us.'

'Look, it's very simple, if I need soap to wash my hands after eating your food, it means the food was oily. And I will cut ten per cent of your fee.'

As Kiran rattled off some final instructions for the man, Radhi began to see her with new eyes. In their earlier interactions, Kiran had come across as timid and unsure, not only of herself but also of her place in the scheme of things. Perhaps it was a result of her partner's personality. It was natural, Radhi supposed, for most people to be overshadowed in the presence of Sarla's confident flamboyance. But now as Radhi watched her talking to the caterer, she could see that Kiran was much more substantial than she had initially given her credit for. There was an obvious and easy adeptness for handling people and getting things done, and Radhi could see why Sarla had invited her to be her partner. Not an employee but an equal. But she knew she couldn't be the only one to have formed a less than favourable first impression of Kiran.

She was mousy and full of nervous tics and had likely always been underestimated. She couldn't possibly have received the same amount of importance or respect that people gave Sarla, and Radhi wondered how that made her feel.

'Oh good, Radhi, you are back.' Kiran turned her attention to Radhi once the man had left. 'I just spoke to Zarna and she told me what a great help you were at the hospital. Thank you so much, dear.'

'It was no problem at all. I just wish he makes it.'

'Yes, yes. I hope so too. Poor boy.' Kiran sighed, suddenly looking tired. 'And for all this to happen when Sarla is away.' She turned to Juhi. 'Juhi, could you please arrange for some tea? Radhi, would you like some? We can sit down in my cabin for a bit.'

'Sure,' Radhi said, walking with Kiran to her office. 'Where is Sarla Aunty?'

'A new client of hers has invited her to visit their farmhouse in Karjat. They are looking to find their son a good match and they want Sarla to meet him.'

'Karjat is beautiful,' Radhi said thinking of the lush, mountainous town on the outskirts of Mumbai where Madhavi and she owned a farmhouse. 'It will be good for Sarla Aunty to get out of the office, she has . . . both of you have . . . been so stressed of late.'

'Oh yes, they'll make sure Sarla has a good time there. They'll ply her with good food and tonnes of compliments on her sari and take her on a tour of their farm where their son will play guide so that Sarla can see for herself how charming and well-mannered he is.'

Radhi grinned. 'You sound like you've seen and done a version of this a hundred times.'

'I haven't. But Sarla has. She keeps getting invited by parents who are anxious about making a good impression on her. And I get to hear her stories.' Kiran smiled.

As Juhi knocked on the door and brought in their tea with bowls of makhana, soya sticks and til laddus, Radhi wondered if she had imagined a hint of bitterness in Kiran's voice. Her tone had been light and yet it had seemed weighed down.

'How come you never go?'

'Me?' Kiran brought her cup down mid-sip, as if the mere thought was absurd. 'I'm not a people's person at all. I get very nervous in social situations. Unlike Sarla, who knows exactly what to say and when from the word go, I get flustered around new people.' She smiled before adding, 'As you may have noticed.'

Radhi took a handful of the makhana and smiled back. 'You prefer to manage things behind the scenes?'

'Exactly. I ensure that this place runs smoothly. Sarla is the one with the hunches and the relationships. She's excellent at networking and matchmaking. But even a matrimonial bureau can't run on those skills alone. Left to her own devices, Sarla can be very disorganized. I, on the other hand, have an eye for detail. I focus on the housekeeping part of things. I make sure that our bills are paid and that the payments due to us come in on time. If the air conditioner is broken or the water filter needs servicing, the staff come to me. I'm the one who ensures that there are always interesting snacks in our pantry to offer our clients.' Kiran drank deeply from her mug of tea before adding, 'On their own these may seem like little things, but they add up.'

Kiran's phone rang, and while she spoke, Radhi, who had missed lunch because of all the running around she had done that day, remembered the kathi rolls that Lila had packed for her. She got her steel lunch box out from her bag and opened it on Kiran's desk. As usual, Lila had packed twice the food Radhi would need. She picked up one of the foil-wrapped rolls and pushed the box towards Kiran to indicate that she was welcome to take one. The roll was full of paneer, marinated in tangy yoghurt and julienned bell peppers. As Radhi ate, she looked around Kiran's immaculately neat cabin and once again her eyes fell on the *WedMe Happy* magazine with Sarla on the cover. She understood that Kiran was introverted and didn't enjoy the social aspect of her business as much as Sarla, but introverted people could also be ambitious.

'Do you miss being in the spotlight, though?' Radhi asked with a nod towards the magazine once Kiran had hung up and accepted one of Radhi's kathi rolls.

Kiran chewed thoughtfully before answering, 'I suppose I do. I envy the attention Sarla receives, even though I know that I'd be terribly uncomfortable around it.'

Radhi, who had expected her to deny it, was surprised at her honest answer.

'Do you know it was my idea to hire a wedding planner and an astrologer, all in-house?'

Radhi shook her head.

Kiran smiled. 'I doubt anyone does. Everyone thinks Sarla is the brain behind the whole thing. But actually, she is the heart of it. I am the brain.'

'Both of you are equally important.'

'Exactly,' Kiran said quietly, as she wiped her fingers with a tissue and began to tap the pens in her pen holder.

There was a knock on the door and Juhi poked her head in. 'Ma'am, Inspector Shinde is here. He'd like to speak to you.'

'Me?' Kiran appeared startled. 'Why me?'

'He was asking for Sarla ben but since she isn't around I suggested he talk to you instead.'

'Of course, of course. Makes sense. Bring him in.'

'I should go,' offered Radhi, beginning to pack up her lunch box, even though she wanted to hear what Shinde had to say.

Fortunately for Radhi, Kiran had the same idea. 'No, no stay please. Don't leave me alone with that horrible man.'

The door opened and Kiran reddened at the possibility that he may have heard.

'Good evening, ma'am,' Shinde said pleasantly and then his eyes fell on Radhi and his expression turned sour.

Radhi smiled at him innocently and took a bite of her roll.

'Would you like some tea or coffee, Inspector?' Kiran asked.

'No, no, ma'am, this is a quick visit.' Shinde took a seat. 'This is about the bike parked below your building. The one the man who came to meet the victim used.'

'Yes, yes, what about it?'

'We did some digging and discovered something strange.' Shinde paused to see if he had the attention of both women.

Radhi, who didn't feel like giving him the satisfaction of asking 'what', took another bite of her roll.

'What, Inspector?' Kiran, however, complied.

'We found that the bike was registered in Hansa's name.' Shinde paused again and this time got the reaction he wanted. Both Kiran and Radhi looked surprised.

'We asked her sister if Hansa ever rode a bike or owned a bike and she insists that Hansa did neither.' Shinde continued, 'So, my question is, had Hansa bought this bike for work? Did you, that is, Soul Harmony, help her purchase it? Is it possible that the man with the gold chain was in her employ, which means in your employ, essentially?'

'No, we have certainly not helped her buy a bike . . . at least, I don't think so. I mean, I'll have to check with my partner, of course, but she'd have told me if we had.' Kiran twirled the edge of her pallu around her finger, looking far from certain. 'Thing is, I rarely worked with her. Sarla would be in a much better position to answer this.'

'Well, where is she? We tried calling her, but she didn't take the call. I hope she hasn't left town when we had expressly forbidden all of you from travelling.'

Before an extremely flustered-looking Kiran could answer, Radhi spoke up. 'They have a brother. Hansa and Jigna ben. Do you think it could be him?'

'We know about the brother. But from what I understand they are not close. We are planning to question him, of course, but that's not a priority. I strongly suspect the man on the bike is related to her work with Soul Harmony. From what we've gathered so far, her work here had her dealing with all sorts of characters.' He narrowed his eyes and frowned accusingly at Kiran as he said this, making the matchmaker squirm.

'Still, maybe you could show the artist's sketch to Jigna ben and see if there's any resemblance to the brother?' Radhi pressed.

'Like I said, ma'am, we'll be looking into it.' Shinde stood up with a long-suffering sigh, as if dealing with bossy, nosy women was a fate far worse than catching criminals. 'And you have Sarla ben call us right away,' he told Kiran.

'Here,' said Radhi handing the cheque to Lila, 'this should cover their hospital bills and some.'

Lila's eyes widened when she saw the figure on the cheque. 'This will be so helpful to them, didi, you have no idea!'

Radhi had just returned home from Soul Harmony and had filled Lila in on what had happened to Jeevan.

'Poor things!' Lila had exclaimed. 'It is just one thing after another for them. First, the younger one's appendix operation and now Jeevan is in the hospital. God knows how they'll manage all the expenses!'

And Radhi, who was ashamed to think that the financial implications of the situation hadn't even occurred to her, had hurried to her study to write out a cheque.

'I have to say, didi, you have a heart of gold,' Lila said as she folded the cheque and put it carefully into her purse. 'But you have one bad habit.' She scanned Radhi's face as if trying to decide how her next words would be taken before plunging ahead. 'You drink too much. I know it is not my place to say anything and I considered going to Madhavi didi instead. But somehow that felt like betraying your trust.' She hesitated, trying to gauge if she had said too much.

When Radhi remained quiet, she continued, hurrying slightly, so as to not lose her nerve. 'I know it's very common abroad for women to drink. And that most modern women do it. But I've seen too many empty bottles over the last couple of months and it makes me wonder if something is troubling you.'

Radhi, who had been too ashamed to respond before, smiled now. 'Nothing is bothering me. I promise. And you're sweet to care. I know I should go easy on the wine. And I will. Try, that is,' she said lightly.

Lila nodded and picked up her purse, getting ready to leave for the day. 'Thanks for not getting angry, didi. But I had to say something, no? After all, we have known each other a long time.'

'We have,' Radhi agreed softly.

When Lila had gone, Radhi stood at the window, smoking one cigarette after another, as she tried to make sense of all the things she was feeling. She could recognize the agitation, the shame and the guilt. There was sadness in the mix as well, but sadness wasn't new. Sadness and she were old friends. It was the other feelings which she didn't know how to process or where to put away. They were swirling in her stomach, making her uneasy and unhappy.

She had been looking forward to the couple of hours she had at home after Lila left and before she had to get ready for her date with Nishant. She had hoped to wind down with a glass of wine, knowing fully well that she wouldn't stop at a glass. But now that Lila had called her out on it, she felt too ashamed to open her bar. And that wasn't all she was ashamed of. Lila had thought she was generous for having helped Jeevan's family, but deep down, Radhi knew that the person she had really been helping was herself. The more she thought about it, the more she felt that Jeevan had tried to harm himself after his conversation with her. And the fat cheque she had written earlier was just a way for her to assuage her guilt.

'Are you still not going to tell me the plan?' Radhi asked Nishant.

They were in Nishant's car on their way to meet his friends and Nishant was driving.

'Nope.' He grinned.

'Why the suspense?'

'Why the impatience?' he teased, turning to her as the car stopped at a signal. 'You look very nice, by thc way.' His eyes lingered on her face and Radhi blushed. She was wearing a deep purple silk dress with a high neck, full balloon sleeves and a bold hemline that stopped several inches above her knees. She had taken extra care with her makeup that evening, doing up her eyes with thick mascara and a dramatic shade of green eyeshadow. It had had the effect she wanted. She didn't look like she had spent the day thinking about murder motives and death. He brushed her cheek with a finger and held her gaze for a moment longer before turning his eyes back on the road.

'You should know, I really don't like surprises,' Radhi tried again.

'Clearly.' He chuckled.

'Nishant,' Radhi asked, suddenly worried, 'we are meeting your *friends*, right? You're not going to suddenly spring your parents on me?' She looked down at her clothes. 'I'm really not dressed for it.'

'No, relax, I'd never do that! Besides, my parents are chill. At least my dad is. You'll like him.' He added with a wicked smile, 'Though I'm glad you're thinking of meeting my parents and all that.'

'Jesus!' Radhi swatted his arm, knowing fully well that he was teasing her and yet unable to help herself. 'I wasn't!'

She leaned forward to increase the volume of the music on the stereo and Mohit Chauhan's voice filled the car with a soulful song about what it was like to always be last in line when it came to love. Radhi looked out of the window. They had just crossed Churchgate and she presumed they were headed to Kala Ghoda, the city's art district. Packed with heritage buildings from the colonial era, restored and converted into cafes, art galleries and stylish bars, the area always bubbled with a kind of creative energy that Radhi loved. She closed her eyes and took a deep breath. How simple life could be if only she let it. If only she knew how. It had been a long, taxing day and every part of her had protested when she slipped her feet into her 5-inch stilettos. But she knew that curling up in bed with a good book and a glass of wine was not an option. If she cancelled on Nishant that evening, it would be rude and last minute, and he'd think she was avoiding meeting his friends. Besides, that glass of wine was now spiked with even more guilt than before. Why in the world did this have to be a surprise? She'd have felt so much more settled if she just knew what to expect. Radhi's eyes flew open as a new possibility occurred to her.

'Is it your birthday? Is that what this is?' Radhi turned towards him, alarmed. 'We've been dating for months, and I don't even know when your birthday is! Is it today?'

Nishant looked at her amused, his brown eyes twinkling.

Radhi clutched her head. 'Oh God, I am terrible, aren't I? Why didn't you tell me? I would've got you a gift.' She leaned towards him and gave him a soft kiss on the cheek. 'Happy birthday.' Then she kissed him again more fully on the mouth. 'And this is an apology for being so completely self-involved.'

'Thank you, Radhi,' said Nishant, his face flushed with pleasure. 'Now I really wish it *had been* my birthday!'

Radhi's eyes widened, and she swung her clutch at his arm. 'You're horrible!' She leaned back into her seat and folded her arms. 'This place we are going to better be worth all this suspense!'

Nishant laughed. They drove in silence for a few minutes.

Then he said, 'April 19th. That's your birthday, isn't it?'

Radhi turned to him and smiled. 'Who told you?'

Nishant shrugged.

'Now you had better tell me yours,' Radhi said.

'Later,' he said, slowing down the car. 'We're here.'

Radhi looked at the almost 12-foot black glass door their car had stopped in front of. She saw the neon sign at the top of the door, and her smile froze in its place.

21

'Shall we?' asked Nishant turning to her as the valet came to help them with the parking.

Radhi shook her head. Her voice seemed to have stuck in her throat.

'What's the matter? Did you forget something?'

'No, I'm sorry, I can't.'

'Can't what?' Nishant looked confused.

'Go in there.'

'Why not?'

'I can't sing.'

'Why? Do you have a bad throat or something?'

Radhi shook her head.

'Didn't you tell me you love singing?'

'I don't sing any more.'

'I don't sing at all, Radhi! But this is karaoke. It's supposed to be just fun.'

The valet was knocking at their window and other cars had stopped behind theirs, waiting their turn. Nishant waved the valet off and drove the car away from the entrance and back onto the main road, where he parked it to the side. Then shutting the engine, he turned to face her.

'What is it, Radhi? Are you feeling shy? Or is it because you don't want to meet my friends?'

'No!' Radhi said, anguished. 'This has nothing to do with your friends!'

'I don't understand then.' Nishant ran his hand through his hair, frustrated. 'When you told me about learning music as a child, I thought this would be fun for you to do. I thought it would be a nice surprise . . .'

Radhi's eyes had teared up. 'I'm sorry, Nishant, I really am.'

'You're crying?' Nishant had an incredulous look on his face as he peered at Radhi in the dark. 'Jesus, what did I do? This was so not how this was supposed to go! I had planned to . . .' His voice trailed off.

Radhi's tears were flowing freely now. She sat there silently clutching her purse so hard that her knuckles turned white. Nishant gently pried her hand loose and held it between both his hands. The gesture made Radhi cry harder.

'Hush, darling, hush.' He kissed her fingers tenderly. 'What is it? You can tell me.'

Radhi shook her head, continuing to cry silently. But Nishant didn't let go of her hand. He sat silently, patiently, waiting.

'It was a singing competition we were coming back from . . . the day . . . the day my parents died in a car crash,' Radhi said finally, her voice barely above a whisper. 'We had travelled to Pune. It was a state-level competition and I'd won . . . I remember everything so vividly from that day. The song playing on the car radio, the peppery makhanas we were eating, the smooth and cool surface of the gold trophy in my hand, the sickening sound of our car being crunched between two trucks . . .'

Radhi choked back a sob. 'After . . . after the accident, when the ambulance had come and taken my parents away, and the police had put me in a different car . . . I was still holding the trophy.' She shook her head, a gesture so leaden with guilt that years of therapy had done nothing to lighten it. 'I threw it into the sea when I got home . . . couldn't bear to look at it, couldn't bear to sing again . . .'

Radhi looked away, seeming to run out of tears and words at the same time. But Nishant squeezed her hand and drew her attention back to him.

'Don't,' he said. 'It wasn't your fault. Don't punish yourself for it.'

Radhi bit her lip. So many people, friends, family, therapists alike had told her the same thing over the years. But she couldn't believe them. Couldn't draw even a smidgen of comfort from their words. How could she when she hadn't told them the whole story? Radhi nodded and allowed Nishant to gather her in his arms. She knew her tears were probably more palatable than the truth.

'Here, let me,' said Nishant, gently prying the zipper from Radhi's fingers.

His hands lingered for a moment on her bare back while he bent forward to kiss the nape of her neck before he helped her zip up her dress.

'Thanks,' Radhi turned to joke about how his proficiency with zippers must mean that he'd had lots of practice, but her voice caught in her throat, suddenly shy under the surprising intensity of his gaze.

After abandoning the karaoke plan that evening, the two of them had gone on a long drive. Radhi had been reluctant to talk at first, but he had drawn her out in that funny, wry way of his until she had laughed quietly at one of his jokes, and he had leaned back into his seat satisfied. They had driven around for more than an hour, reaching the other end of the city, where they had stopped for ice creams on Juhu Beach. Here, leaving their shoes behind a rock, they had walked barefoot on the wet sand until they had reached a quiet, moonlit stretch where the only sound was the lapping of waves against the shore. To Radhi, the sea had seemed like it was coming in for kisses. Desperate, lingering, repeated kisses, as if it was unable to stay away from its beloved, despite being pulled away over and over again. She had turned to Nishant then, and their lips had moved towards each other as if in that moment every hungry desire of the sea had seeped into their own blood.

Now she looked away from him, feeling confused. She had sensed a shift in him; it was subtle, but it had put a charge in the air between them and she was unsure of what it meant. He watched her as she busied herself with brushing the sand off her clothes, her movements becoming slightly flustered as the silence between them deepened. Finally, he took both her hands in his and held them until she stopped moving and looked up. Then very slowly, his eyes never leaving her face, he turned one hand so that her palm faced the sky and put a small, glittering ring on it.

Tuesday

Radhi woke up the next day with a headache so vicious that it eliminated every other sensation from her mind. She had forgotten to draw the curtains the night before, and now her room was flooded with sunlight. Unforgiving, prickly light that had forced her to open her eyes and acknowledge the possibility of morning. From the sound of running water and the sizzle of tempered hot oil, she guessed Lila was at work in the kitchen. It occurred to Radhi that Lila had probably rung the doorbell, but she hadn't heard it. She grimaced as she hoisted herself up on an elbow and reached for her phone. It was almost ten. Her housekeeper who came in at sharp eight every morning had likely used the spare key that Radhi had given her for emergencies.

Radhi frowned as another thought occurred to her. Had Lila come into her room to check on her? The door to her bedroom was ajar, and Radhi couldn't blame her if she *had* looked in — it was unlike Radhi to sleep through the sound of the doorbell or for that matter to even be asleep at this hour. But Radhi hadn't wanted Lila to see the empty bottle of wine rolling on the floor beside the discarded clothes near her bed. Not when they had literally just had a conversation about it. Radhi hadn't planned on drinking last night. She had heeded her housekeeper's words and had promised herself to cut down on the alcohol. But after her conversation with Nishant, she had come home so agitated that she hadn't been able to think of any other way to get through the night.

She lay on her bed staring at the ceiling, unwilling to get up, knowing fully well that even the slightest of movements was going to make her head throb. Snatches of the night came rushing back to her and made her chest hurt harder than her head. What had she done? Was she the world's biggest fool? Or did she enjoy being broken so much that any chance of healing had her running in the opposite direction? Radhi's mouth felt dry as she thought of how hurt Nishant had seemed.

Her therapist in the US had told her that they needed to examine the patterns of her life. Her relationship with happiness and guilt in particular. Radhi had reacted to this suggestion of reflecting on her past by giving up therapy altogether. Scraping new skin off an old wound wasn't her idea of healing.

With a groan she got up and gingerly made her way to the kitchen, in dire need of a sip of water.

'Should I make the tea, didi?' Lila asked when she saw Radhi.

'Yes, please,' Radhi said as she filled her glass from the cool earthen pot by the window.

She leaned against the kitchen platform, sipping on her water as Lila grated the ginger and added the mint leaves to her tea. There was no cheerful chatter today, no questions about her date with Nishant or jokes about how it may have ended. In its place were brisk, efficient movements and a silence that had much to say. Radhi knew Lila was disappointed in her, which to Radhi, who was often disappointed in herself, came as no great surprise.

'Better than popping pills, no?' Renuka chuckled as she put a walnut in her mouth and turned a large seven-day pillbox filled with nuts, seeds and dried fruit towards Radhi.

'Always.' Radhi took a cashew and smiled back.

Radhi had been surprised when Renuka called her that morning, asking for a chat. She was just the person Radhi had hoped to talk to that day and this little instance of serendipity had the effect of lifting Radhi from the fog of her hangover and the general gloom she had surrounded herself in. Now, sitting across from the founder of Pair Perfect, she wondered what Renuka wanted with her, and how she could steer the conversation to what *she* wanted from Renuka — some answers.

'Before we start, tell me what will you have? Tea? Coffee? Cold coffee?'

'Some tea would be great. Thanks.' Radhi brought out her diary and pen from her bag, wishing Renuka would stop offering her things — it was difficult to ask hard questions when one had been plied with tea and snacks.

Once the tea had been ordered, Renuka put her box of nuts away and cleared her table. 'I'm glad you could make it today. There was something I've been thinking I should share with you.'

Renuka appeared to hesitate. But to Radhi it seemed the hesitation was more for her benefit than from any actual reluctance on Renuka's part.

'It's just that a big section of your book is going to be about Soul Harmony, isn't it?'

'I plan to talk to a few other matchmakers in the city as well, but yes, Soul Harmony will feature prominently.'

'Well, I just wondered if anyone had given you the full picture? It's true they are the most successful matchmakers in the city. But are *all* their clients happy with them? What about the ones who get divorced within a year? Or the ones with broken engagements? Or the ones they are unable to help and who continue to remain single even after paying Soul Harmony's hefty fee? I just feel that if you're going to write about them, maybe you want to take a more balanced view . . .'

'I suppose no business or service can be expected to have a hundred per cent success rate. I'm—'

Renuka interrupted her. 'True. But unfortunately, ours is a business of lives; when we fail at our jobs, people's entire lives are impacted . . .' Renuka leaned forward and lowered her voice, 'I heard that one of Sarla ben's clients was so unhappy in her marriage that she committed suicide. To be clear, these are just things one hears. But there is no smoke without fire, no?' Not waiting for an answer, she continued, 'Of course, if this is something you'd like to pursue, I could point you in the right direction.' Renuka leaned back into her seat and smiled at Radhi expectantly.

Radhi studied Renuka for a few moments trying to judge if it was malice in her eyes or something else. 'Is this about your son, Renuka ben?' she asked finally.

'What?' Renuka looked as if she had been slapped.

'I know you'd registered him with Soul Harmo—'

'Has that Sarla been spreading her lies again!?' Renuka hissed with narrowed eyes.

'Sarla ben has told me nothing. At Hansa ben's house I found a folder on your son in which she—'

'All bloody lies!' Renuka said, making an angry ball of the parrot-green tissue paper with which she had been dabbing her mouth and flinging it to the ground.

'You and I both know they aren't lies. A simple Facebook search can confirm that your son is gay and living with his partner in California.'

All colour had drained out of Renuka's face. She pushed herself away from the desk as if Radhi had a contagious virus and she needed physical distance from her. 'Please leave.'

'Look, Renuka ben, your son's sexual orientation is nothing to be ashamed of—'

'Now!' She thumped the table loudly.

She was sweating heavily despite the strong air conditioning. The sharp and stylish businesswoman from a few moments ago had been replaced by a petrified mother. Radhi tried changing tack.

'Why did Hansa ben come to you? Was it about this?'

'No.' Renuka blurted out, then paused, before speaking again. 'I don't know any Hansa.' She walked stiffly to the door, holding it open for Radhi. 'I made a terrible mistake inviting you here to talk. I thought you were one of us, a Temple Hill girl first and then a journalist. But true to your profession, you've gone and dug up the dirt. If you have any decency, you won't repeat these lies about my son.'

'This was never about your son, Renuka ben,' Radhi said coldly, putting her diary and pen away as she got up from her seat. 'I realize that being gay is still a big taboo in our world. Our society can be bloody narrow-minded. So I get why you'd want to lie about your son. But why about Hansa? Why lie that you didn't know her?' Radhi paused at the door. 'And as for digging up dirt, isn't that why you asked me here?'

22

'I know, Ramila ben, I know. But what to do? Young people today don't want to meet with their entire families. They involve parents right at the end,' Kiran was saying into the phone when Radhi peeped into her cabin. She waved Radhi in and flashed two fingers at her to say that she would be free in a couple of minutes.

Radhi had just come up to the Soul Harmony office, where she found Juhi helping a client with his biodata in the conference room and Sarla ben missing from her cabin.

'Let me see if I can convince the boy's mother,' Kiran said in response to the person on the other line. Then saying goodbye, she hung up with an exasperated shake of her head.

'The girl's parents want to accompany her on her meeting and the boy's parents prefer they meet alone,' she said to Radhi by way of explanation.

Radhi smiled sympathetically. 'Wouldn't meeting alone be much more comfortable for the young people?'

'Honestly? There are pros and cons to both. When parents are a part of the whole process, the decisions get made faster. Parents tend to focus on the whole picture — not just the boy or girl in question but also the family, the standard of living, etc. Anyways, tell me, did you want something?'

Radhi shook her head. 'I was just wondering if you know where Sarla Aunty is?'

Kiran's face turned grave. 'We got the tarot cards again today. An awful-looking Devil Card. Sarla was really upset . . . said she was going home. I have never seen her like this. Between the both of us, she's usually the strong one.'

'Oh!' Radhi bit her lip. 'What did the message say?'

'Something about how the devil within us wouldn't go unpunished.' Kiran clutched her head. 'Don't remind me. It's hard to deal with clients with this going round and round in my head.'

'Sorry.' Radhi changed the subject. 'How is Jeevan?'

'Same as before.' Kiran sighed. 'Between you and me? It's not looking good. Zarna had dropped by the hospital this morning. The doctors are worried.' She clicked her tongue. 'Poor boy.'

If Jeevan was in the hospital, then who had delivered the tarot cards this time? Had the culprit found another way to send them? Or had her theory about Jeevan been completely wrong in the first place? Radhi's mind worked furiously as she made her way to Sarla's home.

After leaving Kiran's cabin, she had decided to meet Sarla. Sarla lived just ten minutes away from Soul Harmony, and Radhi had decided to walk in the hope that the fresh air would help with her muddled thoughts. There were many things she wanted to discuss with Sarla — the conversation with Alpa, the terrible argument with Renuka ben and now this confusion about Jeevan. If Jeevan wasn't the one delivering the cards, then how exactly was he involved? He was hiding something, but what?

Radhi stopped suddenly in the middle of the narrow footpath, eliciting an annoyed 'pcch' from the lady walking behind her, as a new possibility occurred to her.

What if Jeevan had seen something or someone he wasn't supposed to see? What if he hadn't spoken up not because of guilt but fear? Could the culprit have threatened him to keep quiet? And when Radhi had insisted that he come clean, had he felt trapped? Had Radhi's questions rattled not only Jeevan but even the person who had threatened him? Was it possible that he was in the hospital because someone had actually tried to silence him? She knew it was far-fetched, but this whole situation had stopped feeling normal a long time ago.

Hurriedly, she turned into the lane where Sarla stayed and made her way into a petite 5-storey building with its own rose garden.

As she rode the elevator, she checked her phone for what felt like the hundredth time that day. There was no message from Nishant. She knew she was wrong to expect it when it was she who had told him to give her some time and to stay away. But a tiny, selfish part of her wished he hadn't listened.

'Damn it!' she swore under her breath as she put her phone away and rang the doorbell to Sarla's apartment.

While she waited for the maid to get Sarla, she studied the spacious living room with its high ceiling and sweeping sea view and marvelled at how all the furniture had changed, yet the colour scheme was exactly the same as it had been almost three decades ago. Maroon, brown and cream. The two chesterfields facing each other had maroon upholstery and cream silk cushions, while the heavy, scalloped curtains were cream with maroon organza frills. All the walls were cream, all the furniture of rich brown mahogany and the carpet a shade of light maroon with a cream and gold paisley print. Everything was colour-coordinated precisely, just like Sarla's outfits every day. Today, however, as Sarla walked in, Radhi could see no sign of the flamboyant matchmaker, just a middle-aged woman who seemed very, very tired.

'That bad, huh?' Sarla asked with a grim smile, noticing Radhi's expression as she took a seat on a wide maroon armchair across from her. 'Most of it is the missing bindi . . . my face looks dull without it.'

When Radhi remained silent, Sarla sighed and rubbed her eyes. 'Okay, fine. I know I look terrible. I haven't slept in two days, I had a migraine last night and now my whole body hurts from the lack of sleep. But I'm telling you, had I remembered to put on my bindi, you wouldn't look so worried right now!'

That made Radhi smile. 'I know the bindi is a big part of your whole look, Aunty, but, and I say this with a lot of love, no bindi in the world can do anything when you look this haggard! I've never seen your hair tied in all the years I've known you.'

A maid came in with a glass of water on a tray and Sarla asked her to wait.

'Have lunch with me, Radhi. You don't mind palak paneer, do you? Please, I don't feel like eating alone today.'

Radhi agreed with a smile and Sarla gave the maid a few instructions. When they were alone again, Radhi said, 'Kiran ben told me you've received another one of those terrible cards.'

Sarla nodded and sighed. 'They keep getting worse and worse.'

'I had a theory about how the cards were coming to you, but now I'm not so sure.' Radhi said, filling Sarla in about her conversation with Jeevan and all the doubts she had about the peon.

Sarla massaged her temples with her fingers. 'My God, what a mess this is. If something happens to Jeevan, that will be another death on my hands!'

'You can't blame yourself, Aunty—'

'Can't I? I didn't go to the police to protect my own reputation. If I had involved them right at the start, when the tarot cards first started coming, who knows, Hansa would be alive right now!'

'But, Aunty, you couldn't possibly have known that things would get this serious!' Radhi protested.

Sarla shook her head, closed her eyes and sank further into the sofa. Radhi contemplated telling her about Alpa but decided against it, seeing how careworn Sarla looked. She'd wait until she was sure or had more information.

'Oh and before I forget,' Radhi dug around in her handbag and brought out the files she'd found in Hansa's brown bag, 'I figured these belonged to Soul Harmony and asked Jigna ben if we could keep them. They seem to be about the Bhavana ben problem.'

Sarla frowned, as if it was difficult to remember that she had once had a life beyond Hansa's murder and the tarot cards. 'Yes, she was trying to get to the bottom of why the boy called off the engagement with Bhavana's daughter.' She scanned the file absently before putting it away.

The maid came in to announce that lunch had been laid.

When Radhi had helped herself to a bowl of cucumber raita, palak paneer and a large spoonful of the nutty carrot halwa, which Sarla insisted she couldn't miss, the maid served her hot, ghee-soaked rotis straight from the tawa.

'Satpadi roti!' Radhi smiled as she broke one of the soft, flaky, multi-layered rotis with its delicately spiced folds. 'I haven't had these in decades.'

'I remember how much you liked them.' Sarla put one more on her plate. 'Just like your mum.'

For the rest of the meal they talked of Soul Harmony's upcoming anniversary party and Sarla's visit to Karjat and the basketful of fresh farm produce her client had given her. When they were done, however, Radhi felt she could no longer avoid telling Sarla about her meeting with Renuka, even though she knew it would distress Sarla further.

'She had a very hard time of it,' Sarla said, shaking her head when Radhi finished telling her about her interaction with Renuka. 'Her son is a dentist and over 6 feet tall. He was considered an absolute catch in our circles. When she first came to me with his biodata, I remember teasing her that she was wasting her time with this whole arranged-marriage process, he was sure to have a girlfriend. And she told me that she'd already checked with him and that he was open to being set up. When I had Hansa look into him, it was a mere formality; we just wanted to be sure that he was actually single like his mother claimed he was. When their then-maid told Hansa that he had a male friend come home for stayovers when his parents were travelling, I didn't think much of it. But Hansa dug a little more and found out that things were not all above ground, so to speak.'

Radhi cringed at the choice of words but didn't comment. Sarla belonged to a different generation and didn't yet have the right vocabulary to speak about homosexuality.

'I am assuming she didn't take it well when you told her?'

'Created quite a scene, actually.' Sarla shuddered. 'Called me a liar and a gossipmonger and threw the file in my face!'

Sarla paused as the maid came in with a tray of mouth fresheners and tall glasses of buttermilk and resumed only when she had left the room.

'And that wasn't even the end of it. A few months later the story came out on its own. There were rumours about how someone had seen him in Thailand holding hands with his boyfriend. Or kissing. Or something. I can't remember now.

People added all sorts of mirch masala to it. But Renuka came to the office to accuse *me* of having leaked the story!'

'But why?' Radhi put her glass of buttermilk down. 'What could you possibly gain from telling the world about her son's sexual orientation?'

'That's what I said! I would never go around gossiping about a client. In our business, that's just not done. But by then she wasn't listening to reason. Threatened to ruin me, etc., etc. Of course, I didn't take any of it to heart. I just felt sorry for her. I mean, I can't even imagine what I'd have done if it was *my* son who'd been caught with another man.' Sarla shuddered.

'Aunty, you can't possibly still think like this in this day and age!' Radhi said, appalled.

'Please, beta.' Sarla held up her hand to stop her. 'I know it's all very normal for *your* generation, but it's difficult for us older folk to accept. We've had a lifetime of thinking in a certain way.'

Before Radhi could protest that educated and aware people like Sarla couldn't use age as an excuse for their prejudices, her mother's friend hurried on, 'Don't get me wrong. I have nothing against them, personally. In fact, I believe in live and let live. People should be free to love whoever they want. But unfortunately, everyone in our society doesn't think like that, no?'

When Radhi held her tongue, she continued, 'Renuka's family had a rough time of it. They didn't step out for social events for almost a year. You know how mean-minded people can be sometimes, no?'

Radhi nodded, reluctantly. She had experienced that side of Temple Hill first-hand. Fresh after her divorce when she had come down to India to visit her sister, hardly a neighbour or member of her extended family had met her without a passing reference to her failed marriage. Even if it was only to make meaningless sympathetic noises devoid of any real concern. Most of this she had chalked down to general thoughtlessness, but some people, her sister's mother-in-law first among them, had gone out of their way to remind her that as a divorced Indian woman nearing thirty she was at the bottom-most rung of the social ladder and that she should try her best to get 'settled' again as soon as possible. If she could find someone, that is.

'Did Renuka know it was Hansa who had dug up the information?' Radhi asked.

Sarla, who had been pacing, appeared to think for a moment. 'I don't know . . . When she came into the office, she only got to deal with me. But I can't be sure . . . why?'

'What if Renuka has carried a grudge all these years? She has this history of feeling wronged by you. She opens her bureau right below yours. Soon you start receiving malicious tarot messages. And then your PI, who she believes ruined her life all those years ago, is murdered. Don't you think that's too much of a coincidence?'

'I suppose it is,' Sarla admitted. 'But I find it hard to think of Renuka as a murderer. It takes a special kind of ruthlessness to kill. Renuka is operating from pain. That sort of pain is supposed to ease and dilute over the years. Not crystalize into something so wicked.'

Radhi nodded. 'I noticed you didn't say she couldn't have sent the tarot cards — just that she couldn't have murdered.'

'True.' Sarla sighed, sitting down heavily on an armchair.

'I don't know about ruthless,' Radhi said carefully, 'but she has been spreading some very malicious lies about you. Something about how a girl committed suicide because she was unhappy in a marriage you fixed.'

Sarla stared at Radhi, her face losing all colour. A tortured sob escaped her, and she covered her mouth with the pallu of her sari. Then before Radhi knew it, the most formidable matchmaker of Temple Hill was crying helplessly in her arms.

23

A blue arched gateway announced the Temple Hill Police Station in a bright yellow Devanagari script as Radhi, Juhi and Sarla made their way into the sprawling complex built with blue basalt. Over a hundred years old, the structure had been labelled a heritage site, its architecture featuring prominently in books on Mumbai's colonial history, and yet Radhi, like most Temple Hill residents, had never set foot inside it. Not because it was inaccessible, but because there had never been any need to. Now, however, as she walked up to the second floor, where they were to meet Shinde, she looked around with surprise at the bright, airy rooms with their white casement windows, high ceilings and neat rows of desks with computers and files. She had imagined paan-stained, grimy walls, unsavoury characters being ferried in and out, and a general air of menace, which would have been a close approximation of what she had seen in Bollywood films, and which she suspected was how police stations looked like in the rest of the country.

But she had forgotten that this was Temple Hill, home to the country's richest and devoutest; here, even cops and criminals were expected to exist and conduct themselves behind a veneer of respectability. As they waited for Shinde to see them, Radhi took in the large portrait of Gandhi smiling benignly on two constables huddled around a phone watching a game of cricket. At a neighbouring desk, a man was reporting on the contents of his lost wallet, seeming more stressed about his various club membership IDs than any money or credit cards that may have been in there. Radhi walked to take a closer look at a large soft board which covered the wall opposite them with government notices, posters of missing people and news clippings that featured the Mumbai Police in a positive light. There were stories of narcotics being seized and stashes of RDX being unearthed and a gang of child traffickers being busted. None of the articles, Radhi observed, had anything to do with Temple Hill or its cops. This would simply never be that kind of place. And yet, she reminded herself of why she was here. Temple Hill was a peaceful neighbourhood, but it could, and had in the past, harbour a murderer.

Shinde had called Sarla an hour ago and reported rather gleefully that the mystery man had been apprehended. He had asked for Juhi to come to the station to identify the man from the line-up, but Juhi had seemed so panicky at the thought of going alone that Sarla and Radhi had agreed to go with her.

When he came to usher the women into his office, Shinde greeted Radhi with a smile. An actual curving-of-the-mouth, stretching-of-the-lips, showing-of-the-teeth kind of smile. It was a gesture so unexpected that for once Radhi didn't know how to respond.

'I have to thank you, madam,' Shinde said, once Juhi had been led away to the line-up of men, and Sarla and Radhi had been plied with steaming cups of tea and Parle-G biscuits. 'For urging us to look into the brother connection. We would have done it eventually, of course, but because of you we got there faster.'

'But her own brother?' Sarla shook her head wonderingly. 'It doesn't bear thinking about.'

'Has he confessed?' Radhi asked, finding her tongue.

'No, of course not. Not so soon.' Shinde smiled. 'We'll need to work on him a little bit.'

His eyes had a cruel glint in them, and Radhi suppressed the urge to shudder.

'But why did he do it?' Radhi asked. 'Surely, it can't be for a few thousand rupees?'

'Only those who have too much of it can dismiss money as a motive, madam,' Shinde said coldly. Then, as if remembering that he had decided to be nice to Radhi that day, he added, 'All I am saying is that when you have hungry bellies to feed, even a few thousand rupees can be reason enough. We've looked into this guy's history. He's got a drinking and gambling problem. Hasn't been able to keep a proper job down in the last five–seven years. His wife works as a beautician in a local parlour, but with two school-going kids, money is always a struggle. So our chap was in the habit of sponging off his elder sister.'

'But why kill her then? If she is his source of income . . .' Radhi asked.

Shinde smiled and took a sip of his tea. 'She didn't want to be. Had forbidden him from coming home. Refused to open the door to him.'

'So he came to her place of work?'

'Exactly. He wanted to embarrass her. He was sure she wouldn't refuse him here.'

'And she didn't . . . that is why there was no money in her wallet,' said Radhi.

'Exactly.'

'But if she gave him the money, then why kill her?' Radhi frowned.

'Because they had an argument.' Shinde smiled again, smug that for a change he did have all the answers. 'He's been pestering them to sell off the apartment they live in so that he can have his share. Says it is his parents' home and he is entitled to a piece of it. Hansa and Jigna have been resisting.'

'He told you that?' Sarla asked.

'No. Jigna ben did, when we went to show her the artist's sketch. She said her parents bought him the rooms he stays in currently so that he'd leave them in peace but since there was no legal paperwork done, he can still make his claim. She said he was becoming increasingly loud and aggressive every time he came by. And that the only way to get rid of him was to give him money.'

'So we don't know if they actually had an argument, but we assume they've had one because of all their past interactions?' Radhi asked thoughtfully, cradling her cup of tea.

Shinde's smile faltered. 'Of course, madam. All cases are built on assumptions and theories to begin with. At this stage, we not only have a suspect who was seen at the scene of the crime but also one with a strong motive and a history of aggressive behaviour, which, in my experience, is an excellent place to start,' he smiled again and cracked his knuckles, 'now, we just have to prove our theory.'

Radhi nodded. She couldn't argue with this logic, but she didn't want to think of what kind of confession tactics he would resort to. 'What did he do for all the time in the middle? We saw him in the office around noon, and then if what you say is true, he came back later in the evening, which is when he allegedly murdered Hansa. So where was he in the interim?'

Shinde positively beamed. 'His wife said he came home at eight that night. He says he was at a bar till about seven. The bartender confirmed he was there, but his shift ended at six thirty and the one who replaced him can't seem to remember him.'

'Weren't there other customers?' Sarla asked.

'Yes, a few, but they are not regulars, we are trying to track them down but no luck so far. We think he left the bar at six thirty and came to the office around the same time that your peon said he stepped down for his vada pav. Which is why nobody saw him.'

'What about the watchman?' Radhi asked. 'How come there is no entry for him in that register?'

'Good question,' Shinde said, dabbing his tea-soaked moustache with a tissue paper. 'But when we questioned the watchman, he admitted that he often leaves his post to get paan or to go to the washroom, etc. Which makes that register unreliable.'

'That's true.' Sarla nodded. 'I've seen him run to get cabs for residents and even carry their bags all the way up to their floors sometimes.'

'And you know what's the best part, madam?' Shinde switched from his broken English to Marathi, as if saying it in his mother tongue would give him more pleasure. 'Our man has a prior. He got into a bar room brawl a few years ago and landed some chap in the hospital.' Shinde smirked. 'Alcohol and aggression. We see the same pattern repeated here again. As far as we are concerned, madam, this case is just days away from being closed. We've got our guy, now it's just a matter of tying up some loose ends.'

All three women were quiet on their way back. Juhi had identified the man easily and now seemed less agitated than before. She had requested Sarla to be dropped off at the hospital so that she could visit Jeevan. Radhi glanced at

Sarla, who was resting her head against the window with her eyes closed, seeming drained. If what Shinde had said indeed proved to be true, then Sarla could rest easy on one account at least — Hansa's murder was not connected to the tarot cards. It really did seem to be all adding up, Shinde sounded like he had thought of everything, and yet Radhi felt uneasy. She wasn't sure if it was because she was uncomfortable with Shinde's answers or because she suddenly felt the full weight of the responsibility that she was the one who had pointed Shinde in that man's direction, and now, if there was even a slim possibility that he had been wrongfully convicted, she would be equally to blame.

When they had dropped Juhi off, Radhi turned to Sarla. 'Aunty, I thought you'd seem more relieved after what Shinde said. Are you still thinking about that unfortunate girl?'

Sarla gave Radhi a small smile but didn't answer.

'Aunty, you couldn't possibly have known that the marriage wouldn't work out or that the girl would take such an extreme step!'

Earlier that day, back at her house, Sarla had admitted to Radhi that the rumours Renuka had referred to were indeed true. Radhi had been shocked, but she didn't see how Sarla could have foreseen how it would all unfold. 'Your intentions were good. In the end, that's what matters,' she had said.

Sarla shook her head. 'Good intentions can't excuse my pride. I was so sure that it was a good match, and when the girl expressed her reservations, I told her to stop being so indecisive and that she'd thank me when she was older.'

Sarla smiled bitterly. 'I know what you're thinking. But this tarot business is unrelated. That family moved to Belgium more than a decade ago. They never blamed me. Her mother was probably too busy blaming herself. But she didn't have to. There isn't a day that goes by that I don't think about that girl.'

Radhi shook her head. She hadn't been thinking about the cards. 'You know, Aunty, it's true there's a lot of pressure on young people, especially women, to make a good match, but I don't think that girl ended her life because she was in a bad marriage. But probably because she felt trapped in it.' Radhi paused to see if Sarla had registered the difference. She continued, 'People choose wrong life partners all the time. But it's because our society makes *leaving* a marriage so difficult that someone might be forced to take such an extreme step.'

Radhi reached out and squeezed Sarla's hand. 'So go easy on yourself, okay?' Sarla smiled wearily before looking away.

The sun had set and there was a rush of cars returning from offices. The vegetable sellers and tea vendors were wrapping up their stalls with blue plastic and string. Their wares were always much better appreciated at the start of the day. The florists, however, were still open despite starting equally early because there was no dearth of people who woke up last minute and needed something quickly for a birthday or anniversary.

As Radhi gazed out of the window, she thought back to their afternoon with Shinde. The inspector had said that Hansa's brother had spent the afternoon drinking at a bar. Radhi could believe that a drunk, aggressive man could kill his own sister. But for that same drunk man to then carefully wipe off fingerprints from the murder weapon and the desk seemed harder to imagine. She continued replaying their conversation with the inspector in her mind until an image of Shinde wiping his moustache with a tissue floated into her head and lodged itself in her mind.

'Aunty, do you think Neetu ben will still be at work?' she asked.

'It's possible,' said Sarla checking her watch. 'Why?'

'I saw Neetu ben pull out a checked, parrot-green tissue paper from her purse when I was in her cabin and then I saw the same kind of tissues in Renuka ben's office. Is it possible the two women know each other?'

Sarla frowned and seemed about to protest that the connection seemed tenuous, but Radhi stopped her. 'I know, I know. It's a far shot. But what if Neetu ben did get it from her? You have to admit, it's an unusual colour. What if we have been looking at it all wrong? What if instead of Jeevan, Renuka has enlisted Neetu's help in delivering the tarot cards? Neetu is not exactly happy at Soul Harmony — you would agree, no? Is it possible Renuka is using her against you?'

Sarla stared at Radhi and slowly gave her a slight nod. It was possible.

'Thank you, Neetu, for waiting,' Sarla said taking a seat across from the astrologer.

They had called her just as she was leaving for the day and had requested her to wait. The Soul Harmony office was empty save for the light in Kiran's room and Neetu's, where the astrologer was waiting for them impatiently, her bag all packed and hanging from her shoulder.

'No problem. So what's this about?' Neetu asked Sarla, but it was Radhi who answered her.

'Why did you go to Hansa ben's house, Neetu ben?' she asked the older woman who stared at her uncomprehendingly.

'When? I've never been to Hansa's house.'

'The day after she died. Her sister told us you visited her.'

'I did no such thing.' Neetu frowned.

'Are you sure, Neetu ben?' Radhi asked.

'Of course, I'm sure! Why would I go there?'

'She said you wanted to see Hansa's files.'

'I . . . what? What files? I don't know what you are talking about.'

'Why would she lie, Neetu?' Sarla asked gently. She and Radhi had naturally seemed to have fallen into a good-cop-bad-cop routine.

'How should I know? Go ask her!' The astrologer's voice had risen now and become shrill.

'What about Renuka ben, then? Why did you go meet her?' Radhi asked, changing tack.

At the sound of Renuka's name, Neetu's face turned pale. 'Who said I did?'

'Renuka ben herself,' Radhi bluffed.

Neetu gaped at them, then with a visible effort she said, 'In any case, that's none of your business.'

'But it is,' said Sarla softly, holding the astrologer's gaze until the latter dropped it.

'Renuka ben offered me a job,' she finally said defiantly, 'and I have accepted. I was going to tell you after the anniversary party.'

'That's it?' Radhi asked.

'That's it,' Neetu said. But she had hesitated for a brief nanosecond of a moment and Radhi wondered why.

Back in the car, Radhi's mind was unusually cluttered. There were all these conversations she'd had, impressions she had formed and ideas she was toying with, but when she put them together, they didn't tell a complete, coherent story. It was as if she had been forced to begin a book mid-scene. Or been given thousands of pieces to a jigsaw without a picture of what it was supposed to look like. When she looked back at her week with Soul Harmony, she could see the minor discrepancies between what people had said and how they behaved and the little gaps between what was and how it appeared. There were enough motives, grudges and backstories to the crimes that had been committed. And yet, despite the close view she'd had of all the proceedings, or perhaps because of it, she was only seeing disparate parts of the whole picture. Her proximity to Sarla, while giving her access to facts and insight into the people she worked with, had taken away her sense of perspective. Radhi was coming to realize that she was unable to distance herself and view the situation without bias, the way perhaps Shinde could, if he could be even half as perceptive as his job required.

Radhi had dropped Sarla home and was now on her way to Jigna's house. Her conversation with Neetu had left her feeling uneasy. Not because she appeared to be lying, but because as far as visiting Hansa's house was concerned, it seemed to Radhi that she was probably telling the truth.

'Ramzan bhai, could you stop here a moment, please,' Radhi said snapping out of her reverie as a shop on the street caught her eye.

She jumped out of the car as soon as the driver pulled to one side of the road and approached the paanwala on the street corner. It was the same man with shiny, oiled hair and impressive handlebar moustache that Hansa had stopped to speak to the day she died. He was busy watching a cricket match on his phone but looked up curiously when she walked up to him.

'A few days ago, this woman had come to you,' Radhi showed him a picture of Hansa that she had found in Hansa's wallet. 'She didn't buy paan or anything that you sell in this shop. But she did speak with you. Could you tell me what that was about?'

As he looked at the photograph, there was a flicker of recognition in the paanwala's eyes, which was immediately replaced with a calculating look as he took in Radhi's appearance and the expensive BMW she had stepped out from.

'She does seem familiar,' he said. 'Maybe she stopped for directions?'

'It can't be directions.' Radhi frowned. 'She was familiar with the area. Could you take another look?'

He shrugged. 'I can't be sure. So many people stop by here every day. What they don't understand is that I have a business to run. Can't be doing charity all day.' He went back to watching the cricket match on his phone before it dawned on Radhi what he actually meant and wanted.

She picked up a pack of cigarettes from a pyramid of boxes on display, took a single cigarette out of it and slid a 500-rupee note towards the man. 'What did you talk about?'

The man raised an eyebrow and pocketed the money with a smirk before pointing at a building across the street.

'She asked me to tell her if I ever spotted a young man from that building with a ladize.'

'What man?'

'Yug something.' The paanwala shrugged. 'Drives a white Honda City.'

Radhi nodded. Sarla had told her that this was the other thing Hansa had been working on, so this made sense.

'Well, did you?' she asked.

He twisted the ends of his moustache. 'It was a week ago, ma'am . . . it's hard to remember.'

Radhi rolled her eyes and handed him another 500-rupee note.

He smirked again as he transferred the money into the pocket of his kurta. 'I did. A couple of times. I took a picture.'

'Could you show it to me?' Radhi asked getting a little excited.

'I don't have it any more.'

Thinking that perhaps the man was angling for more money, Radhi slid another 500-rupee note towards him.

The man stared at it, tempted to pick it up but didn't. 'I honestly don't have it any more. I showed it to your friend and then deleted it. Can't take the chance of my wife stumbling upon it. She'll kill me if she finds pictures of other ladize on my phone.'

Radhi frowned, frustrated. 'Anything else you can remember?'

The paanwala shook his head.

'Well, let me know if you do,' Radhi said, leaving the final 500-rupee note with him, along with her number.

By the time she turned to go back to her car, his eyes were glued to the screen of his phone once again.

Radhi knew she hadn't discovered anything unexpected, yet when she thought back to Hansa's last day, she remembered how subdued and transformed she had seemed after her chat with the paanwala. She wondered if Hansa's last case could possibly have any bearing on her death. Radhi flipped open the pages of her diary and checked her notes. *Yug Desai.* That was the full name of the guy Hansa had asked the paanwala to spy on. Maybe a conversation with him would shed some more light, Radhi thought as the car pulled up outside Jigna's building and she put her diary back into her bag.

When Jigna opened the door, her eyes were red and her hair was dishevelled. She barely glanced at the box of black grapes Radhi had got her as she wordlessly made way for Radhi to enter their living room.

'My sister-in-law just told me . . . the police have taken my brother. They think he killed Hansa.' She sniffled into her handkerchief.

'I know.' Radhi nodded as she took a seat across from her.

'I just can't believe it!' Jigna shook her head.

'He was harassing Hansa ben and you for money, wasn't he? The police said he would drink and get loud and aggressive.'

'Yes, yes. That's true. But he would never have hurt Hansa!' Jigna swatted a fly impatiently. 'They used to be as thick as thieves when they were children. Why do you think she used to keep giving him money even though all of us said not to?'

Radhi frowned. 'But did Hansa ben not warn him to never come here again? Didn't he want to sell this apartment and claim a share?'

'Yes! Yes! Yes! To all of those things. My brother is an awful, greedy drunk! But he is no murderer!' Jigna dissolved into fresh tears as Radhi watched helplessly, wondering if what Jigna had said was true, and if it was, what she could possibly do to rectify the terrible mess she had inadvertently put him in.

'Would you like some tea?' Jigna finally calmed down enough to remember her manners.

'No please,' Radhi said hastily. 'I just needed a few moments of your time.' She dug out her phone and showed Jigna a photograph. 'Was this the woman who visited you the day after Hansa ben died?'

Jigna appeared confused.

'The woman from Hansa ben's office who brought you a bag of oranges.'

'Oh, yes, I remember now.' Jigna's face cleared. She peered at Neetu's photograph. 'But no . . . this wasn't her.'

'Are you sure, Jigna ben? Could you take a closer look?'

'I'm quite sure.' Jigna gave the picture a perfunctory second glance. 'My grandmother used to sport a long sandalwood tikka like that on her forehead. I would've definitely noticed it.'

Radhi nodded, not surprised. Her instinct about Neetu had been right. She had been telling them the truth. She scrolled through her phone with another name in mind. 'What about her?' She showed Jigna a picture of Renuka ben and held her breath. Renuka's name had cropped up so many times during this whole sordid affair that Radhi was sure she was involved in some way. If Jigna identified Renuka now, it would give Radhi a solid reason to accuse Sarla's competitor of mischief. However, Jigna shook her head dismissively when she saw Renuka's picture.

'No, no. I have never seen her in my life.'

Radhi bit her lip in disappointment. She had been so sure that she was right.

'The woman who came here was much younger. And she was pretty,' Jigna added.

Young and pretty. Radhi's mind whirred with this new information. There were plenty of attractive, young women at Soul Harmony. Zarna . . . Juhi . . . Divya. In fact, if one were looking beyond the bureau, couldn't Bhavana's daughter, the jilted Khushi, be described similarly? Sarla and Radhi had worried about how angry Bhavana had seemed but had paid no attention to the young woman who was actually facing the consequences. Could she have come to find out why her fiancé had dumped her? Young and pretty . . .

Radhi quickly scrolled through her phone again, as a new name occurred to her. This time, she was aware of a tingling sensation at the base of her spine.

'What about her?' She flashed her phone at Jigna once again and got a confident yes in response.

Radhi looked down at the picture of the young wedding planner on her phone. Why had Alpa come to Hansa's house on the day of her murder?

24

'Is it true?' Mrs Bansal hissed in Radhi's ear as she took a seat beside her. 'Is it true?'

Radhi looked at her alarmed. Her eyes immediately sought her sister, but she was unable to spot the peacock blue of Madhavi's patola sari in the sea of guests swarming their cousin's wedding reception. Radhi and her family were in the glittering ballroom of the Taj Mahal Palace Hotel, one of the most iconic five-star venues in the city. Up on the stage the newly minted husband and wife were being congratulated by an interminable line of guests. Madhavi had wandered off to get some pictures clicked with Anshul and her girls. While Radhi had sought out this corner table partially covered by a large potted palm, dying for a moment to herself after an hour of air kisses, bent-at-the-waist-namastes and versions of 'we don't see you even though you're in India now' from a gazillion extended family members.

'Is what true, Aunty?' she asked Madhavi's mother-in-law in a bid to kill time, even though she had a fair idea what the woman was on about.

'Don't you play innocent with me!' Mrs Bansal thumped the table, causing Radhi's passion fruit mocktail to spill and stain the white tablecloth. 'Did you really say no?'

When Radhi didn't answer, Mrs Bansal picked up her clutch bag and began to fan herself with it. 'What a foolish, foolish girl you are!'

When Radhi had turned down Nishant's proposal the night before, she had known that her sister's mother-in-law would eventually find out. But she hadn't expected it to happen overnight. Facing Mrs Bansal's obnoxious interfering was beyond her right now. The proposal had been shocking at many levels. That he should ask. That he should be so devastated when she said no. That she should be so miserable at having hurt him and so unsure of whether she had made thc right decision. It was all too much and too soon to process.

'Aunty, please,' Radhi protested, desperately looking for her brother-in-law or Vrinda Fia to extract her from the situation. She wasn't scared of the old tyrant but rather of herself. She didn't want to say anything she'd regret. 'It really was for the best. We hardly know each other.'

'Know? Know?' Mrs Bansal spluttered so close to Radhi's ear that droplets of spit flew on Radhi's cheek. 'You have been meeting him for coffee and dinner and God only knows what else for the last six months and you have the audacity to say you hardly know each other? How much more do you expect to "know" him? May I remind you that you are in India now? Not your shameless America!'

Radhi wiped her cheek with a tissue and answered in what she hoped was a respectful tone. 'Aunty, don't you think this is a private matter between Nishant and me?'

'What did you say?' Roma Bansal's eyes widened to the size of saucepans. A vein in her forehead bulged scarily. 'Look around you, does this wedding look like a private affair?' She motioned towards the hundreds of guests milling about. 'In India, marriages are not private! There are people involved. Families invested. Relationships at stake! When I introduced you to Nishant, I put my friendship with Parul ben on the line! This morning, she called me to tell me that her son has announced that he isn't interested in getting married unless it is with you. She thinks you are ruining his life. And these are her words, not mine! He was completely willing to be set up before he met you. He met every girl his mother introduced him to without any fuss. And now he says he won't meet anyone new! Parul was crying on the phone!'

Radhi's face burned. However offensive Mrs Bansal was, Radhi knew there was a small kernel of truth in her allegations. She *was* holding Nishant back. She had told him she wasn't ready, and he had promised he'd wait. But the truth was she had no idea if she'd ever be ready.

'Aunty, please, don't you think you are overreacting? I've just been honest with him. I told him I am not looking at marriage in the near future.'

'What is wrong with you? You are in your thirties! Divorced! He is younger than you. Good-looking. From a good family. Well-to-do. I have no idea what he sees in you — but he does see something. And what do you do? Tell him you are not ready. What will it take for you to be ready? Another decade?'

A waiter came to offer them some hara bhara kebabs. Radhi shook her head, but Roma stopped mid-tirade, took two on a small plate with a dollop of mint chutney and bit into one, before continuing, 'Why, may I ask, do you not want to get married? Don't you think you have had enough fun in life?' She gave Radhi an unobstructed view into the contents of her mouth.

Radhi didn't reply in the hope that giving the old tyrant a chance to say her piece would rid her of the situation faster than any attempt at defending herself. But Mrs Bansal showed no sign of tiring. 'Do you think people don't know about that gora you were with? For most people, a divorce in itself is a big blot! But on top of it, you were even living with an older white man. Do you think any good Indian family would accept your past easily? And yet — Parul is willing to overlook all of that! As long as her son is happy, she's happy. If nothing else, think of her!'

'Aunty, really, I can't get married to please his mother.' Radhi was beginning to get really exasperated now.

'No, of course not, you are too selfish for that! But think about yourself, at least!! Do you think you are getting younger? Or does the concept of the biological clock not apply to you? Or do you not want to have any children?'

'I do not,' Radhi said, more out of a desperation to shut her up than because she felt that way.

But it had the exact opposite effect. Roma Bansal's nose flared, and her face became redder than the bride's ghagra.

'THIS! This is the problem with a motherless girl. I told Parul that we couldn't expect you to behave sensibly, but she urged me to try. But I was right! You haven't been taught to care for anyone but yourself.'

'I really don't have to listen to this.' Radhi pushed back her chair and got up, but Roma's hand clutched her own in a vice-like grip. 'You've probably ruined a friendship for me, you will now very well listen to what I have to say!' Radhi looked around once more for her sister or aunt or anyone at all who could extricate her from this ghastly conversation, but the quiet table she had chosen was too far away from everyone. She would have to fend for herself. Sighing, she took her seat again.

'I knew your sister was bad news the day Anshul brought her home. I wanted a good Marwari girl from a respectable Marwari family. Conservative and homely, not like your sister, gallivanting about town in the guise of work!'

Radhi's eyes narrowed. It was one thing for the old hag to berate her — that she could ignore and do as her mum had taught her as a child, listen from one ear and let go from the other. But she wouldn't sit there for even a second and listen to her trash talk her sister. 'You do know she single-handedly runs my father's million-dollar jewellery business?'

'Do you know I had selected a Rajput princess for my son?' Roma snapped back at her. 'Had arranged a meeting for them. She would've come with her titles and my grandkids would've become part of a royal bloodline. So don't you throw your father's money in my face!'

'I wasn't throwing—'

'Don't I know why your sister stopped trying after two girls? Didn't want her precious business to suffer—'

'Her doctor told her it was dangerous to try again! Hell, it was dangerous for her to try the second time also! But she did! Because *you* were so keen on a grandson!'

Roma Bansal scoffed. 'Dangerous — phissh. It is just selfish!'

'Selfish?' Radhi's voice had an incredulous edge to it. '*You* are asking my sister to put her life at risk just so you can have a male child who'll carry on your so-called family name! And you have the audacity to call *her* selfish? Are you really so blind?'

Roma's jaw dropped. In all her years of taunting Radhi, never had the younger woman spoken back so freely. They'd had a few close shaves over the years, but Anshul or Madhavi had always been around to navigate the situation. Now there was no one to shield her from the full brunt of Radhi's sharp tongue.

'Look here, now you listen to me—'

But Radhi had had enough of listening.

'You consider yourself aware and educated, but what's the point of your six-monthly London holidays and your book club gatherings if you hanker after a male child like some mother-in-law from a soap opera? Honestly, if you can't see how good my sister is for your son and what a wonderful mother and wife she is, then I find this conversation with you a waste of my time.'

Radhi got up, adjusted the pallu of her rani-pink chiffon sari and walked out of the ballroom, straight-backed and brisk — without a second glance at the shocked and spluttering Mrs Bansal. In the car, however, much to Ramzan bhai's alarm, Radhi covered her face and began to weep. How had things gone so horribly wrong! Just a month ago, she had experienced a rare moment of pride at the progress she had made after returning to India. She had got over a two-year-long writer's block and had completed the first draft of a new book. She had also been able to look past the pain-induced fog of Mackinzey's disappearance and had begun dating again. And she had a new project, the book on arranged marriages, which seemed promising. The move to India had seemed to be working out well for her.

But now she had gone and made a colossal mess of things. To begin with, she knew Nishant was hurt. Even if she hadn't meant to cause him pain, she had, and she couldn't pretend she hadn't known right at the start that that was a possibility. She had entered their relationship with her heart covered in full battle armour. But while the chainmail of caution she'd put around it served to protect her, it was always going to bruise anyone who tried to get through. And still, despite this crystal-clear self-awareness, she had allowed him to come close. It had been selfish on her part. She could always dress the word in different ways, but it was a trait that seemed to constantly punctuate the relationships in her life. Her therapist had tried to tell her otherwise, but she knew her parents were dead because she had only been thinking about herself. If she hadn't insisted on participating in that competition, they would never have been on that highway. Mrs Bansal was right about her in that, though she would never admit it to the old bully. Radhi realized she had also made things harder for her sister. Madhavi's relationship with her mother-in-law was strained at the best of times, and Radhi's outburst that evening was only going to make things worse. But that wasn't all. If only her list of screw-ups stopped there, she could find a way to stow them away in the little box of denial at the back of her mind, as she had done for most of her adult life, and carry on. But she had bungled up at the bureau as well. After her visit to Jigna, she was fast beginning to think that the police had put the wrong man behind bars — and she regretted pointing Shinde in his direction. And to top it all, another man lay in hospital, again probably because of her. She closed her eyes and covered her face with her palms. But instead of shutting out the thoughts, the action did the exact opposite — it trapped her in, surrounded by them.

Wednesday

The next morning Radhi woke up with dry eyes that hurt. She hadn't opened a bottle of wine the previous night, not because she hadn't felt the urge but because there wasn't any left. Upset and disturbed, she had done what she had always done to calm herself — read. She had picked up the book Vrinda had lent her and read it from cover to cover. Immersing herself in theory about obsessive-compulsive behaviour and case studies until the noise in her head subsided and her eyes grew heavy with sleep. Now she stumbled groggily into the kitchen to make herself a simple breakfast of corn poha and a large pot of tea, which she spiced with ginger and mint leaves. She had given Lila the day off — in her mental list of all the things she had screwed up on, she hadn't even given thought to her developing dependency on alcohol, and she didn't need Lila around to remind her of it. The Soul Harmony office would be shut that day in preparation for the anniversary party the next day, so she didn't have anywhere to go — at least not until after lunch, when she was meeting Alpa, and after that, hopefully, Yug, whom she had messaged but was still to hear back from. Piling her plate high with poha, a crisp khakhra and coriander chutney, Radhi settled herself at her dining table with her laptop and notes, resolved to think only of the thing she could control — her work.

George had followed up a couple of times to see if she had considered his feedback. Now she opened her manuscript and concentrated on bringing the detective to the forefront of her mystery. The character wasn't autobiographical, although the mystery surrounding the death of her best friend's father was based on real life. She had given her detective a husband and two kids, along with matrimonial problems and an old flame which continued to flicker. It was a complex character, but George was right; in her attempt to make the character as different from her as possible, she had hidden away all of her thoughts. Radhi worked steadily for a few hours, surprised at how easily she had been able to 'see' her detective once she decided to view her as a separate entity from herself. After a while, she stopped work, poured herself one last cup of tea and went to stand by the window. Outside, the Arabian Sea was glittering in the sunlight. There was not a single person or boat in the near-still water. Just a family of seagulls enjoying the sun on their backs. As she watched the birds frolic, her mind wandered to her phone, which had remained silent all morning. Nothing from Nishant or her sister. The silence, especially from Madhavi, was disquieting. She hoped her sister's mother-in-law hadn't created a fracas in their home that morning. She sighed and turned her mind to the problems at Soul Harmony. Puzzles, she had always found, were easier than people.

Alpa didn't look quite at home in her own house, a large but bare two-bedroom apartment which she shared with her mother. Dressed in a flowy, white chiffon dress with pearl buttons and puffed sleeves, she looked more ready for the Derby than for receiving visitors.

'Not what you had in mind, no?' she asked Radhi who was doing her best not to stare at the threadbare couches and the peeling walls.

'Not at all,' Radhi said hurriedly, trying to put the younger woman at ease. But Alpa knew just how disconcerting her dilapidated home was to anyone who had only ever seen her own polished and sparkly office persona.

'I wouldn't have asked you here if you hadn't threatened me,' Alpa said holding out a tray with a glass of water for Radhi. She took a seat on the couch across from her.

'I wouldn't have threatened you if I hadn't found out that you were stealing clients from Sarla ben,' Radhi said evenly. She had called Alpa with a request to meet, but Alpa had tried to push it to later saying she couldn't step out since she had no one to watch her sick mother.

'What are you talking about? I told you on the phone also that this whole notion is absurd!'

'I saw an exact replica of one of your stage décor designs at a sangeet recently. The one with the orchid peacocks.'

Alpa shrugged, 'Must be a coincidence! Peacocks are hardly a novelty at Indian weddings.'

'The match had been arranged by Soul Harmony, which means they definitely came to you for a consultation.'

'Look, I meet more than a dozen clients each week. Not all of them decide to go with us.'

'And yet they wind up with near identical décor?' Radhi pressed. 'You showed me the folder with your original designs, this one was from there . . .'

'My designs are original, but they are also inspired by magazines and other weddings I attend, I—' Alpa was interrupted by a fit of coughs from one of the inside rooms, followed by the sound of shattered glass.

She jumped up alarmed and cursed under her breath, hurrying towards the direction of the sound.

As Radhi waited for her to rcturn, she looked around the house freely. Situated in one of the poshest buildings of Temple Hill, it had high ceilings, large windows and dramatic views of the Arabian Sea, but the rest of the apartment was so rundown that the effect was jarring. The walls were bare, but dark outlines could be seen from where large picture frames must have hung. Two glass cabinets flanked the couch on the opposite wall, but they were mostly empty, save for a few plastic knick-knacks — as if anything of value had long been removed or sold.

'My mother,' Alpa said, returning after a few minutes, 'dropped a glass while trying to pour herself some water.'

'Has she been unwell long?'

'Long enough,' Alpa said. Then thinking perhaps that she had sounded too bitter, she added, 'Bone cancer . . . Look, as you can see, I have enough problems of my own. Huge hospital bills to pay, no one to look after Mom other than a maid who comes in when I am at work and a house that has been mortgaged — twice. Can you please just let me be?'

Radhi felt sorry for Alpa. It was hard enough to be a caregiver, devoting all that time and energy towards something that was essentially unbeatable. But to do it while grappling with financial problems seemed particularly rough. And yet,

Radhi couldn't leave it alone. Not when it was Sarla's life's work on the line, not to mention a person's life.

'Why did you go to Hansa ben's apartment the day after she died?' she asked, changing the subject abruptly. And was taken aback at the ripple of pure fear that flashed across Alpa's face.

25

'And?' was all Madhavi said when Radhi answered the phone.

Radhi had been nervous about speaking to her sister. She had been wondering about how her brother-in-law had reacted and was hoping that he wasn't too upset. She had always shared a warm relationship with him and would hate for something like this to sour things between them.

'And what, didi?'

'Well, I've heard my mother-in-law's sensational rant about how rude you were, but I'm certain there's more to it. So go on, tell me.'

Radhi was on her way to the Temple Hill Gymkhana to meet Yug. She stubbed out her cigarette and rolled up her window. Almost as if she were afraid that her sister would be able to smell the cigarette on the other side. 'Now I don't know what she's told you, but here's the gist: Nishant proposed. I told him I wasn't ready. Your mother-in-law called me selfish because I refused to think of his poor mother.'

Madhavi chuckled. 'Jesus, Radhi! You really know how to tell a story!'

Radhi laughed and protested, 'But that's exactly how it went!'

'So that's when you called *her* selfish? Or did that not happen? Please tell me it didn't — because it will be much easier to defend you if I can tell Anshul that his mother is imagining things!'

'No . . . I definitely did call her that.' Radhi frowned unhappily. 'I'm sorry, didi, I know it puts you and jiju in a tough spot.'

Madhavi sighed. 'Doesn't matter. You have to defend yourself. Can't let presumptuous old crones walk all over you.'

'But I wasn't defending myself! I was defending you.' Radhi told her how the conversation had gone and how her mother-in-law had insinuated that Madhavi's doctor's advice was just an excuse for her not to have more children.

Madhavi cursed when she had heard all of it. 'I really can't believe that woman. She and her obsession with a male child. As if my two beautiful girls don't matter. Just wait till Anshul hears of this. He'll throw a fit.'

'I am sorry to cause trouble,' Radhi said.

'Don't be daft, Radhi! I would've been upset if you *hadn't* defended me,' Madhavi replied instantly. 'Now you rest easy, love. Best-case scenario, my mother-in-law is so upset that she declares she wants nothing to do with us, returns to Delhi and is never heard from ever again. Worst-case scenario, she calms down after Anshul talks some sense into her, declares herself too stressed and put upon, returns to Delhi, nurses a grudge against the both of us and returns a few months later with some fresh ammunition — to taunt us again.'

'As of now, either scenario sounds fine.' Radhi lit up a cigarette to savour her relief at having cleared it out with her sister, stubbing it out a second later when she remembered who she was talking to. 'As long as it ends with her in Delhi.'

The sisters laughed and spoke of other things for a while, including the happenings at Soul Harmony, then finally,

Madhavi asked, 'And what about Nishant? Where do things stand now?'

Radhi sighed. 'I don't know. I haven't heard from him since. And I haven't reached out either. I just want to give him some space right now.'

Madhavi was quiet for a moment, then she asked, 'Is *that* really why you haven't reached out, Radhi? Or is it because you are scared?'

Radhi bit her lip. If it were anyone else, she'd have denied it but lying to her sister felt like she was being dishonest to herself. She missed Nishant. But she was afraid of reaching out, afraid of giving him hope. Even if their conversation began with a clear disclaimer, he would begin to dream of a future together. Whereas she found herself unable to dream at all. Unable or terrified, she didn't know which. She was just glad when she didn't wake up drenched in cold sweat after having relived her parents' car crash. Grateful for a deep, dreamless sleep, even if that meant there could be no happy dreams. But even more than her fear of hurting Nishant, Radhi realized that the person she was most scared of was herself. She recognized she was being driven by a single-minded, almost ruthless instinct of self-preservation whose only job was to keep her heart safe. Even if the cost of that safety was a lifetime of loneliness.

She was quiet for such a long time that Madhavi wasn't sure if the line had got disconnected.

'Radhi? Are you there?'

'Yes, didi.'

Stout and square, Yug had floppy hair and large, muscular arms — the kind that were not only a product of many hours at the gym but also in front of a mirror, where they were consistently flexed, tightened and admired from every angle. He was already seated at a table when Radhi walked into the cafe at the Temple Hill Gymkhana. From his wet hair and the large duffel bag beside him, it was clear that he had just showered after a workout. Radhi guessed that like most young men on Temple Hill, he probably worked for his father; only a family business could offer the flexibility of a mid-afternoon workout. When they had ordered tea and cheese and cucumber sandwiches and spoken of the new Vegas-themed card room coming up at the club, Radhi brought out her diary and asked him if she could record their conversation on her phone.

'As you already know, I'm doing a book on arranged marriages, but did Sarla ben's assistant give you any details?'

Yug shook his head and smiled. 'Just that you are an accomplished author from New York and that I'm to cooperate.'

Radhi smiled back. 'That's about right. I've spoken to quite a few people over the last couple of weeks, but I keep feeling that I'm getting a very one-sided view of arranged marriages. I understand now how the system works and why it has proven to be so effective over the decades, but what happens when it doesn't? I'd like a more balanced view of things. I understand you've had a broken engagement recently?'

Yug nodded.

'So tell me, what about the system didn't work for you?'

The waiter had arrived with their food on the table. Yug waited until he left, before answering. 'Look, I am in enough trouble with my parents, as it is. They said I had to do this interview with you to get back into the good books of Soul Harmony and Sarla Aunty. But if I tell you my views on arranged marriages, I'm not sure either Sarla Aunty or my parents are going to be pleased with me.'

'We don't need to mention your name or any specifics. I'll just describe you as a twenty-seven-year-old Gujarati man from Temple Hill — there are plenty of those around, aren't there?' Radhi asked lightly.

Yug smiled and picked up his cup of tea. Radhi noticed that he added no sugar and wondered, not for the first time, about the point of a workout if it couldn't afford you a proper cup of tea.

'I only agreed to go the arranged marriage way to get my parents off my back. My mum has high blood pressure, and she used her poor health to blackmail me into my first arranged meeting. You know how guilty mothers can make you feel, right?'

Radhi didn't know about mothers, but Madhavi tended to have that effect on her. She smiled and nodded. The cucumber sandwiches were slathered with spicy jalapeno mayonnaise, and Radhi took an appreciative bite as Yug continued.

'The thing is, I find the whole idea absurd. How can you decide to spend the rest of your life with someone when you've met in such contrived settings? Meaning, how do you feel any attraction when there is pressure from so many quarters? You know?'

Radhi nodded again. He was echoing some of her own reservations about the system.

'But then you met Khushi? And you had a change of heart?'

'Yes. Well, I don't know if it was a change of heart but I thought she was very nice and my parents loved her.'

'So you agreed to get engaged?'

'Yes. I was a bit apprehensive at first, but my mom convinced me. And for a while I thought I had made the right decision.'

Yug took a sip of his tea and fell quiet.

Radhi waited for a few moments to see if he'd say more. When he didn't, she asked, 'What changed your mind? Did you meet someone new?'

'No, nobody new.' Yug put his cup of tea down and clarified, a little too quickly, Radhi thought, 'It's just that I realized that I wasn't feeling any butterflies. After the initial few months, there wasn't much excitement. And I began to think that maybe this wasn't a great way to begin a marriage, you know?'

'True,' Radhi agreed as she switched off the record button on her phone. Radhi thanked him for his time and gathered her things.

Yug was seeing someone else, that much was certain. What the paanwala had told her, combined with his own reaction today, confirmed that much. But she doubted it had anything to do with Hansa's death. This conversation hadn't brought her any closer to finding out what had happened that day, but her meeting with Alpa on the other hand was a completely different story.

'Blackmail, huh?' Sarla ran a hand over her face, covering her eyes for a moment before shaking her head wonderingly. 'You know, I should be shocked. But when I think about how Hansa was . . . I find . . . I can't put it past her.'

Radhi had dropped by Sarla's house to fill her in on her conversations with Jigna ben and Alpa, but she wished now that she had come with better news. In the twenty-four hours since they had last met, Sarla's face seemed even more shrunken in than before.

'And how long had it been going on for?'

'A year. Well, a year since Hansa found out and began blackmailing Alpa. But I suspect Alpa has been doing weddings on the sly much before that.'

'So she was attracting our clients with lower rates than us, and when Hansa found out she asked for a cut?'

'Yes. Twenty per cent of her profit. Or she threatened Alpa that she'd come tell you.'

Sarla seemed to be struggling to digest the information. 'All this was happening right under my nose and I didn't have a clue?' She smiled bitterly. 'I always think I am so sharp. That I read people well. And these women have worked with me for so many years.' She shook her head. 'I feel like such a fool . . .'

'Don't say that, Aunty. Being trusting is not a weakness. Besides, I don't think you were paying attention. I'm sure you'd have caught it otherwise.'

Sarla sighed. 'Kiran and I did talk about this, you know. About how we weren't getting as many weddings as before. But we've been so busy on the matchmaking side of things that we didn't try to get to the bottom of it . . . So what was Alpa doing at Hansa's house?'

'Looking for the file which had their accounts. It seems Hansa maintained a record of all the weddings Alpa planned, the fee that was charged and the commission she was owed.'

'And do you believe her?'

Radhi nodded because Alpa had been in tears towards the end of their conversation. 'I think so. In fact, I did find a sheet of numbers when I looked through Hansa's bag. Didn't recognize it of course but maybe that was what Alpa had been looking for.'

Sarla got up and went to stand by the window, staring intently at the sea as if it held all the answers. After a few moments, when Radhi joined her, she said, 'I've been thinking . . . what if I do what Zarna has been saying all along — sell to investors and be done with it all.'

'But, Aunty, you love your work!'

'It's just that of late I've been wondering if all this stress, first the tarot cards . . . now this . . . is worth it.'

'But what would you do?'

'I don't know. I haven't thought about it.' Sarla shrugged. 'Maybe I'll rest, travel, go on a few pilgrimages . . .'

When Radhi didn't answer, Sarla turned to her and smiled. 'Don't look at me like that, child. I'm a god-fearing person.'

'You are kidding yourself, Aunty, if you think you can be happy without your work.'

Sarla smiled again and turned back towards the sea. 'I've been considering it seriously, Radhi. I don't know if I can keep this up.'

When Radhi returned home that evening, she relished the quiet of her house. She switched on the corner mango wood lamp with its mustard silk lampshade and put on a Prateek Kuhad song about a city of secrets. Then opening up one of the bottles of wine she had asked Ramzan bhai to pick up from the store, she went to the kitchen to fix herself a light dinner. As much as she valued having Lila around, she had lived alone in a foreign country long enough to crave her solitude every so often.

She hummed as she roasted the peppers, zucchini and baby corn for her vegetable wrap. Her conversation with Madhavi, about both her mother-in-law and Nishant, had left her feeling lighter. But she was concerned about Sarla, who had seemed so frail that Radhi hadn't shared the terrible doubt that had been gnawing at her after her conversation with Alpa. The wedding planner had admitted that Hansa had blackmailed her, but what had her own reaction been? Had she simply paid up? Had she not tried to fight it or find a way around it? Alpa's financial problems seemed real enough. What if she had got fed up with paying Hansa and they had an argument? Could Alpa have hit Hansa with the statue in the heat of the moment? Or worse, could it be premeditated? Killing the PI would have put an end to two of Alpa's problems — the loss of much-needed money and the constant threat to a much-needed job. Radhi wondered though if Alpa had it in her to kill. If the detail about the twice-mortgaged apartment was true, she was certainly desperate enough.

Radhi carried her plate with the veggie wraps and a bottle of Tabasco out into the dining room. The window was open, and there was a slight nip in the air now that winter, if Mumbai's mild December could even be called that, seemed to be approaching. She put her plate on the table and went to fetch her jade green shawl with turquoise peacocks from her bedroom, along with her diary and phone, which contained all her notes and audio recordings. As she ate, she listened to the interviews she had conducted over the past ten days. Stopping only to jot down observations and once to put away her plate and shift her wine and things to the couch in the living room. She had more than six hours' worth of conversations, and the wine along with the long day she'd had were beginning to make her drowsy. She was just contemplating continuing the rest the next day when one conversation made her sit up. She stopped the recording and played it again from the beginning. By the end of it, all traces of sleep had vanished from her eyes, and with her heart pounding hard, she opened the photographs she had taken on the day that Hansa died. Swiping quickly on her phone, she came to a stop when she reached the picture of Hansa's dustbin. She zoomed in, bit her lip and stared at the picture for a long time.

She now knew who had killed Hansa and was beginning to form a fair idea of why.

26

Thursday

'Didi, I have good news!' Lila announced as soon as Radhi opened the door to her the next morning. 'Jeevan is showing signs of recovery.'

'Oh, that's wonderful!'

'I know, his mother is so relieved. In fact, all of us are.' Lila walked into the kitchen to wash her hands and put on her apron. 'Do you know we held a prayer vigil for him last night? For one whole hour we sang bhajans, and then this morning, the nurses called saying he had opened his eyes.'

'I am so glad.' Radhi had followed her housekeeper into the kitchen and was leaning against the refrigerator while the latter boiled some water for their tea. Radhi was smiling, not only because she was genuinely relieved about Jeevan's recovery but also because things seemed to have normalized between Lila and her. She had taken care that morning to wash her wine glass and hide the half-finished bottle back inside the bar so that there would not be any signs of her drinking when Lila came to work that day. She asked Lila to fix her bowl of vegetable poha and went in for her shower. She had been up all night. She had finished listening to all the conversations and gone over all her notes to make sure she hadn't overlooked anything. She had looked at the situation from every possible angle and slowly the picture had become clearer to her. She believed now that she had the answers to more than one of Sarla's problems.

'Please, can't we meet this morning instead?' Radhi asked Shinde again in her politest voice, trying her best to keep her fear out of it. She had jumped out of her shower with just a towel wrapped around her and shampoo still in her hair because she had just had an awful idea, which, now that she had thought it, seemed so obvious that she couldn't believe it hadn't occurred to her earlier. She was on the phone now trying to convince the oaf of an inspector that she needed to see him.

'Madam, I'm very busy arranging security for the CM's wife who's visiting Temple Hill today,' Shinde said impatiently. 'If it's so urgent, can't you just tell me on the phone?'

'Fine,' Radhi cut him off; then perching on the bed and dripping water all over her sheets in the process, she told Shinde what she feared and why she needed his help. He scoffed at her at first, incredulous, dismissive and annoyed in turn. And finally, when he came around, Radhi knew it was more to get rid of her rather than because he thought she was onto something. Radhi didn't care. She knew she was right. The tarot reader had told her to trust her intuition and for the first time she didn't doubt herself. She dressed hurriedly. She had one more stop to make before she went to Soul Harmony.

At the matrimonial bureau, preparations for the party were in full swing. Decorators were hanging strings of white jasmine across the doorframes of each cabin. All the desks and chairs in the centre of the room had been cleared out, and the caterers had set up a buffet counter along its length. On one end, a booth announced 'Palmistry & Face Reading', and Radhi guessed that Neetu would be in charge of it. She walked up to Sarla's cabin, where all her staff had gathered.

'And remember, if any of you see Bhavana ben and Yug's mother, Charmi ben, talking to each other, intervene immediately. The last thing I want is a rehash of why that engagement was broken in front of all our other clients!' Sarla was saying when Radhi parked herself in a corner.

'I've also invited Renuka ben to this party,' Sarla continued as a buzz rose from the women gathered around her. 'Just, as a gesture of goodwill,' she told Zarna, who looked surprised and about to protest. 'Don't worry, I've already discussed it with your mum.' Zarna glowered at her, but Sarla had already turned to her partner, who had been standing silently so far. 'Kiran, do you want to add anything?'

Kiran nodded and cleared her throat. 'Zarna has invited some media people to the event, please make sure to say all the right things. Zarna will tell you about the key points we want to touch upon. And, Juhi, please ensure that the security helps all the guests with the parking. Tell the guards they need to be polite. I don't want to hear any complaints.'

'Yes, ma'am,' said Juhi.

'Yes,' Sarla emphasized, 'if I hear even one guest grumbling about parking, tell the guards they can kiss their Diwali bonuses goodbye. Oh, and I have good news. Jeevan is out of danger. The doctors say they're hopeful of a full recovery.' Sarla smiled at the group assembled before her. 'On that happy note, I will see you all dressed and back here at six. Good luck everyone!'

When everyone had filed out of the room and only Radhi and Sarla remained, Sarla closed the door and met Radhi's eye in a sort of silent understanding. Radhi had called her after her visit to the paanwala and explained at length what she had discovered, what she feared and what she wanted Sarla to do. Now it was time for Radhi to set the next phase of her plan in motion. If she was right, the murderer would try to kill again today.

As Bhavana tucked the pleats of her purple organza sari tightly into the folds of her petticoat, she grimaced at the thought of the party she was about to attend. What were the chances that everyone had forgotten about Khushi's broken engagement? And would no longer pry tastelessly or, worse, express false sympathy? But staying at home was not an option. That would mean they were ashamed. No, they had to show up and look good. Besides, she had work to do. She stuck a safety pin into the pleats to hold the sari in place. It was a gesture more vicious than the sari deserved.

Kiran examined the hair extensions the hair stylist had attached to her scalp and admired the full appearance they gave her scanty hair. She had worked very hard for this party, for this moment. She was determined to shine today. Especially since her partner seemed a mere shadow of her former self. Her eyes clouded at the thought of Sarla. She shook her head, she would sort it out, just as she would sort out her foolish, stubborn daughter. Zarna had been keeping something from her. Behaving oddly, stepping out of their office to take calls and refusing to say why. Kiran counted the eleven extensions in her hair and asked the stylist to add one more. She hated not knowing what the girl was up to.

Renuka chose the largest pair of solitaires from her jewellery box for Soul Harmony's party. The invitation had come as a surprise, and she wondered if it had been sent out of spite or as a show of power. In either case, she wasn't going to miss the chance of seeing the great Sarla Seth in action. Worst-case scenario, it would be a learning. Best case, the possibilities were endless. She turned the screw of her earring tighter with a glint in her eye.

27

Radhi lay on Jeevan's bed, her body and face covered under two blankets, sweating profusely despite the air conditioning in the hospital room. She had drawn the curtains, darkened the room and turned to face the wall so that anyone who entered the room would not be able to make out immediately whether the figure under the thick blankets was a man or a woman. As she waited for the door behind her to open, she cursed Shinde for the nth time. The inspector had only partly done what she had asked him to do. He had moved Jeevan out of his room to a new ward on a different floor, but he hadn't stationed any men in the old room to take his place. When she called him again, he had cited a personnel shortage and hung up on her. Now Radhi thanked her stars that she'd had the foresight to ask Lila to be on standby. Her housekeeper was hiding in a utility cupboard in the passage outside, her eyes on the door to Jeevan's room.

The hospital blankets were rough, and Radhi, who had been having a hard time suppressing the urge to scratch, was about to shift to a more comfortable position when there was a slight sound of footsteps outside the door. Her senses on hyper-alert, Radhi froze, but the footsteps passed, and everything was quiet until a few minutes later, without any warning, the handle to the door of the room turned softly and swiftly; a stream of light from the outside illuminated the room for the briefest of moments, and then just as suddenly the door shut again. Radhi knew without having turned to look that she was no longer alone in the room.

Radhi had told Lila to wait a few minutes before following the murderer into the room so that they could catch the person in the act. But she hadn't realized how dangerous that could be. Because though she knew exactly who would enter and what they would try to do, she had no way of guessing how they'd do it. Now as Radhi sensed the person approach the bed, some ancient survival instinct seemed to claw at her to throw off the blankets and reveal herself, but before she could act upon it, a large pillow had descended on her face and begun to suffocate her.

'I still can't believe it was you.' Sarla's eyes were wide with incredulousness and horror.

The woman in front of Sarla seemed shell-shocked herself.

Beside Sarla, Radhi was quiet. Things had moved at such a frantic pace over the past hour that she was only now beginning to appreciate just how much danger she had been in.

Lila had walked into Jeevan's room to find Juhi pressing down on Radhi with all her might, as Radhi hit and scratched and dug her nails into the receptionist's arms to no avail. Juhi had hardly registered Radhi's blows, barely even realized that the person she was trying to kill was not Jeevan. She had an almost crazed expression on her face, and it had taken all of Lila's strength to pull her off Radhi and the help of two ward boys to finally restrain her.

Now Radhi and Sarla were sitting across Juhi in an interrogation room at the Temple Hill Police Station, while

Shinde was standing quietly in a corner. He had quickly become aware that his refusal to spare men from the CM's security detail would have cost them a life had it not been for Radhi's quick thinking. And realizing that even a single misstep at this stage would cost him his job, he was staying out of the way and letting the women do the talking.

'Why did you do it, Juhi? What were you thinking?' Sarla asked. 'You had such a bright future ahead of you!'

Juhi, who was dressed for the party, looked resplendent in a red bandhani kurta, despite her dishevelled hair and smudged mascara. She lifted burning eyes towards her employer's face, the slight crack in her voice the only sign of her fear. 'What future? How high did you think I could really rise? From a receptionist at a matrimonial bureau to a store manager in some shop? Or a secretary in some office?'

'Why? Just look at where you started and how far you've come, who knows where you might've reached!'

'Please, ma'am,' Juhi snapped. 'Do you really think my basic government college degree would take me further than that? Your world is so high above ours that the ceilings we stop at aren't even visible from where you are!'

'And you thought dating Yug would be your ticket out of your world?' Sarla, who had been shocked when Radhi told her Juhi's motive, still seemed to be reeling from the discovery.

When Juhi stayed silent, Sarla asked exasperated, 'Juhi, did you seriously think he would marry you?'

'We love each other . . .'

'Even so,' Sarla interrupted her, 'even so, are you really that naive? Or have you forgotten that his father is a diamond merchant, and your mother is a—'

'A maid! I know my mother washes bathrooms! And my father works at a tea stall! But are we not even allowed to dream?' Juhi's eyes welled up with furious tears. 'Given enough time I knew I could've been honest with him, and he would have been able to look past it.'

'Aah . . . he didn't know. Now that makes sense,' Sarla muttered to herself, as if finally figuring out how such an unlikely relationship could have begun in the first place.

Radhi realized that the economic divide between them was so deeply entrenched in their collective consciousness that Juhi's relationship with a man so far above her station had shocked them almost as much as the fact that she had murdered someone.

'I was waiting for the right moment to tell him!' Juhi said. 'I . . . I . . . he loved me as much as I loved him . . . I just needed time. And that horrid Hansa ben refused to give it to me!'

'She was going to tell Sarla ben, wasn't she?' Radhi, who had been quiet so far, finally spoke.

Juhi turned her blazing eyes towards Radhi. 'She had a picture of Yug and me in his car, at the paanwala's near his house. She was going to show it to Sarla ma'am. I begged her not to! I promised her I would tell Sarla ma'am of my own accord as soon as I was ready. But she refused to listen!'

'So you killed her?' Sarla asked with wide eyes, as if she couldn't recognize the young woman she had known all these years.

Juhi wiped her tear-stained face impatiently. 'What choice did I have? This was my one chance, my only chance at a better life! Do you know what it's like to go back to the one-room hovel that is my home after spending the day in your fancy, air-conditioned office? The place is always stinking, either of sweat or wet clothes or whatever the neighbour is cooking! And there are rats and mosquitoes, regardless of how often my mother sweeps the floor or how many coils we burn. Do you know I often come to work much earlier just so I can use the bathroom in peace? Yug was my ticket out of the shithole that is my life! And Hansa was trying to take it away from me! In one moment, she would've destroyed everything I had worked so hard for! Starting with your trust.' Juhi glared at Sarla. 'What would you have done when you found out? Called Yug's parents and then mine, isn't it? Would you have let me continue in my position even if I had broken it off with Yug?'

It took Sarla a moment to gather herself before she could reply. 'I don't know what I would've done, child. But I would've tried my best to help you. Like I've been doing since you were ten!'

Juhi shook her head. 'You couldn't have! Do you think my parents would've continued to let me work and get an education after you told them I was having an affair? They would've forced me to get married to the first man they could find. In our world, we don't have much — just our reputations! If I got pregnant or, worse, developed a reputation — my life along with theirs would've been ruined.'

'And now, Juhi? What about their life and reputation now?' Sarla ran a hand over her face and sighed. 'How I wish you'd just come to me. Just trusted me, instead of taking this godawful step!'

'I would do it again, you know,' Juhi said glaring defiantly from Radhi to Sarla. 'If faced with a similar choice, I'd kill that bitch again. Only I would be smarter about it.'

The receptionist had not shown a shred of remorse, and yet Radhi pitied her. She knew the desperate picture Juhi had painted of her life had not been exaggerated. It wasn't often that Radhi thought about the privileges of her own birth and circumstances, let alone felt guilty for them, but Juhi's speech had jarred her. And the role she had now played in determining the course of Juhi's future weighed heavily on her conscience. She pushed a glass of water towards her and watched as Juhi drank deeply from it.

Beside her, Sarla stirred and checked her watch. They had been at the station for over an hour; the party was about to start. The matchmaker shook her head, distressed. 'I wish I could stay longer.'

'Don't worry, Aunty.' Radhi pushed her chair behind and rose to walk Sarla to the door. 'I'll stay until her statement is recorded and other formalities are done. And then I'll come to help you with the other thing,' she added in a softer voice.

Sarla nodded, then with one long and sorrowful glance at Juhi, who to her credit didn't look away, she left the police station.

'How did you know?' Juhi asked in a small voice.

'Also how is that peon from your office mixed up in all this?' Shinde stirred, unable to control his curiosity any longer. 'Did he know about the affair too?'

At the mention of Jeevan's name, Juhi's face turned pale and she looked ashamed of herself for the first time.

'It was the Cadbury Eclairs wrapper,' Radhi said, remembering the rustle of the wrapper she had heard when she was listening to her interview with Juhi which had started her thinking in that direction. 'You had a handful of Eclairs in your bag, you offered me one at lunch that day, and I remembered seeing a wrapper in Hansa's dustbin the next day. I knew Hansa had just had a root canal; she had told me she was eating only soft foods that week, so that sticky toffee couldn't have been hers. Which meant someone who had met Hansa that evening had probably eaten an Eclair in her room.' She stopped and looked at Juhi, who gave her an almost imperceptible nod.

'When I asked you if you'd visited Hansa, you said you hadn't, but there was a doodle on her rough pad which—'

'But I tore that page!' Juhi interrupted. 'Hansa was on the phone when I went to see her, so I ended up doodling, but after our . . . our,' Juhi faltered, 'our argument, when I was leaving the room, I wiped the statue and the desk clean, and I tore that page.'

'Yes, but the impression of the doodle remained on the page below.' Radhi nodded at Juhi's incredulous expression. 'I've seen you make that heart-shaped doodle before.'

'Why didn't you say anything to us then?' Shinde asked in a querulous voice, leaving his post by the corner to take Sarla's seat. 'This is what happens when you withhold information from the police,' he began as if seeing his chance to claw out of the hole he had dug himself into.

But Radhi gave him a withering look. 'I only put it all together yesterday. And even then, it was only a hunch. I suspected Juhi was lying, but I couldn't be sure she had killed Hansa until I was sure of the motive. It was only after I showed the paanwala a picture of her and he confirmed that it was the same woman he'd seen with Yug that I knew for certain.'

'You took Hansa's phone, no?'

Juhi nodded, looking almost relieved now that it was all out in the open.

A constable knocked on the door, and Shinde reluctantly left the room.

'I never meant for any of this to happen,' Juhi said, her voice barely above a whisper. 'Not even the relationship with Yug. Never in my wildest dreams did I imagine that someone like him would be interested in someone like me.'

'You met while helping him with his biodata, I am guessing?'

Juhi smiled faintly. 'We connected over music. He mentioned he enjoyed K-pop and I told him my favourite bands. We took more than two hours to make his biodata that day.'

Radhi nodded, remembering the Korean song Jeevan had been listening to, which he said Juhi had sent him.

'It was very innocent at first. He asked for my number so that he could send me the link to an old, little-known song by my favourite Korean band. Then I sent him a news clipping about *his* favourite singer. It went on like that for a few weeks and then, before we knew it, we were friends on social media who knew more about each other's lives than just the music we listened to. I think it helped that I don't post pictures of my actual life on Instagram. Or one look at my kholi and he would have run in the opposite direction.' Juhi smiled bitterly before continuing, 'At one point he got engaged to Khushi, but we continued to remain in touch. But it was only when he broke it off with her that we began dating in earnest.'

Juhi seemed like she wanted to say more but Shinde came back to the room again with some paperwork.

'And what about the peon?' he asked as he took his seat. 'How did he get involved?'

'He wasn't involved. He is completely innocent,' Juhi said, belatedly trying to do right by the friend she had almost killed. 'Yug and I often met in the office after everyone had left. I would tell Jeevan that I needed to study in the office since it was very distracting at home. I'd tell him that I would lock up after I was done and drop the keys off at his place on my way home. Even that day I had told him to leave early and kept the keys for myself.'

'He lied about it when the police asked him, no?'

Juhi nodded. 'I told him we'd both be in trouble if Sarla ma'am found out that he had been giving me the office keys and I had been staying back long past office hours. I knew how badly his family needed this job and I told him it would be all right if he kept his mouth shut.'

'But he couldn't take the pressure,' Radhi guessed.

'He was a mess!' Juhi frowned. 'Jumpy and nervous every time the police questioned him.'

'We knew he was lying about something,' Shinde said, in an attempt to prove he wasn't completely oblivious. 'It was only a matter of time before he spilled it.'

Juhi looked accusingly at Radhi. 'Especially after you spoke to him . . . he made up his mind to come clean to Sarla ben and was urging me to do the same thing — I didn't have a choice but to . . . but to . . .'

'Murder him?' Radhi asked. 'There's always a choice, Juhi.'

'Your whole life is a luxury of choices,' the receptionist's eyes flashed. 'Please don't presume you know what it's like to be pushed into a corner.'

'But how did you know that she tried killing him that first time?' Shinde asked puzzled.

'I didn't,' Radhi admitted. 'Until yesterday, I thought he'd attempted suicide because I put too much pressure on him.' She turned to Juhi. 'But once I realized that it was you who had killed Hansa, it got me thinking about how close you and Jeevan were. The thing he was hiding could well have been to protect you, in which case you might've had something to do with the peanuts he consumed that day. You used to share your dabba with him. You knew about his peanut allergy — which is why you told him not to have that chutney that first day when we ate lunch together. Isn't it?' Radhi asked.

Juhi swallowed but didn't attempt to deny it.

'That's why I asked Sarla ben to announce that Jeevan was better this morning. I figured if I was right and you had indeed tried to silence Jeevan before, then you'd be worried about his recovery now and might be desperate enough to attempt murder again.'

Juhi's voice came out as a whisper, as if saying it louder would make the thing she had done more real. 'I told my mother to make capsicum subzi and add extra peanut powder to it. Then I told Jeevan I wasn't hungry, and that he could have my dabba instead. It was horrible, I just sat there at my desk knowing he was going to collapse any moment.'

Radhi was silent; beside her, Shinde, who was probably used to hardened criminals, too seemed at a loss for words in the face of such wickedness from someone so young.

28

The party was over by the time Radhi returned to the Soul Harmony office that evening. The music was still playing but the caterers were clearing out the buffet counter and the decorators were carrying away the extra tables and chairs that had been brought in for the event. Radhi met Divya, the young wedding-card designer, as the latter stepped out of the washroom.

'How was the party?' asked Radhi.

'Oh, it was wonderful! Everyone loved the décor and the food! Everything went off so smoothly,' Divya gushed. And then added, 'For the most part, that is.'

'Why for the most part? Did something happen?'

'Well, that Bhavana ben showed up and was saying snide things about Soul Harmony to whoever would listen. And then Renuka ben came and made a beeline for the media people, which annoyed Zarna, and the two of them would've gone at it then and there only, but luckily Sarla ben intervened and took Renuka ben into her office for a chat. They were in then for a long time, which was a good thing because Zarna had invited some investors to the party, and from the look on Kiran ben's face, I don't think they were expected.'

'That's eventful . . .' Radhi said with raised eyebrows.

'Yeah, but I don't think the guests noticed all of that.' Divya shrugged. 'They were busy getting their palms read by Neetu ben and eyeing potential matches for their sons and daughters. All in all, it was a success!' Divya yawned. 'I would like to go home now, but Sarla ben has insisted we wait, she wants to talk to us, it seems.'

Radhi, who had called Sarla to tell her that she was on her way, knew what Sarla had on her mind.

'First of all, I want to congratulate all of you on a job well done,' Sarla began when everyone had filed into her cabin and made themselves comfortable. Apart from Kiran and Zarna, there was Neetu, Alpa and Divya and a couple of others from accounting. Someone had asked after Juhi, but when no one seemed to know where she was, they hadn't pursued the matter.

'And I want to say thank you,' Sarla continued. 'This would not have been possible without you.' She looked at her long-time partner and friend who smiled back encouragingly. 'This party has been about celebrating our successes, but I think I would be remiss if I didn't admit the mistakes I have made as well. For instance, there are some here whom I should have acknowledged better and much earlier. Neetu, I'm sorry you thought your work here was not valued. I should've been more expressive in my appreciation for what you do.'

The astrologer blushed and smiled, and Radhi marvelled at how much younger she looked without the permanently bitter expression on her face.

'And I want to thank you for your loyalty,' Sarla continued. 'I know now that Renuka ben asked you to pass along information about our clients and you refused. Even though you have agreed to join her at Pair Perfect . . . But we'll come back to that later.'

Sarla paused and smiled, 'There are others here I should've talked to more. Alpa, I didn't know your mother was so unwell and that you had such grave financial problems. If you'd only come to me first, we'd have worked out a different arrangement. There was no need to steal our clients.'

The wedding planner had turned pale when Sarla addressed her, and now she hung her head in shame. She was about to respond, but Sarla continued, 'And then of course there are those I wish I hadn't trusted so blindly.' She turned to where Zarna was standing with Kiran and stared in silence.

'I was not betraying you!' Zarna erupted. 'Yes, I've been talking to investors and, yes, I took some files from the office the day Hansa died because I wanted to show some numbers to the investors, but in the end, you would've benefited equally from it!'

When Sarla didn't say anything, Zarna added, 'I am sorry I went behind your back and invited them here, but honestly, you are so closed to new ideas, what choice did I have?'

'I meant your mother, Zarna,' Sarla said softly and Zarna, who had been about to launch into another explanation, looked at her mother and Sarla in confusion.

'I know you have been sending me the tarot cards, Kiran.'

Sarla's partner had gone completely still. 'What are you talking about, Sarla?'

But it was Radhi who answered. 'It was the purple cat in the dustbin that gave it away, Kiran ben.'

'What cat? Is she insane?' Zarna asked Sarla.

When Sarla remained silent, she turned to her mother. 'Mummy?'

But Kiran didn't look at her; she was staring intently at Radhi, her face pale, yet fearless.

'I kept wondering what that cat was doing in the bin,' Radhi continued. 'Until I realized there were six cats in that line, and you'd thrown away the seventh one because you need everything to be an even number. I've seen your office, the number of cushions, the frames on the walls, even the number of plants, everything's even. I didn't put it together at first, but then I read a book about obsessive-compulsive behaviours and realized that when you were tapping things like the pens on your desk you were actually counting them.'

'Yes, so? Mummy is a little particular, we both are, but what's that got to do with anything?' Zarna asked, confused.

The rest of the staff gathered in the room had begun to buzz with questions and confusion. But Radhi ignored them. 'That day, Sarla Aunty told you that she had enlisted Hansa's help to find out who had been sending the tarot cards and you panicked. You were afraid that the PI would discover that it was you, and so you went into her room to check her files and see if she'd found something, isn't it?' Radhi paused to study Kiran's expression, but it was difficult to read. 'That is when you arranged the cats. But when the police asked you if you'd gone to Hansa's room, you denied it. Which got me wondering why you'd lie.'

'If you are seriously suggesting that my mother was sending tarot cards to herself, I'm assuming you have some proof.' Zarna's voice was laced with sarcasm.

'No proof. Since she touches most things with the pallu of her sari, there were no fingerprints except Hansa's on the cats. But I do have an idea of how it started.' When Zarna didn't object, she continued, 'Sarla ben and I have been wondering what happened two months ago that could've resulted in the tarot cards coming in. At first, we thought it was Renuka ben with her new bureau or Bhavana ben with her daughter's broken engagement, but then I kept seeing that *WedMe Happy* magazine around the office with Sarla Aunty on the cover and I realized that even that interview probably happened around then. I checked with Sarla Aunty, who confirmed that the cards began coming exactly a week after the magazine people visited the office.' Radhi paused and Kiran folded her arms across her chest. She was yet to say a single word. Radhi continued, 'I think that interview really rankled you, didn't it?'

A fleet of emotions crossed Kiran's face. She seemed to be contemplating denying everything. She knew Radhi didn't have any actual proof. But another, more desperate instinct looked like it wanted to own what she had done. To finally use the words she had kept bottled in for so long.

'But what I don't understand is why, Kiran?' said Sarla into the silence. 'Why stoop so low?'

A floodgate seemed to open up at Sarla's words and Kiran's eyes blazed with barely repressed fury. 'Are you really so self-involved, Sarla, that you can't even fathom why I'd be angry at you?' Kiran's voice was so biting that an instant hush descended upon the room.

'You have a problem that they featured me? But you've always shunned the spotlight!' Sarla frowned, as if genuinely trying to understand what had upset her partner so much. 'Haven't you always pushed me forward at events?'

'Yes, I don't like attention, but I could do with a little credit, you know!'

'I asked you if they could interview you, but you refused!' Sarla looked around at the employees assembled there to see if someone could explain her partner's reaction to her.

Kiran rolled her eyes. 'They wanted someone who bore witness to your journey in becoming the best matchmaker in town. As if I was some bystander who had watched it from the sidelines, instead of walking with you every step of the way! You know, Sarla, I didn't mind that they called you the best.' Kiran smiled bitterly. 'I have a problem that you let them. Where was the acknowledgement that we had built Soul Harmony as a team?'

Sarla fumbled around the things on her desk and picked up the magazine. 'I say it right here, see, on the first page, that this would not have been possible without your support!' She thrust the magazine at Kiran, who took it and flung it aside.

'I am not mere support, Sarla!' she yelled. 'I am your partner, your equal, and you've never actually believed that! I may not have your instinct for setting people up, but what I lack in instinct I make up for in hard work!'

'And I've always valued that! Always valued your opinion on things!'

'On what food to serve at the party? Yes! But never when I suggest a match!'

'Because I just prefer to go with my gut. You knew how I worked before you joined me!' Sarla turned to Zarna. 'Do you think your mother is being fair? Do I not treat her like an equal?'

Zarna shook her head. 'Honestly? You don't. But I think that's more my mother's fault than yours. She forgets she has a spine when she's around you.'

The employees gathered around them were shifting on their feet, looking distinctly uncomfortable, and Radhi wondered if this conversation could have happened at another place at another time. But Sarla had been so livid at the thought of Kiran sending her those tarot cards that she had insisted on doing it like this, in front of everyone.

Kiran turned furiously towards Zarna. 'You brat! I did this for you too, you know? You had all those dreams and plans for expansion, and I thought if I could manage to shake Sarla enough with the tarot cards, she'd get off her high horse a little and be open to your ideas as well!'

'Well, you've succeeded in that at least. I am shaken, all right. But not by your ridiculous threats,' Sarla said softly, as if she had suddenly lost the steam to fight, 'but by your betrayal.'

The two partners looked at each other with such distaste that it was a wonder to anyone present in the room how they had ever managed to work together.

'So, what is Kiran ben going to do now?' Vrinda asked Sarla before taking a bite of the ghee-soaked carrot halwa that Radhi had sprinkled with generous quantities of cashews and raisins.

The two of them and Madhavi had gathered for a traditional Gujarati lunch at Radhi's house and had just served themselves kadhi, a stuffed potato subzi and a cucumber and lentil salad, along with what was clearly the highlight of the meal so far, delicately rolled patras, which Radhi had spent a week perfecting.

'This is delicious, Radhi, why haven't we said what a good cook you are on your biodata?' Sarla said licking her fingers, before replying to Vrinda. 'I suppose she and Zarna will start the online matrimonial service for Gujaratis abroad that Zarna's been going on about.'

'Do you think they'd work well together?' Radhi asked thinking of the prickly relationship the mother and daughter shared.

Sarla smiled wickedly. 'Honestly, I don't think they'll last more than a month.'

'And what about you, Aunty?' Madhavi asked. 'You aren't quitting matchmaking, no? Radhi told me how stressed you were.'

'No, no, not quitting,' Sarla grinned. 'I did try imagining life without it and got such a migraine that I couldn't get out of bed for two days.' She put her spoon down with a more serious expression on her face. 'We will be closing Soul Harmony, though.'

Vrinda raised her eyebrows and Sarla shrugged. 'I didn't want Kiran to use the name, and she'll certainly not let me have it. So we've both agreed to give it up. Besides, my new partner probably wouldn't want to use it either.'

Radhi leaned forward, surprised and delighted. 'You mean she agreed?'

'Almost. We've still got a lot to figure out, but it looks promising.' Then turning to Vrinda and Madhavi, she explained, 'Radhi convinced me to invite Renuka from Pair Perfect to our party and speak to her candidly. Let's just say, one thing led to another and now we are thinking of collaborating.'

Radhi nodded. 'She is quite impressive. Why waste all that energy competing when it would be far more rewarding to work together.' Radhi took a bite of the carrot halwa before adding, 'And what about the rest of the staff?'

'Well, Neetu has agreed to stay back, at least until I figure things out with Renuka. By the way,' Sarla's spoon paused mid-air, 'Renuka offered Hansa a job! That's why Hansa had Renuka's card in her purse. But Hansa declined it. I don't know if it was out of loyalty to me,' Sarla smiled, 'but I'd like to think it was.'

'And Alpa?'

Sarla shook her head and sighed. 'She apologized profusely, but I can't keep her on. I've agreed to bring her on as a freelance consultant for some of our weddings. But we'll see. She'll have to earn my trust again.' Sarla paused to mix her kadhi with her rice, before adding, 'I told everyone that they were welcome to join Kiran and Zarna if they wanted to. One of the accounting people will be going with them, but other than that everyone is staying with me.'

'How is Jeevan?' Radhi asked, pushing her plate away and dabbing her mouth with a napkin.

Sarla smiled. 'Oh, he's much better. Almost as good as new. He'll resume work next week.'

The women got up from the dining area and moved towards the sofa, where Vrinda promptly put her feet up and closed her eyes. They were feeling full and drowsy after all that rich and delicious food.

'What about that girl, the one who committed the murder?' Vrinda asked. 'What happens to her?'

Radhi frowned. 'I spoke to Shinde as well as a lawyer to understand her chances of making bail. But the second time she tried to kill Jeevan really stacked the cards against her. The first one could've been committed in the "heat of the moment" but the second attempt was clearly premeditated.'

'Poor girl,' Madhavi clicked her tongue, sympathetically.

Sarla sighed. 'I know. I'm helping the family while they wait for the trial.'

'I'd like to help too,' Radhi said immediately.

'You are a good girl, Radhi.' Sarla gave her a fond smile. 'Jeevan's family told me how you helped them as well. Not to mention, me! I'm not sure how I can thank you.'

Radhi blushed. 'You don't have to—'

'By finding her a good boy!' Madhavi said.

'Didi, please!' Radhi blushed even more deeply.

'But I thought she was already seeing someone?' Sarla asked, looking from one sister to the other.

'Not any more,' Madhavi said. 'She's single and ready to mingle.'

'Please, no! I'm not mingling,' Radhi protested with a half-hearted smile.

A few weeks ago, she'd had a long and painful conversation with Nishant. He had wanted to continue dating. Had looked into her eyes, kissed her hands and promised her that they could keep things light, that she could take things as slow as she wanted to. And Radhi had almost agreed. The gullible part of her that she could easily delude had found much-needed solace in his words. But the other part, the one that was routinely racked with guilt and shame, and which bore the brunt of her actions, had been able to perceive the truth. Because despite his assurances otherwise, it was apparent to her that Nishant was deeply invested in their relationship. He was already planning a life with her, even if he refused to admit it. She had turned him down then, taking comfort in the fact that however hurt he may seem now she had spared him a worse fate in the future.

'How is Roma?' Vrinda asked, well aware of the drama her sister's mother-in-law had caused.

'Sulking in Delhi. But she'll come off it, unfortunately. And then she'll want to visit us again.'

Madhavi made a face, and the four women laughed.

Radhi, you gorgeous, brilliant thing. I love it! I can see her clearly now — your detective. She is such a fox! Not at all what I had in mind — not at all like you and yet so believable. I am going to pitch this out to a couple of publishing houses that would be perfect for this, but tell me, you mentioned you wanted to turn this into a series — is that still something you are considering? Do you have any ideas?

George XOXO

Radhi grinned as she blew smoke rings out of the window. The light from her phone illuminated her face as she replied to George's email with the title she had thought for the next book in her series — A Matrimonial Murder.

Acknowledgements

This mystery was harder to write than the first one. Maybe because unlike *The Death of Kirti Kadakia*, this one was written to an internal deadline. But despite all the writerly anguish, or perhaps because of it, it was all the more satisfying.

A big thank you is owed:

To Mekhala Moorthy, my wonderful editor at Bloomsbury, for her intuitive understanding of Radhi and for her faith in the Temple Hill Mystery series.

To Mekhala again and to Jaishree Ram Mohan for their detailed, thoughtful and sensitive editorial inputs.

To Kanishka Gupta, my literary agent, for his continued faith and guidance.

To Goa-based artist and tarot reader Darpan Kaur, for her insight into the practice of tarot.

To Swati, Deepti and Suchitra, my beta readers, for their unfailing honesty and kindness. Our many conversations about life and writing keep me afloat.

To Meera, the sun of my existence, and to Mum for always being my true north.

And finally, and always, to my husband, Maulik, for making *all* of this possible. And for being so fiercely proud of me that I can't help but want to write better.

About the Author

Meeti was longlisted for the prestigious CWA New Blood Dagger in 2022 and for the *Times of India* AutHer Awards in 2023 for *The Death of Kirti Kadakia*, her first Temple Hill Mystery. Her first book was the critically acclaimed memoir *Do You Know Any Good Boys?*, a funny guide to the Indian arranged marriage, which was an Amazon bestseller in 2016 and has since been optioned for screen. Before turning to full-time writing, Meeti was a creative consultant and copywriter with an award-winning career in advertising spanning over sixteen years. Meeti graduated from St Xavier's College, Mumbai, and has a master's in English literature from Mumbai University. She writes from a small, blue desk in Mumbai, where she lives with her husband, daughter and a dozen astonishingly sturdy houseplants.